AS LONG AS IT TAKES

ALSO BY EE SAMPLE:
The Last Siren
info@eesample.com

AS LONG AS IT TAKES

EE SAMPLE

LUMINARE PRESS
WWW.LUMINAREPRESS.COM

Luminare Press
442 Charnelton St.
Eugene, OR 97401
www.luminarepress.com

LCCN: 2021904431
ISBN: 978-1-64388-575-9

For my son, Sean

TABLE OF CONTENTS

PROLOGUE

The woman behind the telescope adjusted the optics until he came into focus. The perfect haircut, the navy overcoat, the chiseled features of an impossibly tanned face. It was him. She watched as he strode purposefully along the winding sidewalk across the manicured lawns of the park. Her heart beat faster, she felt her pulse in her ears. A shot rang out from somewhere outside and above where she stood in the study of her Hyde Park apartment. She saw the man's head explode and his crumpled body fall into a dark, blue heap among the leaves on the green grass. The woman recoiled in horror. Horror turned to shock, and with shock came numbness. She willed herself away from the window and across the room.

Nine nine nine. What is your emergency?

"I've just witnessed a murder."

Chapter 1

29 OCTOBER

He could make himself invisible when he had to. He could be in a room with you for half an hour without you knowing he was there. That's how good Chance Kincaid was. His special skills had been honed by the best black ops instructors in the world and by years of experience practicing his lethal trade, but today he was very visible. A six-foot-two-inch, two-hundred-pound man was hard to miss sitting on an airplane at thirty thousand feet above the South China Sea.

"Sir, we are on our final approach to Manila right now. I'll have to ask you to finish your drink and fasten your seatbelt at this time." The flight attendant, a slim, brown-skinned woman of about thirty-five with silky, raven hair stood over him as he swallowed the last of his bourbon. She smiled as she took his glass. "Thank you, Mr. Kincaid." She turned and swayed through the first-class cabin toward the galley.

His thoughts, as his eyes followed her down the aisle, must have been obvious.

"She is beautiful, isn't she?"

"What? Oh yeah, I guess she is."

"Polynesian people are some of the most attractive on earth, I think. Would you agree?"

"I wouldn't disagree," he said.

He first noticed the woman across the aisle from him when they left Guam four hours ago. She was in her early thirties, probably, with hazel-green eyes and a honey complexion bordered by long, light-brown hair that fell softly onto her shoulders. Perhaps a little young for him but pleasant enough to look at just the same.

"Are you going to Manila on business?" she asked casually as she removed her earbuds.

"No and no. I'm going to El Nido on holiday." His voice was low and raspy, barely audible over the jet's engines.

On holiday, she thought. A decidedly British term, yet he sounded like an American. "You're not staying in town then?"

"No, I have a reservation on one of the islands." He didn't perceive this young woman as a threat, but he never divulged more than was needed to anyone. Habit. He had probably said too much already. "Do you know the area?"

"Yes, quite well. My father has a business in El Nido. I'm going there to visit him as a matter of fact."

So that's how an attractive young woman happens to be travelling alone in first class to a remote part of the world.

The chatter in the plane had subsided. It was the usual nervous quiet that precedes the touch down of every commercial flight. The plane taxied to the gate and the passengers began standing and pulling luggage from the overhead bins.

"Maybe I'll see you around. El Nido is a small place."

"Yeah, maybe." But he didn't mean it.

He pulled his shoulder bag from under his seat, thanked the smiling flight attendant and strode down the ramp and into the cavernous Terminal 3. The Ninoy Aquino

International Airport serviced more than twenty million passengers per year. To Kincaid, it looked as if they had all arrived at once. He elbowed his way through the jostling crowd and pulled his duffel off the carousel. After some searching, he located the baggage window to claim the small, locked case that contained his firearm.

Chapter 2

OCEANIA

From Manila, it was an hour and a half to El Nido by puddle jumper. The fifty-seat AirSwift ATR-42 was almost empty, but he edged down the aisle to the back row anyway. He stuffed his bag under the seat and ordered a bourbon. The flight attendant was male, and the young woman from the 747 wasn't onboard, so he was alone with his thoughts and his old friend, Jim Beam.

Ten years and two dozen different countries as a mercenary had left him craving solitude, and the province of Palawan might be just what the doctor ordered. A few years ago, he had done a job for the Philippine government when some senators got into trouble in Manila, and he promised himself that he would return someday as a "tourista." *Condé Nast* listed these pristine beaches as the best in the world. Probably because they were a twenty-three-hour plane ride from the United States.

He was happy to finally land in El Nido. From the airport, he took a taxi to the ferry docks just outside of town. The last leg of his journey was a forty-five-minute boat ride to the Oceania Resort. Aside from the crew, the only other people on board were a young couple whom Kincaid guessed to be honeymooners and an affluent-looking, older gentleman with a British accent. He was accompanied by a woman who appeared to be his much younger wife. She seemed annoyed with the steward. "I find it implausible that you don't have prosecco!" she screeched as she ran her hands through her blonde hair. "I don't even know what we're doing on this stupid boat."

Kincaid ignored them all and opted for a seat well down the aisle. It was late afternoon, and the catamaran was cool and comfortable. He stared out the window as they motored out of the marina into open water where the captain cut the engines and the deckhands hoisted the sails. The elegant craft slipped silently by a towering rock formation rising from the sea like The Colossus of Rhodes. The fiery sunset glinting off purple limestone cliffs, the turquoise sea, the tawny whiskey—all were colluding to affect Kincaid's senses. He was beginning to relax.

The bell captain greeted them at the dock, and a young Filipino took his thirty-pound duffel. "Is this all your luggage, sir?"

Kincaid nodded and smiled. If not for his Wilson Combat .45 and several boxes of ammo, it would weigh half that and he would still have everything he needed for the rest of his life.

The *Oceania Resort* was the way he remembered it: nestled at the foot of a jagged mountain on one side and a deep, primordial forest on the other. The crescent, sandy beach wrapped around a crystalline cove that was tempered on the seaward side by a natural coral breakwater. The resort itself was a modest yet luxurious ecological sanctuary comprised of twenty rooms situated among the trees and fifteen cottages on pilings over the water.

The bell captain led the way up a long wooden pier to the main clubhouse. The entrance was beneath an archway bounded by dense stands of bamboo and fronted by an expansive, gray portico where several members of the staff had gathered to welcome them upon their arrival. "Kamusta," they said, smiling and bowing to each passenger in turn.

Kincaid mounted the stairs to the lobby. Massive koa timbers supported the high teak ceiling. The salt air combined with the smell of old wood and tropical plants, creating a sweet ambiance as the sea breeze wafted through the open doors. He waited patiently behind the old gentleman from the boat, then stepped to the desk and handed a striking, exotic woman his reservation and passport. She was the color of amber and looked to be in her twenties. Dangling gold earrings peeked out beneath shining, black hair bobbed just at her chin. She smiled, revealing perfect white teeth framed by deep-red painted lips.

"Good evening, Mr. Kincaid. Welcome to Oceania." She spoke with the typical Filipino accent.

"Kamusta." It was about all the Tagalog he knew.

She seemed amused. "You will be staying with us for a week?"

"At least." He noticed the small gold pin over her left breast. "Lucia. I may want to stay longer if you can accommodate me." He smiled.

"I don't think that will be a problem," she said matter-of-factly. "Just let us know as soon as you have decided. We don't have many units, and they can fill quickly."

"I will keep that in mind."

Lucia ran his American Express card and handed it back to him. No ring on her left hand.

"Ricky will show you to your cottage. I hope you have a wonderful evening."

"Thank you, and you as well."

He followed the boy, who was still carrying his bag, out along the sidewalk. Adjacent to the lobby was a wall of windows overhung with a thatched awning. "This is the restaurant and bar." Ricky gestured. They crossed the lawn onto the boardwalk that ran beside the whitest sand he had ever seen and out over gin-clear water. The last vestiges of sunset were streaking toward the beach, leaving soft, golden trails behind them. They walked past three cottages before turning up the ramp to a set of polished mahogany double doors. Ricky swung them open. On the opposite side of a spacious but spartan room where a wall should have been was a stunning view of the cove.

"There are sliders on that wall if you want to close them," Ricky said, "but no one ever does. And if you want to order food, there's a menu by the phone." He paused for a moment before adding "But don't try to call anyone outside the resort, because it's not that kind of phone."

Kincaid took the bag and handed Ricky a twenty-dollar bill. He always tipped well and early to insure good service for the duration of his stay.

"Thank you, sir!" Beaming, he turned and ran back the way he had come.

Entering the room, Kincaid observed a teak writing desk and chair to the left. Beyond it was a small sofa with thick, white cushions and a flat screen TV. Across the wood plank floor on the right was a king-size bed. The duvet was turned down to expose high thread count linens and four fluffy pillows. Through the door past the bed was a small hallway with a bathroom on the right and a kitchenette to the left. There were a few plates, some flatware, a coffee pot, and an assortment of cookware. Everything one would need to cook a meal on the small, two-burner stove. Most importantly, there was a small refrigerator with an icemaker for his drinks. The window over the sink afforded another view across the water.

Kincaid took off his shoes and stripped off his shirt, stepped out onto the terra-cotta tiled veranda, and sat in one of the three wicker chairs that surrounded a round glass table. He put his feet up and stared out at the sea as day faded slowly into dusk. The lights came on at the clubhouse, and their white beams glimmered and danced on the rippling water. He could smell hibiscus blossoms on the breeze, mixed with what he was sure was charcoal smoke. He called room service and ordered a T-bone steak and a bottle of wine that arrived a half hour later. He drank half the wine with his dinner and the rest as he sat in the salty breeze. It was warm and quiet as he drifted off to sleep in his chair.

It was dark when he woke and glanced at his watch. A couple of hours had passed. He stared out toward the now ink-black sea beyond the breakwater where gentle but persistent waves tried to infiltrate the still lagoon. Gradually, he became aware of an approaching engine somewhere in the darkness. At first, he wasn't sure he really heard anything. It had been a long trip, and except for the time on the catamaran, he had been listening to engines all day. Maybe this was just residual noise that had found its way from his subconscious to blend with reality. Kincaid strained to see into the darkness for any sign of movement. In a few seconds, he made out the silhouette of a speeding skiff bobbing from side to side in the surf. It displayed no running lights as he watched it make a sharp turn toward the shore. It looked, for a moment, like it might crash into the breakwater, but instead it slowed and crawled cautiously along parallel to the rocky barrier. Something didn't feel right. This wasn't a fishing boat, and it seemed a bit too stealthy.

Now he could make out men dressed in dark clothing. They definitely weren't fishermen. Eventually, the craft found the barrier's opening and turned into the channel that led into the cove. Kincaid's hackles were up now. His paramilitary experience was prodding him to act, but exactly what needed to be done was unclear. Until the craft reached the dock. Three men leaped out carrying assault rifles, and a fourth remained at the stern, his hand still on the tiller. The motor idled quietly. Two of the men were now crouching and moving across the dock toward the clubhouse.

Kincaid grabbed his pistol and a couple of spare magazines. He ran out the door, down the ramp, and along the boardwalk. As soon as he reached the beach, he jumped off onto the firm sand at the water's edge to avoid being spotted. As he sprinted, he saw the two men enter the building. He figured the third invader was waiting somewhere on the dock. This didn't look good.

Chapter 3

TERRORISTS

The end of the boardwalk rested on a seawall made of cement and coral rock. Kincaid scaled it, ripping his bare feet on the coral and barnacles. He ignored the pain and laid on his stomach. Floodlights on the building illuminated the terrace and lawn. He could see the scene clearly, but anyone standing in the light would have trouble seeing him out in the shadows. Two short bursts of gunfire. The unmistakable sound of an AK-47, the preferred weapon of terrorists the world over. The two men emerged through the door of the dining room. They were dragging someone with them. Their captive was struggling to escape. A good sign—captured but alive. He could hear angry voices screaming something, but he couldn't make out what was being said or by whom. Just then another figure appeared at the door. Another short burst from an automatic rifle, and the figure disappeared. Kincaid took advantage of the distraction. He jumped to his feet and ran full speed toward the kidnappers. He stopped just short of the courtyard lights and knelt behind a large coleus bush. They were unaware of him until his first round struck one of them between the shoulder blades. The man fell squarely on his face, losing his grip on the prisoner. His partner spun and fired in Kincaid's direction, but the rounds couldn't find their darkened target. Kincaid emptied his automatic at the shooter who must have been wearing body armor, because he kept firing wildly. The third attacker was chasing their abductee back toward the door. Kincaid slammed another magazine into the pistol, but before he could pull the trigger, his man fell to the ground. *Maybe he wasn't wearing a vest after all.* Kincaid jumped up and ran toward the third man who now had his arms around the hostage. He had dropped his rifle in the skirmish and was hiding behind his human shield. Or so he thought. His target was about the size of a saucer, but Kincaid didn't hesitate, though a prudent man might. Kincaid had never been described as a prudent man. He stopped running and shot. His bullet whizzed past the captive's ear and hit his assailant in the forehead. At the dock, the boat roared to life and sped away. *So much for loyalty.* Kincaid sprinted to the dock and sent the rest of his ammo in the direction of the fleeing craft.

The shooting had stopped. Blue smoke and the acrid stench of gunpowder lingered in the air as a few diners cautiously came out to the terrace. Three men were lying in expanding pools of blood. An old man was leaning with his back pressed against the wall, and Kincaid was walking back toward them, calmly holding a .45 caliber semiautomatic pistol at his side.

"Please don't shoot!" a man shouted.

"The shooting is all over," Kincaid said. "Someone should call the police or the militia, whoever's charged with keeping the peace around here." He was sure all three men were dead but checked each of them anyway. The one with the jagged hole in his forehead was clutching a Browning 9 mm, a gun long revered by the Filipino military. Kincaid took the gun, stuck it in his belt, and turned his attention to the man against the wall. He was the old gentleman from the catamaran. His ashen face was spattered with the kidnapper's blood. He was sweating and breathing heavily. "This man needs a doctor."

"That's the ambassador." The blonde from the boat was weaving her way through the gathering crowd. She seemed more annoyed than frightened as if she resented the fact that her dinner had been interrupted.

"The ambassador?" The question came from a dark-complexioned man in a deep-blue polo shirt emblazoned with the golden Oceania logo. Kincaid thought, due to his demeanor that the fellow must be more or less in charge.

"Yes, the British ambassador to Vietnam" She paused, then added "Well, he used to be the ambassador a long time ago, I guess. He still likes to be called that."

"Are you his wife?"

"You must be kidding. My name is Lisa Kettering. I'm his traveling companion." Lisa looked to be about thirty-two or thirty-three years old. An expensive-looking diamond necklace hung from her graceful neck. She was wearing an elegant, scarlet evening gown with a slit up one side, revealing a long, shapely leg. No shoes.

Kincaid jerked his thumb in the direction of the old man. "What's his name?"

"It's Earl Grey."

"You mean like the tea?"

Lisa rolled her eyes. "I guess you think we haven't heard that one before. Try about a thousand times." She turned and crossed toward her consort who was staring blankly at the bloody corpse at his feet.

"I'll have someone help you get him to his cottage until

the doctor arrives" the man in the blue polo said. He spoke softly into a radio and then to Kincaid, "I'm Marcus Tejada." He extended his hand. "I'm the director of operations here at Oceania." Tejada was a small but stout Filipino with black, neatly coiffed hair punctuated by gray at the temples. It was hard to say how old he was, but Kincaid guessed him to be in his late fifties.

Kincaid shook his hand. "Kincaid. I just checked in this evening."

"How fortunate for us. Kidnapping has become a serious threat in the Philippines, and foreign nationals in particular are being targeted," he explained. "But we have never had a problem here." He was speaking to Kincaid but staring at the bodies bleeding on his terrace. Like he was preoccupied. Maybe he was thinking it was going to be hell getting the stains out of the concrete.

"Well, it seems like you have a problem now. I'd hire some security people if I were you. Any idea who they were?"

"There are several extremist groups operating here." He motioned to one of the dead men. "Judging by their clothing, I'm guessing they are terrorists, part of the Abu Sayyaf Group, but they could be anybody."

"Were," Kincaid said.

"Were?"

"They were terrorists. Now they're just dead."

"Yes. I was coming to that. Where does a man acquire the skills that you demonstrated this evening?"

"Here and there."

"I don't suppose you'd be interested in helping set up a security team for us?"

"No, I don't suppose I would. I'm here on vacation, and if this gets to be a regular event, I won't be here long. Any thoughts on how they knew the ambassador was here? He and his girlfriend arrived today when I did."

"I can't imagine. We're fairly isolated here, and the resort respects the privacy of our guests. We never make such information available to anyone. It's our policy."

"Okay. I'm sure the police will want to talk to me. I'm in Cottage 4. In the meantime, I'm going to try and get some sleep. It's been a long day." He started to walk away.

"Mr. Kincaid, were you shot?" Tejada called.

"No, why?"

"Because you're leaving a trail of blood behind you."

Kincaid looked down. His right foot was bleeding badly. "I cut my foot on the seawall. It's not a big deal."

"It looks like you need stitches. I'll send the doctor over to have a look at it after he's seen to Ambassador Grey."

"Don't bother. I can take care of it myself." Kincaid turned and walked toward his cottage, leaving a bloody footprint with every other step.

It was 3:00 a.m. when Kincaid was awakened by a knock on his door.

"Who's there?" he called without raising his head off the pillow that covered his Wilson automatic.

"The police. We have a few questions for you."

"Come back later. It's the middle of the night, and I'm sleeping."

The knocking became banging. "All right, I'm coming." He was more than a little annoyed. He climbed out of bed and went to the door wearing a pair of olive-green boxers and a white T-shirt. He didn't bother to put on his pants. He opened the door to find a slight Filipino man in a rumpled,

EE Sample

tan sport coat who identified himself as Sergeant Cutro. Cutro was about five foot six with close-cropped, black hair and wire-rimmed glasses. He spoke English with no discernable accent and was flanked by two bigger men in similar dress. The biggest of them looked like a sumo wrestler. They said nothing.

"Come right in." Kincaid hoped they detected his sarcasm.

"There was a shooting on the grounds here tonight, and three men are dead," said the sergeant.

"Yeah, I heard."

"Several witnesses have identified you as their killer."

"I would hardly call myself a killer."

"But you did shoot three men who were armed with automatic weapons?"

"They were shooting at me. What would you have done?"

"We are talking about you right now, not me. You're registered here as Mr. Kincaid." It was more a statement than a question.

"That's right."

"Do you have a first name, Mr. Kincaid?"

"Yes."

"You are trying my patience with these smart-ass answers, Kincaid. Do you realize the trouble you're in?"

Kincaid had dealt with local police before. And he had been questioned by interrogators more skilled than this guy, that was for sure. In fact, he considered himself a more effective interrogator than Cutro. "Look, I saw four men try to kidnap a British citizen. When I interrupted them, they fired AK-47s at me. Now they're dead. End of story. I don't think I'm in trouble at all. In fact, maybe you should be thanking me for doing your job for you."

The sergeant ignored the last part of the reply. "You said four men."

"That's right. One of them stayed in the boat and used it to escape."

Cutro sat down on the sofa next to Kincaid and took a small notepad from his coat pocket. "How is it that you were here tonight?

"I'm here on holiday."

"On holiday? What do you do for a living?"

"Whatever I need to do."

"You're going to answer my questions, Kincaid, one way or another. I have a report to make."

"I feel for you, but you're just going to have to look me up."

Cutro leaned forward. He clenched his jaw and stared for a long moment. He was getting nowhere. He decided to change gears. "Where is your weapon?"

"I put it away."

"I'm going to need that gun."

Kincaid remained defiant. "I don't think you are."

"Turn over your weapon, Mr. Kincaid, or I will take you in right now."

"If that's what it takes to get rid of you." Kincaid retrieved his pants and produced the pistol he took from the dead man. He handed it to Cutro.

"Do you expect me to believe you used this piece of shit to take down three men with assault rifles?

"Believe whatever you want."

One of the big cops noticed the bloody bandage on Kincaid's foot. "What happened to your foot?"

"I cut it on some barnacles."

"You should see a doctor. You could get blood poisoning." Was the big man trying to play good cop? That would get him nowhere.

"Your concern is touching, Fat Boy. It's fine," he said dismissively to the now glaring sumo.

There was a long moment of tense silence. "Don't leave the island. We may need to talk to you again," Cutro ordered as he stood to go.

"I don't plan to. Now if you don't mind, I'd like to get some sleep." He followed the men to the door and closed it behind them. Kincaid was sure they would want to talk to him again. If they ran ballistics on the old Browning, they'd know it wasn't the gun he'd used on the three terrorists. That gun probably hadn't been fired since World War II, but if Cutro wanted to play games, he'd play them. No need to give the locals more information than he had to. Policy. He never gave up his gun to anyone. Period.

Chapter 4

THE SECRET LAGOON

The sun was up hours before he woke to the sound of a small outboard motor. He rolled out of bed and walked through the open doors onto the veranda. A small skiff was heading directly toward him. *Not again*, he thought as he rushed inside to retrieve his weapon. Back outside, his eyes were having trouble focusing in the sun that reflected off the sparkling azure water. As he squinted, he could make out a single figure at the stern of the boat as it motored up to the ladder that connected the veranda to the sea. Lucia de la Rosa, the desk clerk, was seated at the helm. She cut the engine and stood to wave.

"Good afternoon," she called. She looked to be about five foot six and maybe 115 pounds. She was wearing a white tank top over a blue-and-white-striped bikini that was held together by thin blue string. Silken, black hair blew across her face as she smiled up at him. He could smell the coconut oil that shone on her shoulders and floated on the breeze.

"Hello," he said tentatively.

"You seem surprised to see me."

"Well, I've never been visited by a desk clerk in a boat before."

"We've never had a hero staying in one of our cottages before."

"What are you doing out here?"

"I thought you might let me show you around the islands today. Besides, I'm not really a desk clerk. My uncle is the DO here, and I help out wherever I'm needed."

"DO?"

"I'm sorry. The director of operations."

"Tejada is your uncle?"

"That's right. We want to show you our appreciation for what you did for us last night."

He caught himself staring at her oiled legs gleaming in the sun. "I just did what any man would do in that situation. I'm far from being a hero, and I wasn't expecting a reward."

"Oh, I'm not here as a reward, just as a guide."

He smiled down at her. "I just woke up. I haven't had my breakfast yet. Will you come up?"

"I've packed us a lunch, and I know a good spot for a picnic. Put on some pants and come down here."

Kincaid hurried inside, found his shoes, pulled a pair of khaki shorts over his boxers, and stuck the .45 in the waistband. He went back out and climbed down the ladder into the boat. No sooner had he stepped aboard than Lucia gunned the engine, causing him to fall clumsily onto the deck. "Better get your sea legs," she laughed. "It could get a little bumpy out there."

He pulled himself up onto the bench that spanned the skiff mid hull and faced her as she navigated to the channel that led out of the cove. They passed the breakwater and turned north, paralleling the beach for about eight hundred meters before slowing to maneuver between two imposing cliffs. The narrow passage opened onto the most spectacular sight Kincaid could have ever imagined.

"This is called the Secret Lagoon," she shouted over the drone of the outboard.

It was about six hundred meters wide, twice as long, and bordered on three sides by lush greenery spilling over rocky limestone escarpments. The water was, in turns, turquoise and emerald green until he looked straight down. Then it was so clear that the boat seemed to be floating on air. It was impossible to ascertain its depth or the size of what appeared to be large, purple rocks that dotted the white, sandy bottom. The air was still and silent, giving the place an ethereal, otherworldly feel. It may have been the most beautiful place Kincaid had ever seen. They sat without speaking for several minutes as their little boat drifted slowly toward the cliffs. He reached for the anchor resting at the bow.

"Oh, no," Lucia said sternly. "We do not use the anchor. It will destroy the coral." She produced a paddle that had been hanging under the gunwale along the hull. "Just give us a couple of strokes with this."

He realized that what he thought was merely limestone rock was actually living coral. *How stupid. I should have known that,* he thought as he paddled back out to the middle of the lagoon. He slipped his shoes off and leaned on his elbow. Being here with this inscrutable woman in such a stunning place was mesmerizing. He could feel the tension ebb from his body.

Lucia noticed his bandage. "Your foot! Uncle told me you had injured it. How is it? Did the doctor stitch it up last night?"

"No, I didn't see the doctor. I stitched it myself."

"Let me see."

He stuck out his foot, and she took it in both hands and pulled on it to get a closer look.

"Hey!" he cried as he almost fell off his bench. "Take it easy."

She carefully removed the bandage. "That's a pretty professional-looking job. What did you use to do this?"

"I have a first aid kit."

Lucia wondered what kind of first aid kit included instruments for suturing.

He read her thoughts. "I like to be prepared for anything."

"Exactly what is your line of work that requires a first aid kit, Mr. Kincaid?" she asked playfully, though she was only half teasing. She and her uncle had thought it odd that he happened to be there last night, shot three men, and then acted so cavalier about the entire incident.

"I'm a consultant."

"What kind of consultant?"

"A very good one."

"Who do you consult with?"

"Anyone who has a problem and can afford me."

She was getting nowhere with him, so she decided to drop it for now. She opened the cooler that had been stowed under her seat and started taking out sandwiches and beer.

"San Miguel Pilsen. I haven't had that in a long time."

"You've been to the Philippines before?"

"Yeah, I guess I've been just about every place at one time or another." He grabbed a beer, twisted the cap, and took a long drink. It was cold and tasted good going down his parched throat. "I didn't realize how thirsty I was. Thanks."

"Drink up. I brought plenty." She handed him a sandwich wrapped in white paper. "It's roasted pork. I made it myself. I hope you like it."

"It smells delicious," he said in anticipation.

Time crawled past as they drifted on the calm, diaphanous water of the lagoon and enjoyed the food and each other's company. Kincaid was becoming entranced by the place and by the woman. He had just leaned forward with the intention of kissing her when they were interrupted by laughter mixed with yelling and screaming accompanied by the low hum of a diesel engine.

"That will be the tourist boat," Lucia said without turning around. "It comes several times a day to bring sightseers from town to visit the lagoon. Don't worry. It only stays a short while. They'll be gone soon."

"Several times a day to the secret lagoon?" he mused. "Not much of a secret if you ask me."

The boat was big enough to accommodate at least fifty passengers on its two decks. The captain cut the engine, and the hull drifted to a stop, pushing a rolling wave that moved through the still water and bounced Lucia's little skiff like a cork in a bathtub. Kincaid, who was still edging forward, lost his balance again and this time, fell into her lap. She stiffened.

"Sorry." he said. I wasn't ready for that." He moved back to his own bench and gave her an apologetic look.

"Neither was I." He could tell she doubted his sincerity by the tone in her voice.

As predicted, the tourists were gone in a few minutes, and all was quiet again. "Tell me about yourself," he said, mostly to break the silence.

She gazed over his shoulder at the trees that stood in the distance. "I was born in Davao City."

"Mindanao?"

"Yes. My father worked for the government, and my mother was the chef in a restaurant. When I was nineteen, my father was killed under mysterious circumstances, and my mother and I moved to Manila to live with my uncle."

"Mysterious circumstances?

"Mysterious to us because the air force wouldn't give us any details. They only said it was an accident. We never believed it."

"Why not?"

"Don't you think they could have told us about the accident? No, there had to be more to it than that. Something the government didn't want us to know. We weren't allowed to see his body."

"Now, that's odd. What about your uncle? Tejada, right?"

"Yes. Marcus Tejada, my mother's brother. He was a bartender then and lived in a poor neighborhood. Money was scarce, and my mother couldn't find a decent job. She was forced to cook and sell food on the street to pay our bills."

"Where is your mother now?"

"She's dead. One night when she was working, she was raped and killed by a street gang. There are many violent gangs there. That's when Uncle Marcus said we should get out of the city because it was so dangerous. We came to El Nido, and he got a good job at Oceania. He was eventually promoted to director of operations. I've been on his staff here ever since."

"That's a pretty sad story, Lucia."

"It's not so bad." She changed the subject. "It is beautiful here, don't you think?"

"Yes, I do."

She grew quiet again and bit her lip. She looked delicate and, for a moment, more than a little sad. He wanted to kiss her. To comfort her. He tried to make eye contact, but she looked away. "I think we should be getting back." She gave the starter rope a yank, and the little Yamaha outboard sprang to life. She pushed the tiller, the boat spun around, and they headed back to the resort.

Chapter 5

AN AMERICAN

Several kilometers away in the city, Sergeant Cutro was sitting at his gray metal desk in the El Nido police station, peering at his computer screen. He had punched in the name "Kincaid." The results were unsatisfying. A furniture company, a restaurant, several doctors and dentists, but no wisecracking American gunman. His phone rang.

"Cutro. My office."

The captain was not a large man, but he wasn't small either. A stocky, hardened veteran of police work, Jaime Belka was known to his officers as a tough, no-nonsense authoritarian. Dressed in a white shirt, black tie, and a dark, cheap suit worn slick at the elbows and knees, he was pacing between a bank of beige file cabinets and the glass door when Cutro walked in. The air in the room was thick with smoke curling from a stubby cigar clenched between the captain's teeth.

"There was a shooting out at Oceania last night."

"Yes, sir. We believe the subjects were terrorists."

"Who got shot?"

"The terrorists. There were three of them. All dead."

"All three? Who killed them?"

"An American. He calls himself Kincaid."

"Why haven't I seen your report?" Belka demanded.

"I'm still working on it, sir. There are some details I haven't nailed down yet." Cutro flipped open a small notebook and recounted the events as he understood them, including his interview with Kincaid.

"What do we know about this Kincaid? What's his first name?

"Unknown, sir."

"Unknown? It had to be on his passport."

"I'm afraid I neglected to get it."

The captain grunted. "What did you get?"

"He's a big man. Dangerous looking, probably military or ex-military. Dark hair, in his thirties or early fourties. Good with a gun and very cocky. We have his weapon, a Browning. I'm guessing it's government issue. I'm waiting on the ballistic report."

"Chance Kincaid."

"Sir?"

"Sounds like Chance Kincaid."

"Who is Chance Kincaid, sir?"

Belka was getting impatient. He bellowed, "That's your job, Cutro. Find out. Get out of my office and do your research."

Cutro hurried toward the door. The captain called out behind him, "And get me that report."

Sergeant Cutro's phone was ringing as he sat heavily in his thinly padded desk chair. "Cutro."

It was the lab. "Sergeant, just wanted to let you know the gun you brought us was not the weapon that was used in that shooting last night."

"You ran the ballistics already? That was fast."

"No need to test it, sir."

EE Sample

"Why is that?"

"This is a government issue 9mm Browning."

"So?"

"All three victims were shot with a .45."

Cutro's face reddened. He realized he had been had, and he didn't like it. He thanked the tech, swiveled in his chair, and rolled up to his computer. He typed "Chance Kincaid" and hit return. A picture of the man he had questioned the night before popped up on the screen. Chance Kincaid enlisted in the American army in 1997. He went to paratrooper school and later became a Ranger. Served in Iraq and Afghanistan. He trained as a sniper before being honorably discharged as a warrant officer in 2008. Since then, he had worked for several paramilitary companies or "security firms" around the world. His current whereabouts were unknown.

Cutro did know Kincaid's whereabouts. If he hadn't skipped yet.

Kincaid hadn't skipped.

At that same moment, Lucia was skillfully guiding her little boat up to his cottage. She reversed the motor and used it as a brake to stop precisely at the foot of the ladder to the veranda. Kincaid stood at the bow and grabbed the ladder to steady himself and hold off the skiff.

"It was an amazing afternoon, Lucia. Thank you."

"It was a pleasure." She didn't move but stayed seated at the stern. The outboard idled quietly as the craft bounced on its own wake.

Kincaid was struggling to keep hold of the ladder. "Maybe we can do this again sometime," he said artlessly.

She beamed up at him and said, "Yes, let's."

He stepped onto the ladder and climbed to the veranda.

Lucia reversed the motor, and the boat pirouetted on its stern. "Have a good evening," she called before speeding off toward the clubhouse.

It was late afternoon. Kincaid thought about his trip to the Secret Lagoon with Lucia as he sat at the teak writing desk and disassembled his pistol for cleaning. It had been fired several times and exposed to the salt air since he had last cleaned and oiled it. He had learned from experience that a gun needed constant attention to remain reliable. Not unlike most of the women he had known. So, what about this woman, Lucia? She was attractive enough and a very pleasant companion, although she had been sending mixed messages all afternoon. Or was that wishful thinking on his part or maybe just his imagination? He recollected their conversation, including the account of her grim past, and wondered what her game really was.

His thoughts returned to the British ambassador and the events of last night. Was he the random subject of a kidnapping because he was a Westerner, or was he the specific target of terrorists? If it were the latter, how did they know precisely where he was? And who, exactly, were the kidnappers? These questions needed answers and soon. He figured he was in for more trouble from these guys, whoever they were. After all, he had dispatched three of their number. It was inconceivable that the three dead men had acted alone. The driver of the boat had lived to tell the tale, and somebody somewhere was going to be pissed. He wanted to talk to the ambassador and his girlfriend, and he hoped the police knew something more about the terrorists and were going to be a helpful resource rather than an interference.

Chapter 6

JOLO

M eanwhile, an old, battered Toyota Land Cruiser was lumbering north on the Taytay-El Nido Highway. Land Cruisers were large, rugged SUVs often used by UN forces in the Middle East and North Africa. This one was black except around the edges where it had oxidized to a rusty red. It had a dented left fender and was missing the front grill. It was pulling a long, flat-bottomed boat sporting a large outboard motor and five bullet holes in the stern. They were in a neat cluster just above where the waterline would be.

At the wheel was a dark-skinned man in his twenties with black hair and a matching goatee. He was wearing desert camo pants and a white T-shirt with broad, green stripes. A black shemagh was draped loosely around his head and covered part of his face. He was called Jolo because he came from the volcanic island of that name. Jolo had spent several hours last night finding the boat launch and loading the green aluminum boat onto its trailer. He had slept in the back of the Toyota until the heat of the sun made it too hot to sleep. Now, he was reluctantly returning to the camp of the Philippine Islamic Separatist Front. As the only survivor of last night's failed mission, he knew he was going to face harsh disciplinary action, but if he ran, they would find him and probably kill him. He had obeyed orders and stayed with the boat but being the lone survivor of a battle was never viewed as honorable. Orders or no orders, he was going to be perceived as a coward and a disgrace. His only hope was to go back and beg for mercy. It was a calculated risk.

He drove slowly along the highway until he came to an obscure turnoff and carefully negotiated the right turn onto a narrow dirt road. A few kilometers down, he left the road and turned right again through a stand of pine trees. He drove past two sentries and into a modest encampment of the PISF. This particular unit was comprised of about forty men. They had no uniforms but wore whatever they happened to own. Combat boots, flip flops, basketball shorts, jeans, Pink Floyd T-shirts, BDUs, you name it.

Jolo climbed out of the truck and was immediately escorted into a military-style, olive-green tent that served as the HQ. He was met by several men standing around a makeshift table. Seated at the table was Mohamed el-Fasil, the company commander. Slightly older than Jolo, he was of medium build and wore woodland camo pants, a green field tunic, and a black bandana tied low around his forehead. Several ammo pouches and a walkie-talkie hung from military webbing strapped across his chest. A Russian AK-47 was slung over the back of his chair. He was unsmiling as he stood. "Come in, Jolo." His voice was smooth as honey but sounded threatening just the same. "Tell us about the mission last night. Where are the others?" He peered through the group mockingly.

"I'm afraid the news is not good."

"Do you think I don't know that you fool? Do you think we don't listen to the news here?" el-Fasil stormed.

"Yes. Forgive me."

"Forgive you? I lost three men last night, yet you come back unscathed and ask forgiveness?"

"There was nothing I could do, sir. I was told to stay with the boat."

"You sat in the boat while the others were killed by one man?" el-Fasil's fists were clenched, and he stared at the man through cold, unblinking eyes. "Could you not help them?"

"I did not think I could, sir." He realized he had greatly miscalculated the risk of returning. The face glaring at him across the table evinced no mercy.

"Then what good are you to me? We are all expected to sacrifice for the cause, not cower in a boat while others are killed. It was a simple task, Jolo—go and get a man who wants to be captured. A child should have been able to accomplish this."

"We weren't expecting resistance, sir, but a man came from out of nowhere. He killed them all in seconds. What could I have done?" Tears welled in Jolo's eyes. He wiped his sleeve across them.

"You should have left the boat and helped your brothers. You bring shame on us all."

el-Fasil turned to one of his lieutenants. "This man disgusts me. Take him. You know what to do with him."

"No, please," Jolo pleaded. "I beg for your mercy, please. My wife. Who will take care of my wife?" He sobbed.

"We will take care of her."

Jolo was sobbing now. He was dragged into the trees and behind a stand of bushes where he was unceremoniously shot in the head. They left him there as a warning to any others who might hesitate to die for Allah and the cause.

el-Fasil heard the single gunshot. He sternly said, "We must find this American, and we must kill him."

Chapter 7

QUESTIONS

At the police station in El Nido, Sergeant Cutro carried his laptop to the door of the captain's office. He knocked and heard a gruff voice call, "Come in."

He held the screen over the desk to show his boss the results of his search. Belka took it from him. There was a link to an old issue of a paramilitary magazine. In it was an article about Chance Kincaid that read in part:

> Kincaid is a serious man, steeled by experience and tempered in battle. He sees everything in black and white. For him, there are no shades of gray. ...Kincaid possesses no discernable weakness.

"I thought that might be the guy," said Belka. "He was out here during the Pork Barrel Scandal, although it wasn't exactly clear who he was working for. I always figured he was one of Marcos' men."

"His background explains a lot," Cutro said. "A Special Forces officer in the US army and now a mercenary soldier. Just another day at the office for a man like that."

"Yeah, well, he may have bit off more than he can chew this time. Did you find out who the bad guys were?"

"The people at the morgue think they are PISF."

"That's what I was afraid of."

"It could be worse."

"How so?"

"They could've been Abu Sayyaf."

"Go back out there and pick him up."

"Do we have enough to charge him?" Cutro seemed skeptical.

"Think of something, Sergeant. Charge him with murder, illegal possession of a firearm, anything. It's for his own good, or else he'll be dead by tomorrow morning, and we'll have even more paperwork to deal with."

At Oceania Resort, Kincaid decided to check on the British ambassador. It turned out that the ambassador's cottage was only two doors down from his. He knocked on the large double doors of Cottage 6.

The blonde who had identified herself as the ambassador's travel companion opened the door. She was wearing a bikini or something that might pass as a bikini somewhere. It consisted of three small triangles of maroon material held together with lots of orange string. Her hair was piled on the top of her head and pinned in a wild bundle.

"Hello, Ms. Kettering."

"Come in, ace. I guess you want to talk to the ambassador."

"That was the original idea." He tried not to stare as she turned and waved for him to follow her. From behind, she was all golden skin and orange string.

She led him through the main room of the cottage. It looked similar to his own. Same layout, same furnishings, different color scheme. Mostly greens and grays. She stopped at the triple sliding doors to the veranda, motioned like a model on a game show, and said simply, "He's right out here." Then she disappeared down the short hallway.

Ambassador Grey was an older man, probably in his seventies. He looked reasonably fit if a little paunchy. About a hundred and eighty pounds and a little under six feet. He was wearing a white terrycloth robe, the kind they have in expensive hotels, and he was reclining comfortably on a wooden chaise lounge with a thick, green cushion. His hair was thin and gray, almost white. Kincaid figured there was probably more hair on his chest than his head. He was holding a champagne glass in his right hand. "Welcome, sir. Would you care for some champagne?"

"No, thank you."

"Something stronger? Scotch, perhaps?"

"Scotch would be nice. Thanks."

The ambassador called out, "Lisa, please bring our guest a glass of scotch." He looked up. "You're Mr. Kincaid. Am I right?"

Kincaid nodded. "You had quite a night last night."

"Quite right. If not for you, I'd probably be dead by now."

"Not likely. They probably wanted you for ransom money. They would have demanded the British government give them a couple of million, but if they didn't get it, they would have beheaded you and put the video on the internet."

Grey rubbed his neck gingerly. "In any case, I owe you my life, and I'm truly grateful."

Kincaid nodded again, as if to say *you're welcome.*

Lisa Kittering appeared at the door with a glass in her hand. She looked annoyed. "I hope neat is okay. We're out of ice."

"Neat is perfect." He looked her up and down. He couldn't help himself. Her body was amazing, and it was definitely on display. He walked over to her and took the glass from her hand. She spun around and went back inside.

The ambassador saw how Kincaid had ogled the girl. He was pleased. He had met her at a government function in London, and Grey was mildly surprised that she had shown an interest in him. He was much older than her, but then again, he still had the same charm that had always attracted beautiful women. The difference was that now all he could use a woman for was arm candy. "Why don't you come out and join us, darling? Take some sun."

"It's too late to get sun, and I'm bored. You're boring." She yelled from somewhere inside the cottage. She sounded like a petulant child. "Why don't you take me somewhere?"

"We are somewhere," Grey yelled back. He winked at Kincaid and shrugged his shoulders. He suddenly realized he hadn't invited his guest to sit. "Where are my manners? Won't you please have a seat?"

Kincaid grabbed a wicker chair from the table and slid it toward Grey. It left thin white scratches in the terra-cotta tile. A cooling breeze was blowing in from the sea. The scent of salt air mixed with the aroma of the scotch as he took a long draught from his glass. It had the smooth, sweet taste of a fine whisky. "I'd like to ask you a few questions, if it isn't an imposition."

"Not at all," said the ambassador.

"Something doesn't add up. Who knew you were coming here?"

"Just my secretary and, I guess, the travel agent."

"What about your girlfriend?"

"Lisa? Of course, but I assure you, she is above suspicion."

"Do you trust your secretary?"

"Implicitly. She's been with me for ages. Do you think the travel agent tipped someone off? I'm quite well known in Britain, you see."

"It's a possibility, but how did the kidnappers know you would be in the dining room?"

"I suppose they assumed. It was the dinner hour, after all, or maybe it was just coincidence."

"I don't believe in coincidences. Besides, the operation was too well planned to have to depend on coincidence."

A look of panic crossed Grey's face. "You don't suppose they'll try again, do you?"

"Probably." He paused. "Unless you were just a random tourist. The first person they could grab."

"That must be it. I was just in the wrong place at the right time." He looked somewhat relieved, but Kincaid couldn't help but wonder, *shouldn't he and his girlfriend be more upset after such a narrow escape?*

The sun was setting as Kincaid walked back to his own cottage. He went inside to the kitchen and picked up the wine bottle from the night before. It had exactly one swallow left in it. He drained it, plopped across the bed, and fell asleep. When he woke, the room was dark. His first thought was of the ambassador's scotch. One drink had been just enough to make him want more. He called room service. "Send me over a bottle of scotch."

"What brand would you like, sir?" the woman asked politely.

He didn't know anything about scotch. It wasn't his usual drink. "Surprise me, but make sure it's top shelf."

"Certainly, sir. Will there be anything else?"

"Yeah, two club sandwiches." *One for now and one for later.*

"Right away, sir."

A quarter hour later, Ricky knocked on the door with his dinner. "How are you this evening, Mr. Kincaid?" He grabbed a furtive look around the cottage.

"I'm good, Ricky. Put the tray on the table outside, will you?" He motioned toward the veranda.

The bellhop did as he was instructed. Kincaid slipped a five-dollar bill into his palm and walked toward the door. He opened it, signaling the boy to leave. "Thanks, kid."

Ricky kept glancing around the room. He was wondering who the second sandwich was for. "Enjoy your sandwiches, sir."

"I'm sure I will. Goodnight, Ricky."

As soon as he was alone, Kincaid went outside to the table and poured himself a glass of the scotch. The label said it was Glenlivet, distilled in the Scottish parish of the same name. It tasted good with his club sandwich. He felt the warm breeze on his face and caught the salty, poignant scent of the sea out beyond the breakwater. Several kilometers farther out, chain lightning clawed at the ebony sky. The spectacle took him back to other shores and other times. Harder times. Afghanistan, Iraq, the Middle East, North Africa. Kincaid had been pretty much everywhere there was armed conflict. He pondered how he had come to be a soldier of fortune and why fate had spared him his life and steered him to this place. His perilous, frenetic line of work seldom allowed him time to pause and appreciate the beauty of his surroundings, but here he was, and it felt good. He swirled the rich, amber liquid in his glass. For the moment, there were no wars to fight, no covert missions to effect, just a premium single malt that, like him, was a long way from home. It had been an interesting day.

But his day wasn't over just yet. As he contemplated all these things, a loud rap on his door jolted him from his reverie. "Who is it?" he shouted.

From outside, Cutro shouted sharply, "The police. Open up."

Kincaid put down his glass, sauntered to the door, and opened it. Cutro and the two big cops from last night were standing there. They were trying to look menacing.

Kincaid exhaled a long, loud breath. "What now?"

"We need to talk. Can we come inside?" The big cops edged closer to the door.

"I'd just as soon you didn't. What's on your mind?"

Cutro stiffened but stood where he was. "A couple of things. First, you lied to me and made me look like a fool."

Kincaid knew the answer to his next question before he asked it. "How did I do that?"

"That gun you gave me wasn't yours."

"No, it wasn't, but it was evidence. I took it off one of the dead guys. Did you get any prints off it?" Even in the dim porch light, he could see a vein pulsing in Cutro's brow.

"You know I didn't, asshole. It was handled by a dozen guys by the time it got to the lab. Why did you tell me it was yours? That's withholding evidence, which is illegal. I'm taking you in." He took a step back and the two big guys filled the doorway. The menacing act was becoming more convincing.

"Withholding evidence? You just said I gave you the gun."

"Are you coming peacefully, or do you want to go the hard way?"

Kincaid looked at Cutro and his deputies. He could probably take them, but then what? "I'm under arrest?"

"Not yet. The captain wants to ask you some questions."

"All right let me get my phone. I may need to call a lawyer."

"While you're at it, you can bring me your gun."

There was no use arguing. Kincaid would take it up with the captain.

Chapter 8

THE POLICE STATION

C utro's launch was waiting at the dock. It was a thirty-minute boat ride across a small bay and a fifteen-minute drive to El Nido in an unmarked Crown Victoria. The car probably had left the factory in the color Ford called "Norsea Blue" but years in the sun and salt air had faded it to a steely gray. It must have had a hundred thousand miles on it. Kincaid sat in the back with the cop he had called Fat Boy. The cloth seat was stained and dirty. Fat Boy took up most of it, so he sat leaning against the left-hand door behind Cutro.

The police station in El Nido was a white, two-story building trimmed in blue. It was desperately in need of a paint job. The blue was chipping off the metal roof, leaving large spots of gray primer peering through. Above the door, neat lettering read El Nido Municipal Police Station. The station was bordered by a six-foot, chain-link fence stretched between blue concrete posts. Inside, it looked like any small-town police station. There were four wooden desks topped with computers and strewn with newspapers, notebooks, and random ephemera. Only one of the desks was occupied. A gaunt policeman of about forty was talking on the phone. Two rows of plastic chairs were lined up in front of the back wall. To the left there were two wooden doors inset with pebbled glass. One of them sported gold lettering that read Captain Jaime Belka. That was the door Kincaid and Cutro entered. The captain was smoking a stubby cigar and had his feet on his desk. Belka stood and leaned across to shake Kincaid's hand. Pleasantries were exchanged, then the captain got down to business. The tip of his cigar glowed bright orange before he blew a cloud of blue smoke into the already stale air. His eyes narrowed as he leaned across his cluttered desk. "Tell me in your own words what happened out at the Oceania."

Kincaid wondered who else's words he could possibly use but patiently recounted the events leading up to and including the shooting of the three suspected terrorists.

Belka listened in silence, then asked, "How is it that you just happened to be there and were able to kill three men with AK-47s without incurring any injuries yourself?"

"Just lucky, I guess."

"Aren't you Chance Kincaid, the hired soldier who was here working for Aquino during the Pork Barrel Scandal?"

"I'm not at liberty to discuss that."

"But you are a mercenary." He spit out the word *mercenary* like it was a bad taste in his mouth.

"I prefer security professional, but you can call me what you will."

"I don't suppose you want to tell me who you are working for right now?"

"I'm presently on vacation, so I'm not working for anyone."

"That's good, because I'm going to hold you here for a few days."

"Like hell you are," Kincaid protested without raising his voice. "On what charge?"

"Protective custody or, if you prefer, illegal possession of a firearm or suspicion of murder. Take your pick."

"That's out of the question. I'm not staying here, and if you try to hold me, I'll make a couple of phone calls and be out in five minutes. I have contacts in Manila. You can explain it to them." This was strictly a bluff. If he'd ever had friends in the government, they were probably long gone by now, but Belka didn't know that.

The captain stared and rubbed his chin for a long moment like he was deliberating with himself. He shifted the cigar from the right corner of his mouth to the left. "I'm going to let you go for now" he said, "but don't try to leave here without checking with us first."

"That's very generous of you," Kincaid said sarcastically, "but you have my gun, and I want it back."

"I'm afraid I can't do that. You are not permitted to have firearms in the Philippines."

"Tell that to the people who are killing your citizens and kidnapping tourists. Besides, you've probably heard of Resolution 3228. The exception for security personnel."

"You don't qualify as security personnel under that law, and you know it."

"I damn well was security the other night. Doing your job, actually. If I hadn't been armed, you would have lost a foreign dignitary to kidnappers, and who knows how many people would have been killed. That would have sparked an international incident, you can be damned sure of that. And like you said, I may be in danger myself. I sure don't trust you to protect me."

"He does have a point there, Captain," Cutro said.

Belka considered his options for several minutes. "All right. I'll let you have your pistol, but I'd advise you to watch your ass. And, if there is any more killing, you'd better not be involved. Stay out of things that don't concern you. Understand?"

Kincaid ignored the question. "Who's going to give me a ride back to the resort?"

The captain said nothing, but Cutro offered, "If you give me a few minutes, I'll take you back."

"Thanks, Cutro. I'm beginning to like you." He stepped through the captain's door and saw a young, fair-haired woman sitting on one of the plastic chairs. It was the girl he'd met on the plane, and she looked worried.

As he approached, she stood. "Mr. Kincaid?"

"Hi. I remember you from the airplane. I don't think I got your name." He wondered why she was there.

"I'm sorry. I'm Jillian. Jillian Welde."

"So, Jillian Welde, what brings you to the police station?" She was more attractive than he remembered. Her hair was several shades of honey-brown and blond. It spilled onto the shoulders of a white knit shirt with a scooped neck. She was wearing a short, tight skirt. It was tawny tan with six gold buttons in two vertical columns, one over each sinewy leg.

"I read about what happened at Oceania Resort. It was in today's paper, so I came here looking for you."

"You thought I'd be locked up."

"Actually, I'm surprised you're not."

"And you came to bail me out?"

"I thought you were locked up, and I would have bailed you out if I had to. I need your help."

"Thanks, lady, but sorry. I'm through playing Boy Scout. I've got troubles of my own." Kincaid walked past her and headed for the door. She followed him out to the sidewalk.

"I can pay," she persisted. "Will you at least listen?"

"Okay but make it snappy. I'm meeting the sergeant for my ride back to the resort, and I doubt he'll wait for me."

"Remember I told you my father lives here? He was flying to Manila, but he's gone missing."

"You don't need me. Call the airline and see if he made the flight."

"He didn't fly commercial. He has a helicopter."

"So, you were really here talking to the police. Good. Sounds like a job for them."

"They won't do anything. He hasn't been gone long enough to be considered missing, I guess."

'Did you check with the airport in Manila?"

"Yes, but they don't know anything. He didn't file a flight plan. The plant foreman says he never does."

"The plant foreman?"

"Yes. As I told you on the plane, he has a computer factory."

"What else does the plant foreman say?"

"He said not to worry. Dad stays in Manila, sometimes for days."

Cutro pulled up to the curb outside the fence and honked.

"Well, there you go. Nothing to worry about. He does it all the time. He'll probably be back in a couple of days." Kincaid started toward the Crown Vic.

Jillian grabbed his arm. "Please" she said, "something is wrong. I can feel it. He wouldn't have stayed gone this time. He knew I was coming. We were both looking forward to spending some time together."

"Look, I can't help you, I'm just a guy on holiday. There's nothing I can do for you."

"You're not just some guy" she insisted, "Anyone can see that, and I need help. Help from a man like you." She was still holding his arm. Her voice softened but her grip tightened. Cutro honked the horn again. He was clearly getting impatient.

Kincaid laughed. *How could she know what kind of man I am?* "I've got to go. This cop's my only way back."

She leaned against his arm. He could feel her warm breath on his neck. "Come home with me. We can talk about it. You'll find I can be very persuasive."

He believed her. Besides, what else did he have to do? He went to Cutro's old Ford, bent over, and stuck his head in the window. "Thanks, officer, but I guess I won't be going back tonight after all."

Chapter 9

THE WELDE HOUSE

cross the parking lot, Jillian slid behind the wheel of a white Toyota Camry and clicked the passenger door unlocked for Kincaid. It was the typical rental car—four doors and cloth seats that smelled of cigarettes and upholstery cleaner. They navigated the narrow Calle Real and turned onto Rizal Street, passing small shops and bars. The street itself was narrow. Barely wide enough for two cars, it was primarily travelled by scooter or on foot. Tonight, it was mostly empty and silent. Kincaid had buzzed his window down and was listening to the hiss of the little sedan's tires on the concrete. Rizal Street eventually became the Taytay-El Nido National Highway.

Jillian increased her speed, and soon he could see the beach on his right. As they came around a sharp curve, they turned into an obscure, sandy driveway. There was a cement wall and a gate, which Jillian opened with the small remote she had in her purse. Beyond the wall was a swimming pool beside a two-story stucco house painted white. The bottom floor consisted of a garage on the back end and living space on the front. An old jeep occupied a third of the garage. Its faded, bronze paint was scratched and abraded here and there, testament to a life of arduous duty. Apart from the jeep, the garage was empty except for a couple of surfboards and a neglected wave runner.

Concrete steps led up to a porch that ran the length of the main part of the house. From there, the stairs continued to the rooftop, half of which was covered. The rest was an expansive cement deck. A small, orange windsock fluttering from a tall pole told Kincaid the deck was a helipad.

Jillian parked in front of the garage, and he followed her up the stairs. The view was breathtaking, even in the dark. The property was on a private beach. There must have been a million flickering bright stars in the sky, each one reflected on the rolling, ebony waves. The wind whipped around them, blowing errant strands of the woman's hair against his bare arm, a subtle hint of the power of the sea. As Kincaid stood mesmerized, Jillian moved to the door and slipped her key into the lock. He stepped inside behind her as she switched on the lights to illuminate an expansive room.

Two large Persian rugs covered patches of a glossy koa floor. Rattan sofas and chairs were arranged around them to form two intimate seating areas. The rest of the room was sparsely furnished except for a wet bar to the right of the door and an imposing grand piano standing in the far corner. It was situated so that the pianist could look out onto the beach while sitting at the keyboard. The walls were covered with art and photographs. The photos were of a family, presumably the Weldes. In one was an attractive, blonde woman and a tan, wiry man about five feet ten standing behind two girls. They were all smiling the way families do when the photographer prompts them to say "cheese." One of the girls was definitely Jillian. Besides the photographs, there were three large paintings signed by Gauguin. They could have been originals, but Kincaid didn't know anything about art. Two antique rifles were centered over the windows that made up the front wall.

"This is my father's house," Jillian said.

"A man of wealth and taste."

"I suppose you could say that."

"Mick said it first."

Jillian didn't smile. "Something has happened to him, Mr. Kincaid, I just know it."

"What kind of something?"

"I don't know. He may have crashed his helicopter or been kidnapped or...I don't know." Her voice trailed off like she suddenly got lost in thought. She collapsed on one of the wicker sofas. He sat down beside her.

"Does your mother or sister have any ideas about where he could be?"

"He lives here alone."

"Oh?"

"He was stationed at Clark when he was in the air force. By the time he was discharged, he had fallen in love with the islands. He wanted to buy this house and stay here permanently, but my mother hated the Philippines and wanted to move back to the States. They argued about it for months and eventually split up. I left with my mother, and my sister stayed here."

"Where's your sister now?"

"Allison. She's studying psychology at Durham University."

"When was the last time you saw them?"

"When I graduated high school, I came to live with them for a while. That was six years ago. Things were a little tense then. I guess that's because I wanted to be on my own, but I was accepted to Yale, so I moved back to Connecticut. The last time I saw my dad was two years ago. We all met at my sister's apartment in London. He was there on business, but we saw the sights and had a wonderful time. I promised to come here to visit, and we'd been making plans ever since. He bought me a plane ticket in August. I just now was able to get away. There's no way he would have missed my return."

"You said he has a helicopter. Like a Bell helicopter? What kind of business is he in?"

"It's a Eurocopter, I think. I only flew with him once. It's pretty big. As I said, he has a technology company that makes motherboards and things for computers. He uses the helicopter to fly orders to Manila. From there, they go all over the world."

Kincaid was starting to get interested. "Okay. Who are his customers?"

"People who build computers, I guess."

"Where is his factory?"

"I'll take you there tomorrow."

He gazed at her lissome form as she leaned into the thick, ivory cushion of the sofa. The soft light of the lamp behind her was diffused by her windblown hair, imbuing her with an angelic aura. Kincaid was reminded why he had come out here with her.

"It's only midnight now. What are we going to do until tomorrow?"

"What do you want to do, Mr. Kincaid?" Her expression shifted from troubled to tantalizing.

"First of all, you can stop calling me mister."

"I don't know your first name."

"It's Chance, but Kincaid is fine. I got used to being called by my last name in the army."

"All right. Kincaid." Jillian abruptly jumped to her feet. "How about a drink? We have whiskey, vodka, wine. Whatever you want."

"I'll have what you're having."

"There are some interesting bottles of red wine here." She crossed behind him.

"Sounds fine."

She selected a bottle of Beaujolais from the wine rack behind the marble-topped bar and struggled to open it. Kincaid watched her fumble with the corkscrew. It was a walnut-handled sommelier's type, not the kind women buy at the liquor store. He took it from her and read the label on the bottle. Chateau de Beauregard. "This is a fine wine; we should let it breathe." he said. She poured two glasses and handed him one. "Who has that kind of time?" She laughed.

He followed her back to the sofa. It took less than an hour for them to finish the bottle. He watched as she wedged herself against the cushions and closed her eyes, lulled by the susurration of the waves breaking on the shore outside. All her stress was melting away as she slipped into a deep sleep.

Kincaid got up, took off his shoes, and wandered around the room. There was mail on a small end table. He looked through the thin stack. Mostly bills. There was one envelope addressed by hand to James Welde. The crudely scrawled return address was a post office box on Siquijor Island, wherever that was. He searched a small chest near the piano. Some sheet music. Nothing of interest.

He walked down a long hall that opened into the back of the room. There was a kitchen on the right. A big marble island with a double stainless steel sink stood in the middle of the room. There were four stools opposite the sink, and the whole thing was flanked by a cadre of commercial appliances. A large gas stove like the kind you'd see in a fine restaurant took up half a wall. The refrigerator was six feet tall and had glass doors that revealed a meager assortment of foodstuffs and several bottles of beer and white wine. The walls were covered by rich mahogany cabinets.

On the left side of the hall were two identical bedrooms. They looked like guest rooms. Both were neat and tidy, except the second one had an open suitcase lying on an unmade bed. He felt underneath the clothes in the suitcase, trying not to disturb its contents. Lingerie and other women's apparel. Obviously, Jillian's. He opened the closet door. Dresses and a jacket. At the end of the hall was what must have been the master bedroom. A large bank of windows looked out over the beach. He stood for a moment, again taken by the view. The white sand was sparkling like a bed of sequins in the bright moonlight. Gentle waves were grasping in vain at the shore before being pulled back into the vastness of the sea. Kincaid turned back to searching the room, but this time he was much more thorough. There was a massive mahogany dresser. One of the three larger drawers contained a Smith & Wesson .38 revolver. Snub nose, for carrying in a pocket or a boot. Nothing else of note. There were three small drawers that comprised the top row. He pulled them all the way out. There was a roll of cash in one of them. Maybe a few hundred dollars. A slip of paper was taped to the back end of the same drawer. A number that could have been a bank account number was printed on it. Kincaid replaced the cash, tucked the paper into his pocket, and slid the drawer back into its slot. He walked into a large closet. Behind a tangle of hanging garments were five rifles leaning against the back wall, all military-grade automatics. Two M16s, a Russian SV-98, and two Heckler & Koch MP5s. But the weapon that chilled his blood was a Barrett M95 .50 caliber rifle. It was in a hard case that bore the logo of Barrett Firearms, the little Tennessee company that made the most lethal shoulder-fired weapon in the world. Six boxes of blacktip, armor-piercing shells. Several boxes of 9 mm cartridges and tracer rounds were stacked on top of the case. When he opened the lid, Kincaid could hardly believe his eyes. The big sniper rifle looked as though it had never been fired. In addition to the guns were several pounds of PE4 plastic explosive with detonators, primers, and detonator switches. Mr. Welde's interests evidently ran to activities more stimulating than desktop computing.

In the living room, Jillian was beginning to stir. "Kincaid?" She started down the hall. "Kincaid, where are you?"

Kincaid put the Barrett back in its case then ducked into the master bath and flushed the toilet before emerging into the hall. "Just using the bathroom. How are you feeling?"

She rubbed her eyes, trying to adjust to the dim light. "I must have passed out. I'm sorry."

"It's fine, really. I was enjoying watching you sleep."

Jillian took his hand and led him into the guest room with the suitcase. She swept it onto the floor with her arm and sprawled on the bed. She was still dressed, but her skirt was riding up her tanned thighs. Kincaid took off her shoes and lay down beside her. He pulled the sheet over her shoulders, and she sighed contentedly as she drifted back to sleep. He put his hands behind his head, listening to her breathe, and wondered what her father was up to.

Chapter 10

31 OCTOBER

Kincaid opened his eyes. The sun cast its soft, golden glow over his face, gradually bringing the room into focus. It took a moment to remember where he was. He tossed his arm toward Jillian's side of the bed. It was vacant. He looked around the room for her, but she was gone. A sweet aroma was drifting from the direction of the kitchen. He slid off the bed and padded down the hall. She was standing over the stove with a spatula in her hand. She had taken off her skirt, and turquoise panties were peeking from beneath her white top.

"Good morning, sleepyhead," she teased. "Would you like some pancakes?"

"Sure. They smell delicious." He walked over to her and tried to hug her from behind, but she shrugged him off and went for the coffee pot. She poured two cups and handed one to him. It was just the way he liked it: strong and black. Jillian plated three pancakes for him and one for herself. There was maple syrup and butter on the island along with silverware. Kincaid sat on one of the stools and slathered on the butter before pouring a generous helping of syrup on his stack. He was ravenous but waited until Jillian had taken her first bite before digging in himself. After they had finished the pancakes and Kincaid had drunk his third cup of coffee, she announced that she was going to shower in one of the guest bathrooms.

"You can use the master bath if you like, and feel free to take some of dad's clothes from his closet." She looked him up and down. "If they fit."

He already knew her father's clothes would be way too small for him, but he didn't say it. Nothing in that closet would accommodate his six foot two, two-hundred-pound physique. "Okay. Meet you back here in thirty minutes."

He showered and put his own clothes back on. A half hour later, they were out the door and heading north in the Toyota. Thirty minutes after that, Jillian parked the car in front of a long, low, nondescript building on the outskirts of El Nido. The parking lot was big enough for maybe fifty cars, but only eleven spaces were occupied. A chain-link fence separated the lot from the street. There was a concrete helipad behind the fence, and three cargo trucks were parked alongside it. There was probably a loading dock on the back of the structure. The steel front door bore a small sign reading Welde Technologies.

Jillian rang the bell. No answer. She rang again, and a voice came over an intercom set in the wall. "Can I help you?"

"It's Jillian Welde."

A buzzer sounded. She pulled the door open. Inside was a capacious room with a concrete floor. It was immaculately clean and uncluttered. Large lights were suspended from the trusses that supported the corrugated metal roof, casting pools of light on rows of long tables. The tables were in neat, straight lines and set up as soldering stations. Soldering irons, spools of solder, and sponges were placed four to a table. Large, lighted magnifying glasses were mounted at each station. Eight Filipinas worked at four of the tables, the rest were unused. The workers were soldering components to green circuit boards and placing the completed boards into cardboard boxes that were stacked in the aisles. Two young Filipinos waited to shuffle the full boxes from the tables to the loading dock on the back end of the building. No one was talking. Despite a six-foot fan set high into the far end of the room, the heat was formidable.

To the left of the front door, a concrete block wall stretched the width of the structure. It was windowless, but there were three metal doors spaced evenly along its span. Steel stairs led up to what appeared to be an office above the wall. The office had one door and a large glass window overlooking the floor of the plant. A man was descending the stairs, his boots on the steel steps echoing off the concrete walls. He was short and stocky, wearing dark denim jeans and a white, sleeveless, collared shirt. As he drew closer, he appeared to Kincaid to be in his late forties. His face was pockmarked, and his black hair was slicked back, plastered to his head. The name embroidered on his shirt was Marco.

Jillian got right to the point. "Good morning, Marco. Any word from my father?"

"No. I'm sorry, Miss Welde. We have not heard from him, but you shouldn't worry. I'm sure he'll be back soon." Marco's English was good, but his accent was thick. He eyed Kincaid warily.

"This is a friend of mine, Mr. Kincaid."

Marco nodded but said nothing and did not offer to shake hands. He turned back to Jillian. "Is there anything I can do for you?"

"Yes. Mr. Kincaid would like to take a look around while we're here."

"There is nothing else to see besides this." He gestured around the room.

"How about the office?" she asked.

"Ah, senorita, it is only an office like any other one."

"We'd like to see it anyway. I want to find out anything I can about my dad."

"You have seen the office before, Miss Welde. It hasn't changed."

Kincaid was growing impatient with Marco's cagy act. His suspicion deepened. "What's in these rooms down here, Marco?"

"Those are just storage rooms, I'm afraid."

"Let's open them up."

"I don't have the keys for those rooms, sir." Marco shifted nervously from foot to foot.

"Aren't you the manager here?"

"I am, sir."

"You're the plant manager, and you don't have access to the storage rooms?" Kincaid's voice rose. Did Marco think he was that clueless?

Jillian stepped between the two men. "Let's go up to the office and see if we can find the keys, Marco," she said firmly.

They followed a reluctant Marco up the stairs, through the door, and into a small, cluttered office. Stacks of cardboard file boxes flanked a large oak desk. The desk was strewn with papers, books, and a couple of empty pizza boxes. Kincaid opened the top drawer of the desk and sifted through its contents. Then he searched the rest of the desk. No keys. He turned his attention to a pair of metal vertical files standing against the far wall. There was a magnet on the side of one of the cabinets, and a hook on the magnet held a ring of keys. "Maybe this is what we're looking for." He glared at Marco and headed for the stairs with Jillian right behind him. As soon as they left the office, Marco picked up the phone.

Kincaid tried two keys before he found the one that unlocked the first door. The room was completely empty. The same key fit the second door. The second room was filled with cardboard boxes. They were folded flat and wired together in bundles of fifty. There must have been ten thousand boxes but nothing else. The space was filled front to back. The same key didn't fit the lock on the third room. He tried one of the remaining keys, and the lock clicked open. More flattened boxes but not a roomful. Kincaid flipped on the lights to get a better look at the rest of the space. Behind the boxes were two wooden crates, each about four feet long. They were sturdily built and had been marked in grease pencil with handwritten numbers. One of them had a paper shipping label stuck on its side. The addresses had been blacked out. He opened the heavy lid. The crate was empty except for a bed of excelsior, the wood wool used for packing. There were wooden cross members at each end with notches carved at evenly spaced intervals. He opened the other crate. It was the same. But then he noticed something. The smell of oil, or plastic. Kincaid recognized that smell. It was PE4—plastic explosives, aka C4, the same material he had seen in Welde's closet. The size of the crates would be perfect for shipping rifles. He looked at Jillian. "I think we'd better go."

"What is it, Kincaid?"

"I'll tell you on the way."

Marco was standing at the foot of the stairs, glaring at

Kincaid as they made their way to the front door. Kincaid tossed him the keys. "We'll see ourselves out." he said.

When they were on the road back to town, Jillian could stand it no longer. "What is it, Kincaid? What did you see that I didn't?"

"I'll tell you, but you're not going to like it." She stared across the car at him. "Your father is an arms dealer."

"That's ridiculous. He builds computers."

"The plant is running at a fraction of its capacity" he explained. "There was only a fraction of the workforce present today, and they weren't turning out a hell of a lot of product. The trucks weren't running at all. Your father can't possibly be supporting his lifestyle with the profits from that operation."

"Maybe this is the slow season. Maybe they do a lot more business normally. We don't know."

He told her about his discovery in the bedroom closet. He pointed out the suspicious behavior of the plant manager. He explained his theory about the shipping crates and how they had been secreted in the storage room that Marco hadn't wanted them to see. He made a convincing argument.

But Jillian pushed back. "As far as the guns in my father's closet, he has always had guns, and he taught us all to shoot. He was in the military, for God's sake. We used to go target shooting all the time. He wanted to make sure we were all good shots. How can you be sure what was in those crates? Couldn't it have been golf clubs or something?"

"Listen, honey, I've been in enough war zones to know what plastic explosive smells like, and I've been in enough combat to know rifle crates when I see them. The guns in your daddy's closet? Those aren't target rifles except one of them, and it was made to shoot one target only. A man."

Jillian listened as he laid it all out for her, although she didn't want to believe it. Her stomach knotted up and she clasped her arms around herself. "If Dad is mixed up in something like that, he could be in serious danger. That would explain why I haven't heard from him."

Kincaid heard the alarm in her voice and tried to reassure her. Maybe he had said too much. "Don't jump to conclusions, Jillian. We don't know anything for certain yet. Besides, even if he is doing something illegal, it doesn't mean he's in trouble."

He wondered if she was buying it. He sure wasn't.

"What do we do now?"

"I need to go back to the resort. I want to make a few phone calls. I may still have a few friends out here who could help us. And besides, I need some fresh clothes."

"Then I'm coming with you."

"No, you're not. You need to be at your father's house in case he comes home."

"Does your phone even work here? I only have service about half the time."

"I have a satellite phone. It works anywhere on the planet. Give me your number, and I'll call you later."

There was no point arguing with him. He had an answer for everything. So, she drove him to the docks downtown where he could catch the ferry back to Oceania. They exchanged phone numbers, and he kissed her cheek before jumping out of the car. The next ferry was due to leave in ten minutes.

Chapter 11

A MURDER MOST FOUL

The moment he stepped off the ferry at Oceania Resort, Kincaid knew something was wrong. The dock was deserted. There was a strange stillness in the air as he walked up the pier toward the clubhouse. Why was no one around? He hoped Lucia was on duty at the front desk. He wanted to find out what, if anything, had been going on in his absence. But he never got to the lobby. Halfway there, he spotted an ambulance in the parking lot. Its back doors were open. He looked to his left and saw a small crowd gathered at the end of the boardwalk to the cottages. They were restrained there by a stretch of yellow police tape. Several of El Nido's finest were on the other side of the tape, milling around the cottages. He made his way down the boardwalk and through the crowd. He started to duck under the tape when he was stopped by one of the uniformed policemen.

"That is my cottage right there, officer. What's going on?"

"What is your name, sir?"

"Chance Kincaid. I'm a guest here."

"Wait here." The cop hurried away and came back with Cutro.

Cutro looked tired in his wrinkled sports jacket and loosened tie. His hair was disheveled, and there were dark circles under his eyes. He was wearing latex gloves. "Where have you been, Kincaid?"

"I've been with the girl you saw me leave with last night. Why? What's happened?"

"Come with me."

Kincaid followed him to his cottage. One of the heavy wooden doors had a large indentation in its center and the wood was splintered around the lock. Cutro pushed it open, and they stepped into the room. It had been ransacked. The writing desk was smashed, its drawers had been thrown against the wall. The sofa cushions had been torn open and tossed on the floor. The bed was overturned, and the mattress was slashed open. His duffel had been turned inside out; its contents strewn across the room. Jagged bullet holes formed a straight line across two walls.

"I don't suppose I could gather up my stuff? I want to see if anything is missing from my bag."

"As soon as they are finished photographing the scene, okay?

Kincaid nodded. He hoped the articles from his duffel were innocuous enough to avoid scrutiny.

"Any idea who might have done this?" Cutro asked.

"None."

"You don't think this has anything to do with the fact that you shot three men to death here last night?" Cutro asked rhetorically. He pressed on. "What were they looking for?"

"Your guess is as good as mine." He stood for a long moment and gazed at the damage. He was sure this was the work of the kidnappers' friends. *But why would they tear up my room?* "This is pretty bad," he said finally.

"It gets a lot worse."

Cutro led the way outside and down the boardwalk past Cottage 5 where the newlywed couple from the catamaran was being questioned. The woman was sobbing. Her husband had his arms around her in an attempt to console her. The doors to Cottage 6 were open, and men were hurrying in and out, some in police uniforms, a couple in civilian clothes. A stretcher from the ambulance was standing just inside. They walked around it and out to the veranda. The ambassador's girlfriend was lying on the table. She was on her back with her head hanging off one end and her legs off the other. She was nude. Her wrists had been duct taped to the table legs and she had been stabbed several times in the chest. Blood covered her entire torso and pooled on the table and floor. Her empty eyes stared up at the blue sky. Her bikini was in her mouth.

"Her name is Lisa Kettering. The coroner says she was raped, probably multiple times, before she was killed. He thinks it happened around two this morning. The maids found her at ten fifteen."

Kincaid contemplated how pretty she had been in life and how grotesque she looked now. He had seen it many times before. *When life leaves a body, it takes beauty with it.*

"Where's the ambassador?" His voice was solemn and soft.

"Gone without a trace. Aside from the girl, there's no sign of a struggle."

"Kidnapped without a struggle? He was struggling plenty the last time they tried it."

"Maybe he witnessed the killing and decided to go peacefully."

"Maybe, but why wouldn't he try to stop the attack on his girlfriend?"

"I guess everyone isn't as gallant as you."

Kincaid wasn't sure if that was a gibe or a compliment, but he didn't spend a lot of time thinking about it. His mind was racing. Why would someone kill the girl, kidnap the Englishman, and then shoot up his room? He figured things must have happened in that order. If they had strafed his walls first, the gunfire would have alerted the ambassador to the danger. He needed to talk to the honeymoon couple.

Their names were Debra and Wilber Canlon, and they were from Nebraska. They told him that they had not seen or heard anything. No gunfire, no screams, nothing. "We're on our honeymoon, ya know?" was Wilber's explanation. Debra just trembled. She didn't speak.

Kincaid was more than skeptical. An AK-47 was a loud weapon, and this one had spewed at least a dozen rounds right next to their bedroom. They would have had to hear that. He was wasting time. They were lying, probably out of fear. The police could deal with them. His thoughts turned to Jillian. He took out his satellite phone and punched up her number. She answered on the third ring.

"Jillian, where are you?"

"I'm at home. Why?"

"Home as in your dad's house?"

"That's right. Why?"

"I want you to get out of there right now."

"Why would I do that? First you say I should be here in case Dad comes home, and now you say I should leave. What's wrong with you?"

"Nothing is wrong with me, but there's been some trouble at the resort, and I'd feel better if you weren't there alone."

"What kind of trouble? You think I'm in danger?"

"Probably not. Call it an abundance of caution in case we touched a nerve this morning."

"I guess I could go to a hotel."

"Good idea. Why don't you go there right now? Call me when you're settled in. Please."

"If you really think I should."

"Trust me."

He clicked off his phone. A thought occurred to him. Where was Tejada? The manager of the resort should be here. But he wasn't. Kincaid checked his own cottage again, and then went back to the ambassador's. A man in a dark suit was taking photos of the body. No Tejada. He spent the next several minutes wandering down the boardwalk to each of the other cottages. Guests were standing around outside their doors, craning their necks to see what was going on. Several people tried to stop him, thinking he might know something. He ignored their questions and kept searching, but there was no Tejada. He backtracked the way he had come. Back in front of his place, the cops were dispersing the crowd when Cutro approached him again.

"You're still here. Good. The captain wants to talk to you. He's up in the director's office. I'll walk you up."

They made their way through the dwindling crowd, past the ambulance, and up the steps to the lobby. Just beyond the front desk was the door to Tejada's office. There he was, smoking a cigarette and talking to Belka, who was chewing on his usual stubby cigar. The room was full of smoke. Both men stood and shook Kincaid's hand. The captain didn't mince words but asked the same questions Cutro had. Kincaid gave the same answers he had given the sergeant. He wasn't at the resort last night, and he didn't have any idea who the killers were or what they were looking for.

Belka took a long puff from his cigar before saying, "Any idiot would know who did it. The PISF."

"The PISF?" Kincaid repeated.

"The Philippine Islamic Separatist Front."

"I never heard of them."

"Maybe not, but you killed three of them the other night. I told you not to get mixed up in any more trouble."

"I can't help it if someone breaks into my room, can I, Chief? Hell, I wasn't even here." He paused. "Maybe I should have been," he added.

Belka squinted, took the cigar from his mouth, and pointed it at Kincaid. "I'm just wondering. You show up in our quiet little town, and immediately one person is kidnapped, and four people are dead. How do you explain that?"

Kincaid shrugged. "Coincidence?"

"This is no time for joking, Kincaid."

Kincaid knew this was no joke. At first, he had promised himself he would stay out of these local matters. He just wanted to sit on the beach and relax, but now it was personal. They had violated his privacy, and they had killed a woman in an obscenely violent way. Either of those two things was reason enough to get involved. The line had been crossed, but he wasn't about to say anything to the local constabulary. He had his own way of handling problems. His way was immediate and direct, unencumbered by annoyances like the law.

"I'm sorry, Captain. I'll try to stay out of your way from now on."

"Yes, you will." Belka looked at Tejada but he was speaking to both men. "I'm posting men at this location for the foreseeable future."

"I appreciate that, sir," said Tejada. Then to Kincaid, he said "I am truly sorry that this has happened, Mr. Kincaid. I will see that you are moved to other accommodations immediately."

"Thanks, Tejada." Belka stood, shook hands with both men, and disappeared out the door.

Kincaid stayed behind. "I'd like to talk to you if you can spare the time."

"Certainly, Mr. Kincaid. How can I be of service to you?"

"I was wondering how the kidnappers knew the ambassador was in the restaurant the other night. I thought maybe he wasn't necessarily a target. Terrorists have been known to kidnap people at random. Especially Westerners, you said."

"That's right, they have" Tejada said.

"But last night, that wasn't random. Somebody knew exactly where he was, and they came for him. And they killed an innocent girl. How do you explain that?"

"Mr. Kincaid, if you are implying that someone at Oceania is working with terrorists, I can assure you that none of my people would ever be guilty of such a thing."

"I'm not implying anything, Tejada. I'm just considering all possibilities. Obviously, you're willing to vouch for all your employees?"

"Sir, we have a strenuous vetting procedure here. No one is hired before submitting to a thorough background check. Under certain circumstances, we use a lie detector to ascertain a person's veracity. This is an exclusive resort, and we demand the highest standards of conduct and discretion from all our staff."

"Okay. I understand, but you may not like my next question. The door to Cottage 6 wasn't damaged the way mine was. That means that either someone had a key, or else the ambassador or the girl let them in. I'm trying to picture either of them opening the door to armed strangers. It doesn't make sense."

"I'm sure I can't explain the workings of the Caucasian mind, Mr. Kincaid."

"You're not alone there, Tejada, but someone sure as hell let the murderers in, and I don't believe for a minute it was Ms. Kettering."

"Please leave this office, Mr. Kincaid. I've endured enough of your insinuations. It's insulting. Good day." He opened the door and Kincaid walked out.

As he crossed the lobby, he noticed Lucia was at the desk. She smiled at him as he approached.

"Hello. How are you?" he asked.

"As well as can be expected, I guess."

She looked shaken. "That business at the cottages is terrible. That poor woman!"

"Did you see the body?"

"God, no. I couldn't bear it. Just hearing about it gives me chills."

"Lucia, has anyone on the staff been acting strange lately?"

"Strange like how? Do you think one of them was involved?"

Kincaid leaned in close to her face. His voice was soft. "I don't think anything, Lucia. I'm just asking, that's all."

"I was off for a few days, but since I've been back, I haven't noticed anything suspicious, if that's what you mean. After the shooting, everyone has been on edge, of course. There has never been a terrorist attack here before. Our staff is very trustworthy, I promise you." Her voice had taken a defensive tone. She averted her eyes.

"I'm sure they are, and I'm on your side, but if you notice anything out of the ordinary, let me know. Okay?"

She moved away, took a key card from the desk, and encoded it. "We're moving you to a Woodland Suite. The view isn't as nice as the cottage, but it's much bigger, and it has a bathtub."

"A bathtub? Is that a special amenity?"

"Here, it sure is. I'd give anything if I had a bathtub. I'd put in lots of bubbles, light some candles, and soak for hours." She scrunched up her shoulders and smiled seductively.

"Well, I don't do baths, but you're welcome to come and use the tub anytime." He smiled.

"Be careful what you say. I might take you up on it." She reached across the desk and handed him the card. "It's number twenty. Go across the parking lot, and you'll see it on the hill."

He took the key from her and said goodbye. Out in the parking lot, the EMTs were loading Lisa Kettering's body into the ambulance. She was in a black body bag, zipped up tight. Kincaid wondered if her mother knew where she was.

Chapter 12

HALLOWEEN

He eventually found the walkway to the Woodland Suites in a large stand of bamboo that had overwhelmed a rustic sign marking the entrance. He walked up the ramp onto the long porch that stretched the length of the building. Suite 20 was at the far end. He swiped his card and stepped into a foyer that led to the living area. It was quite a bit larger than the cottage. The walls were painted pale blue, and all the woodwork was brilliant white. The floor was tiled with slate, and it had a high, wood-beamed ceiling. There was a fan over a white chesterfield centered on the wall opposite a large, louvered door set on tracks. The door opened onto a veranda with a mosaic floor and stone columns. The view from there consisted of a stand of low shrubberies and a large swimming pool. Beyond the pool were the cottages and the beach. Apart from the veranda and lounge was the bedroom. It was finished the same as the living area and was closed off by two more white, louvered doors. The bathroom was all white tile with a shower. In the corner by the window was the prized bathtub. Outside the window, more dense bamboo provided plenty of privacy for the bather. The suite must have been eighty square meters, and although it had no kitchen, there was a coffee pot and a microwave. It was like a treehouse. It was perfect.

His duffel and the bottle of scotch had already been delivered from the cottage, which was good, because the cottage remained taped off and was currently under perlustration by the police. He took a quick inventory of the bag. In addition to his first aid kit, three magazines for the Wilson and a box of .45 ammo, there were a couple changes of clothes, a multi-tool, two energy bars, a burner phone, sunglasses, a steel ink pen, some paracord, and a shemagh. The sunglasses shared their case with a few waterproof matches. He also had a pack of cigarettes and a few lighters; Kincaid wasn't a smoker, but these items had other uses. He checked the straps for his concealed wire saw, razor blades, thumb drive, and handcuff key. He was satisfied that everything was there and surprised he hadn't been quizzed about any of it.

It had been a stressful day. He settled onto the wicker settee on the veranda. A breeze was blowing onshore, bringing the salty breath of the sea and low, dark clouds with it. An afternoon storm was imminent. Nothing unusual about that, but for some reason, it reminded him of Jillian. He hadn't heard from her yet. He found his phone and called her number. She answered on the first ring. "Jillian, are you at the hotel?"

"I'm still at Dad's house."

"I thought you were going to a hotel."

"I changed my mind. I don't know what kind of trouble you're expecting, but I feel much safer here than anywhere. What has happened anyway?"

"A woman was killed at the resort last night."

"What does that have to do with me? Are they killing women at random?"

"I don't think so, but there's more. Whoever did that also ransacked and shot up my cottage. I think it was associates of the three kidnappers from the other night."

"You mean the men you killed."

"That's right. I think they were looking for me."

"I hope you're wrong, but even if they are, how does that put me in danger?"

"You were seen with me at your father's plant this morning."

Her voice rose half an octave. "And you think Dad is mixed up with terrorists? That's just crazy."

"I'm not saying that, but we need to find out where he is. In the meantime, I don't want anything to happen to you."

"That's the first sensible thing you've said. Will you meet me at the docks in the morning and help me look for him?"

Kincaid exhaled loudly. He resigned himself to the fact that Jillian was not leaving her house. "Fine. I'll take the first ferry. In the meantime, make sure the gate is locked, and don't open the door to anyone."

"See you in the morning. And Kincaid?

"Yeah?"

"You be careful."

"Always. Goodbye."

"Bye." She hung up.

It turned out the veranda was a nice place to hang out. There was a view of the sea and, more interestingly, the crime scene. He could smell the rain in the air as distant thunder signaled its impending arrival. He found his scotch and a glass. There was no ice, so he drank it neat. He felt the familiar, warm sensation of the whisky flowing down his throat as it made its way to his stomach. He might have stayed there all afternoon if his curiosity hadn't gotten the better of him. There was plenty of activity at the cottages. Maybe the police had found something. A clue as to who the attackers were or what the mission was.

Kincaid wasn't a man who could sit on the sidelines. In college, he got a degree in criminal justice, but he didn't want to be a cop. After graduation, he joined the army with an eye toward serving as an MP. The army had other plans for him, however. His technical, combat, and physical assessments were off the charts, so he was assigned to the Seventy-Fifth Ranger Regiment and sent to Fort Benning where he excelled in the most demanding training of any armed force in the world. His marksmanship and mental evaluations earned him a spot in sniper school. But being a sniper was too dull for him. He preferred being an assaulter. Even nine years of combat duty in the Middle East wasn't enough for Kincaid, so after his discharge, he went to work for a private military company. Now he wanted to find these terrorists and eliminate them.

He refilled his glass and headed down to the boardwalk. The wind was up and gusting to maybe fifteen knots. He counted the seconds between a lightning bolt out over the water and the subsequent thunderclap and reckoned the storm to be about eight kilometers offshore. He ducked under the yellow tape at the entrance to Cottage 6 where he was met by a uniformed officer. Cutro waved the cop off and greeted Kincaid with a handshake.

"Have you found anything yet?"

Cutro shook his head. "No prints and nothing left behind. The lab guys are here, and we're looking for trace evidence now." He glanced at the glass of scotch Kincaid had brought with him.

"You're looking for trace evidence with all these people here?"

Cutro ignored the question. "Your place yielded nothing but the caliber of the bullet holes—7.62 x 39 mm."

"An AK. Did you find the casings?"

"Yes."

"You should be able to lift a print from one of them. And what about Grey? Anything on him?"

"We're working on it, Kincaid. By the way, you aren't supposed to be here. Belka will have my ass if he finds out I'm sharing information with you." He was following Kincaid now, back toward Cottage 4. "Did you hear me? I need you to leave this area."

Kincaid wasn't listening. He wanted to check out his old place for himself. The door was open. No one was inside. The two men strolled around the main room. The spent shells had already been collected. Small, numbered cards marked the places where they were found. The furniture had been left broken and strewn about to be photographed. It started to rain. Slowly at first, a soft pattering on the thatched roof, but it soon turned into a torrent. The roar of the deluge on the roof made conversation difficult. Kincaid stood at the open doors to the veranda and watched giant raindrops, like rocks, splashing into the South China Sea.

Cutro stood at his elbow. "You seem to be quite fascinated by the ocean."

Kincaid took a drink from his glass.

"You know, it's hard to fathom how you managed to take out three violent men that night. I'm not sure I could have done that." Kincaid didn't respond. Cutro raised his voice. "I mean, even if I had the skill, I don't know if I'd have the nerve."

Kincaid turned. "Well Sergeant, the Ranger code says, 'I will never allow a comrade to fall into the hands of the enemy.'"

"You're not a Ranger anymore, Kincaid."

"Maybe not by profession, but I'll always be a Ranger in spirit. And I'll always do my best to live up to those ideals."

"I can respect that, but how do you summon that kind of courage?"

"I didn't think about it. I saw a situation, and I ran to it. Once I got there, I acted. I attacked and neutralized the threat. Simple as that."

"You have my admiration, Kincaid, but to be clear, I don't want you interfering with our investigation."

"I have no intention of interfering, but you and I both know that these people are going to keep coming after me. And now they've killed a woman in a very ugly and violent way. So, I don't know how I'm not going to be involved. I'll keep you informed of whatever I find out, but don't expect me to sit on the beach and wait for you to protect me."

"I can't imagine a world where that would happen. And I wouldn't mind if you wanted to help me out with this case, but don't let Belka find out. He clapped Kincaid on the shoulder and smiled. "Keep me in the loop, okay?"

"I'll do my best."

He left Cutro to his work and headed back toward his new accommodations. The rain had turned into a light drizzle. He didn't mind getting wet. His glass was empty, but he was still thirsty. On the way up the hill, he ran into Lucia, who was holding a large golf umbrella over her head. She asked him if he had found out anything more about the murder or the kidnapping. He told her what Sergeant Cutro had told him and asked her if she'd like to have a drink with him on his veranda.

"Thanks. I'd really love to, but I have some things to do tonight. It's Halloween, you know."

"Actually, I didn't realize. I haven't trick or treated in years, believe it or not."

Lucia laughed. "It isn't too late. There's a party in the clubhouse this evening. Costume optional."

"Thanks, but I think I'll just stay in and drink."

"Have fun." She smiled, turned, and headed toward the parking lot.

Chapter 13

NEW TERMS

Several kilometers down the Taytay Highway and down a sandy backroad, Mohamed el-Fasil sat across a metal field table from an ashen Ambassador Grey. The ambassador was wrapped in an olive-green, wool blanket and grasping an aluminum coffee cup.

"Who are you really, Mr. Grey? You say you are James Welde's partner, and you have come here to sell us guns. But we have already negotiated with Mr. Welde for guns. If you were his partner you would know that."

The ambassador's voice was shaky. "I assure you I am his partner."

"Then, where is Welde, and where are the guns?"

"I told your contact at the police station. Mr. Welde, unfortunately, has been detained." Grey was starting to sweat. The men stared at each other. Grey said, "Would you be kind enough to fill me in on the terms of your agreement? Do you have paperwork, perhaps?"

el-Fasil laughed. "Do you suppose that is how our business is done? That Mr. Welde signed a contract for the sale of five hundred stolen rifles?"

"First of all, the arms are not stolen. I have documents to verify ownership of all our product."

"I'm sure you do. But the question remains. Who are you, and where is our merchandise? We know the Kettering woman was working with the British government. I think maybe you are too." el-Fasil was fishing.

"That's preposterous. I was the British Ambassador to the Republic of Vietnam, and Lisa was my aide and travel companion. Her murder is an outrage. I should walk out of here right now." But Grey knew that would be impossible. "I don't know why your men had to kill her. You're all barbarians. Animals. I came here with honest intentions, to help you by supplying you with weapons. I was given to understand that you were sincerely fighting for a cause. I didn't know that included rape and murder." His voice was hoarse and raspy. He had said too much, and he knew it. His situation was growing desperate.

"What did you expect us to do with an American informant?" el-Fasil demanded.

"I don't think she was an informant. She was a sweet girl."

"She was an agent of the US government. The Bureau of Alcohol, Tobacco, and Firearms to be precise. And she wasn't looking for alcohol or tobacco."

"I don't believe you."

"You are a fool, old man. Did you think she was attracted to you?" He sneered. "Lisa Kettering has been known to our people in London for some time, and she has been overheard talking to MI5 on her satellite phone at the resort. Her job was to stop people like you from trafficking guns to people like us. That is why she approached you in London and that is why she wanted to come here with you. She would have known about our plan soon enough." el-Fasil paused and stared at Grey through narrowed eyes. "Unless you had already told her" he said accusingly.

"I didn't tell her anything" the ambassador insisted.

"No? Maybe you didn't, but what you did do caused three of my best men to get killed. You resisted too much. The American had time to intercept you because you resisted. You put our entire operation in jeopardy."

"I only tried to give the appearance of resistance. I would have gone with them. I wanted a meeting with you, but your men came in with violence and shooting. Even after the first incident, I believed you to be a reasonable man. When your "soldiers" came to my door, I let them in, thinking they would just bring me here. I didn't travel all this way to be a party to killing and cruelty. I am a man of peace."

el-Fasil grinned broadly at the idea of an arms dealer proclaiming himself a man of peace. "In any case, it is done. Now we must talk about the guns."

The ambassador pressed on, his outrage overshadowing his fear and, perhaps, better judgment. "I don't want to talk about the guns right now. Your men brutalized that poor girl and stabbed her to death. It was the most horrific thing I've ever witnessed."

"They were not instructed to kill her. She would have been much more valuable to me alive. Those men have been dealt with I assure you."

"Even so, how can I trust you after this?"

"It is not important that you trust me, Mr. Grey, and I do not need to trust you. You are now my prisoner." He smiled. "But when we have finished here, of course you will be free to go."

"No, sir, I am not your prisoner. I'm a businessman, and you need my guns. Those AKs you have are worn-out pieces of shit, no match for the army's M4s. And, the army is well supplied by the Americans, believe me. No, sir, you need me much more than I need you."

"Then stop pretending you are saddened by the death of one woman. The weapons you are going to deliver to me will be used to kill many. And make no mistake, you will deliver the guns Mr. Welde owes us."

Grey's burst of adrenaline had subsided, leaving a chill he could feel in his bones. "I'm telling you if Welde made a deal with you, it was before he and I became partners. I don't know anything about that."

"We have a bargain for five hundred rifles. AK-47s. I gave him a deposit to demonstrate our good faith. They were supposed to be delivered by now. When you contacted my man, I assumed you were coming here with them. Instead, you are telling me there are no AKs, that you do not have my money. And now I am to believe you are offering me something better."

el-Fasil stood and walked to the door of the tent. Two men were standing guard outside, and several more of his ragtag soldiers were milling around the camp. He turned back to Grey. "Tell me again how you came to possess so many American M16 rifles."

"When the United States leaves a war zone, it usually abandons its munitions. It's cheaper to manufacture new ones than ship the old ones home. When the war in Vietnam was over, they left thousands of rifles behind. When I became the ambassador, I made contacts with the people who have them now. We can deliver as many as you want. For a price."

"What condition are these M16s in today? They are very old weapons."

"They're the same as new. Packed in grease and stored in a climate-controlled facility for fifty years. An expert couldn't distinguish them from the ones made today."

"We will still be overmatched by the M4s."

"M16s are six inches longer, but that means better accuracy, and they run cooler than M4s. You'll be happy with them."

"Okay. If they are as you say and packed in their original crates, we will forget about our deal with your partner and make an exchange."

"The price hasn't changed. Three hundred per gun, cash in US dollars, non-negotiable. That's the exchange. You give me the money, and they'll be delivered to any airfield you choose within the week."

el-Fasil thought for a moment. To Grey, he seemed angry. He replayed the savage murder of Kettering in his mind. Was he about to meet a similar fate? He clutched his cup of cold coffee tighter. The aluminum began to bend. Neither man spoke. Finally, the terrorist said "I'm afraid you misunderstand, Mr. Grey. We are talking about your life. We will exchange your life for the weapons."

"I'm sorry, but you don't understand. The weapons do not yet belong to me. I'm merely the middleman. I can get them for you only when I have the money. The people who control them will not care if you kill me or not."

"Then you will have to come up with the funds to purchase them yourself. What is your life worth to you?"

The ambassador was perspiring heavily and wiped his forehead with the tail of his shirt. "I'll need my phone to see if I can obtain the money."

el-Fasil handed him his phone.

"I'll need some privacy."

"I think not, sir. I will be right here in case you decide to try to betray us."

Grey punched in the number for Sasher Global Investments. When he got Sasher on the line, he tried to sound composed. "Hello, Bruce. Grey here. I'm afraid I've run into a bit of a snag out here. I need you to wire twenty thousand pounds to my contact in Ho Chi Minh City."

Sasher sounded puzzled. "Why would we do that? I was under the impression that when you made the sale, the money would go there, and then you would bring the purchase price back here."

"Well, you see, Mr. el-Fasil is now saying that he'd like to make a trade instead."

"A trade? What kind of trade?"

"The rifles for my life." The ambassador's voice cracked as he said the words.

Sasher laughed. "That's absurd, he's bluffing, Grey. He has nothing to gain by killing you. He's obviously bluffing. Tell him there is no possibility of such a deal. You'll be okay."

"Easy for you to say. You're safely tucked away in London while I'm in the thick of it out here in the jungle. These men are ruthless, I tell you. They've already killed Miss Kettering."

"Who the devil is Miss Kettering?"

"She was my assistant." Grey was anxious to get back to his own predicament. "Call it a personal loan to me, Bruce. I need that money. At least enough to procure the merchandise."

"I can't do it, Grey. I'm already out too much money. Sit tight. You're a diplomat, for God's sake. This Fossil guy will come around when he sees you won't give in. He has nothing to gain by killing you, believe me." With that, Sasher hung up.

"Okay, thanks," the ambassador said to the dial tone before clicking off.

"What did he say?" el-Fasil asked.

"He said it might take some time to make the transfer."

"Fine. But I warn you, I don't have much time, and you have even less." He turned abruptly away from the old man and said something to the guards outside. They entered the tent, and one of them stuck the barrel of his pistol in the ambassador's ribs and pushed him outside.

Chapter 14

A FAVOR

When he got back to his suite, Kincaid refilled his glass and found the SAT phone. Settled in his comfortable seat on the veranda, he searched through his contacts. It took a couple of minutes, but he found the number he was looking for: a man he had served with in a private military company in Basra. Most of the people in his line of work had satellite phones, and their numbers never changed. Otherwise, finding work would be next to impossible. He keyed in the number.

"Yeah?"

"Alex, this is Kincaid."

"Kincaid, you old bastard, what are you up to?"

"I'm in the Philippines, and I need a favor. Do you still have connections at INTERPOL?"

"Sure. What do you need?"

"I need any information you can get on a guy named James Welde. He is from the States but currently living here. Also, one Ambassador Earl Grey. He's a Brit. Before you start with the tea jokes, yes, that's really his name."

Alex chuckled. "I know who that guy is. He used to be the envoy to Vietnam. The word is that he's in the arms business now."

"That's the guy. See what else you can dig up on him, okay?"

"Can do, buddy."

"Call me back." He switched the phone off.

"Yeah, you're welcome," Alex said to the dial tone.

As he sipped the last of the scotch, Kincaid recounted the events of the last three days. There was the attempted kidnapping, the visit to the police station where he met Jillian. The trip with her to her father's plant, the ransacking of his cottage, Kettering's rape and murder, and the eventual abduction of Grey. All this, and he was on vacation.

He was staring out toward the beach when he saw two men approaching the hedges to his right. They were dressed in robes and wearing shemaghs. Kincaid reached for his pistol. It was locked and loaded. He clicked off the safety. The men were guffawing and talking loudly. He thought for a moment that no terrorist would be in robes and then he remembered it was Halloween. They were probably going to the party at the clubhouse. He closed his eyes and laughed at himself.

Chapter 15

1 NOVEMBER

I t was eight-thirty exactly when he stepped off the boat in El Nido. The white Camry was waiting for him. He slid into the passenger seat. Jillian looked fantastic and smelled better. She was wearing a pale-pink dress that made her look tanner than he remembered her to be. Or it might have been a tunic—he didn't know anything about women's fashion. It was short, sleeveless, and made of a lightweight cotton fabric. Whatever it was, Kincaid liked it a lot.

She greeted him with a smile. "Good morning. Have you had breakfast?"

"Are you kidding? I barely got up in time to make the ferry."

"Great. I know a place."

They drove a few blocks before Jillian parked the car. "It's easier if we walk the rest of the way."

The street was narrow, probably too narrow for a car, but several scooters zoomed past them, leaving their pungent, oily exhaust behind. Following the scooters was a tall man in a white tuxedo and top hat. His face was painted white with black paint around his eyes and covering his nose. Behind him were a dozen or more people in various costumes and masks. They shared a single theme: skeletons. It was a small parade with noisemakers and tambourines.

EE Sample

"What is this all about?"

Jillian laughed. "I forgot. Today is the Day of the Dead. People visit their dead relatives in the cemetery and celebrate in the street. It's a Spanish tradition that spread here."

About fifty meters down, they entered a little café. The red neon sign in the window proclaimed it Brett's. The room was about ten meters long and half as wide. The counter separated the room into two parts. The kitchen occupied the back half, and the front was filled by tables and booths. Bare incandescent light bulbs were suspended from the ceiling by their wires. Over the counter, a large blackboard listed numerous breakfast items and their prices. Kincaid guessed it was changed in the afternoon to the lunch and dinner menu. The two girls waiting tables were locals and could have been twins. Both were slight Filipinas with brown eyes and straight, black hair.

Kincaid ordered three eggs with a stack of pancakes and two sausage patties. Jillian had an egg white with mushrooms on a muffin. "Bring lots of coffee," she said. The waitress returned with two cups and a carafe.

Several people wandered in carrying bouquets of flowers. A young woman with raven hair and white face paint approached them. "Would you like some flowers for Dia de los Muertos?" she asked.

"Sorry, we don't have any dead relatives here," Kincaid said. The girl moved on to the next table.

"Tell me about the woman who was killed at the resort the other night. I heard about it on the news and it sounds dreadful."

"It was bad. She and an old man were staying two doors down from my cottage. Apparently, they let someone in who subsequently raped and killed her. The man has disappeared. Then, the killers broke into my cottage and shot the place up. The police suspect it was an act of terrorism."

"What about the old man? Do you think he did it and tried to make it look like something else?"

"I thought about that, but honestly, I don't think he was physically capable. She was probably stronger than him. Also, he was the same man that was the victim of the kidnapping attempt the first night I was here. But I'd be surprised to find out he wasn't involved in some way."

"You killed those kidnappers, Kincaid."

"I killed some of them."

"Aren't you worried about your own safety?"

"Not much, but I am concerned that I may have put you in danger."

Jillian stirred her coffee and took a sip before replying, "I think that's highly unlikely."

"All right let's talk about your dad," he said.

"Shouldn't we discuss your fee first?"

"Probably, but it just seems so untoward."

"Seriously, Kincaid."

"I'm not working for you, Jillian. Maybe it started out that way, but that was before Kettering was killed. I'm in it now and I think your father will lead me to the men I'm looking for."

"You keep saying that, but you're wrong. This whole thing about my father being mixed up with terrorists and gun smugglers is too hard for me to believe."

"Just tell me what you know. Anything that might be relevant."

"Honestly, I don't know that much about him. I've only seen him once in the past five years. I can tell you he's a good father. He seems happy, and I think he loves my sister and me."

"We also know that he owns a factory that assembles computer parts, flies a helicopter, appreciates art, and lives at the beach. That tells me he's doing well financially."

"I guess so."

"Does he send you money?"

"He did when I was at Yale, but I don't need help now. I'm a real estate attorney."

"Impressive."

"Are you making fun of me?"

"Not at all. Your sister is in England, right?"

"That's right. She's going to school in London on a scholarship, I think."

"You told me your dad lives alone. Does he have a girlfriend or anyone special that might know where he is?"

"I don't know. He hasn't mentioned anyone to me."

The waitress brought their food. Jillian watched as Kincaid attacked his eggs. He poured syrup on his pancakes as he finished off one of the sausage patties.

"I suppose a big man like you needs a lot of calories just to keep going," Jillian said.

"I couldn't live on egg whites and mushrooms, that's for sure."

They finished eating, and Jillian paid the check. They decided to go to the beach and talk to the neighbors. Maybe they knew something about Mr. Welde.

Just before the driveway to the Welde residence was a mailbox. It bore no name but marked the entrance to the adjoining property. Jillian turned right and drove through a stand of palm trees to a white frame house. It was modest compared to the Welde house and dissimilar in style. Kincaid thought it would look more at home on a farm than a beach. He followed Jillian up three wooden steps that led to the porch where two well-worn rocking chairs sat, looking forlorn. They rang the doorbell twice before a petite woman in an emerald housedress opened the door. She had short, gray hair and piercing blue eyes. Kincaid reckoned she was in her sixties.

"Yes?" she said. She appeared to be slightly annoyed, as if she had been interrupted from something. But then suddenly, her expression changed. "Jillian. What a pleasant surprise! My goodness, you look so grown up."

"Mrs. Garland. I wasn't sure if you still lived here."

The two women stood smiling at each other for a couple of moments before Mrs. Garland said, "I'm sorry. How rude of me. Won't you come in?" She stared at Kincaid.

"This is my friend, Chance Kincaid. Kincaid, this is Mrs. Garland. I used to come visit her when I was staying with my dad."

Kincaid smiled and dipped his head. He pulled the screen door open and held it for Jillian. They stepped into what appeared to be a sunroom. The plank floor was painted a glossy gray, and all the furniture was made of wood and painted yellow. The two women sat down together on a long bench, and Kincaid sat opposite them in a big Adirondack chair.

"How is your dad, my dear?"

"That's why we're here, actually. I don't know where he is. He flew to Manila a few days ago and hasn't returned."

"Oh my. You don't think something has happened to him, do you?"

Kincaid said, "Probably not, ma'am, but we wanted to ask you a couple of questions."

"Okay."

"When was the last time you saw Mr. Welde?"

"I don't know. It's been a while. Maybe a month or more."

"Did he look healthy when you saw him a month ago?"

"Well, of course. James has always been very fit." She sounded amused by the question. Jillian sat quietly, so Kincaid persisted.

"Did Mr. Welde have a lot of company over there in the past couple of months? Anyone who looked suspicious?"

"Heavens, no. James is kind of a loner. He stays to himself most of the time." She hesitated for a moment as if she was unsure if she should say more. "He did have a woman friend at his house one night, I think."

"Why do you think that? Did you see her?"

"I didn't see her, but I could hear them talking and splashing in the pool. You can't see his pool from here because of his fence."

"Were they arguing at all?"

"It wasn't like they were arguing. Quite the opposite... you know." She glanced at Jillian and blushed slightly.

"That was the only time you know of her being there?"

"I may have seen her in the car with James once or twice. We sit out on the porch at night sometimes."

Jillian finally spoke up. "What did the woman in the car look like, Mrs. Garland?"

"It's hard to say. It was always dark, so you could barely make out it was a female. You know, long hair, big earrings. I'm sorry, that's all I can tell you." There was an awkward pause as she stared first at Kincaid, then at Jillian.

Sensing the conversation was over, Jillian stood and extended her hand. "It's been so nice to see you again, Mrs. Garland. Thank you."

The woman shook hands with both of them. "I hope I have been helpful. I'm sure your father will show up soon."

That's what I'd say too, Kincaid thought.

They got in the Toyota, but Jillian didn't start the engine. She stared out the windshield. "At least we found out he's been seeing a woman, but that's all. That doesn't help us much."

"If the person in the car was the same woman. He may be seeing more than one woman. Hell, we don't even know the person in the car was a woman. Long hair? Earrings? I'm afraid we got nothing."

"We know there was a woman in the pool. She might know something."

"That's if we can find her. We need more to go on. Let's go talk to the other neighbor."

The house to the south of the Welde home was a sprawling, two-story stucco structure with a circular drive. The woman who answered the door was a middle-aged Filipina wearing a gray maid's uniform. She looked tired but smiled at Kincaid just the same.

"Hello," he said. "We're looking for the homeowner."

"I'm sorry, sir, he isn't in right now. They have all gone to the cemetery. Is there something I can do for you?" The maid looked past him at Jillian.

Jillian stepped forward. "Hi, I'm Jillian Welde. My father lives next door."

"How do you do, Miss Welde. I'm Linda Cerqueda."

"We were wondering if you had seen my father lately. I've come for a visit, but we're unable to locate him."

"I'm afraid I can't help you, ma'am. I haven't seen Mr. Welde for a week or more."

"Have you noticed any unusual activity next door, Linda?" Kincaid asked.

"No. It is very quiet here most of the time."

EE Sample

"Was Mr. Welde alone the last time you saw him?"

Linda put her index finger to her chin thoughtfully. "I think the last time I saw him, he was on the beach with a woman."

"Do you know who the woman was?"

"No, I didn't recognize her."

"What did she look like?"

"It was hard to tell from a distance." Linda turned to Jillian. "I'm not the nosy type."

Jillian smiled. "Of course not. Did you notice anything at all about her appearance?"

"Well," she hesitated, "she was wearing a bikini. It was red, what there was of it, if you get my meaning."

"Yes, I know what you mean. Is that all you can tell us?"

She wrinkled her brow. "That is all I know, senorita."

"Thank you for your time." Jillian turned and headed for the car. Kincaid smiled at the woman and followed.

Back in the Toyota, the optimism had drained from Jillian's face. "We're getting nowhere, and the more time that passes, the more anxious I'm getting."

"Try not to worry, Jillian. We'll find him. I'll think of something." Kincaid was silent all the way back to town. When he finally spoke, he said, "We need to go to Manila."

Chapter 16

A LEATHER JACKET

The ferry was scheduled to leave for the resort at one o'clock, so they sat at a sidewalk café and had coffee while they made plans. Jillian called the airline to make a reservation. She was told there were no seats available from El Nido to Manila for the next three days. The reservationist suggested leaving out of Puerto Princesa instead.

"We can't wait, Kincaid. We have to go tomorrow."

It was a six-hour drive to Puerto Princesa and then an hour and twenty minutes to Manila by air. Jillian made a reservation for the next day, departing Puerto Princesa International Airport at three o'clock. It was agreed that Kincaid would take the same ferry in the morning to make their flight to Manila. Kincaid said goodbye at the dock and caught the boat back to Oceania to get ready for the trip.

This ferry was a 170-foot catamaran. The aircraft-style seats were arranged four abreast in the center of the deck, and the perimeter was lined with two-seat units. Each pair of seats was configured so that the occupants faced each other. Aft of the seating was a section devoted to cargo since the ferry also delivered goods to the island. There were large crates stacked five high and held in place with heavy cargo netting. Forward, a wide set of stairs led to the upper deck and the wheelhouse. Aside from the wheelhouse, the rest of the upper deck was outfitted similarly, but it was shorter than the main deck and didn't extend over the cargo area.

As soon as he was aboard, Kincaid could feel that he was being watched. He scanned the passengers quickly. Some were obviously tourists, and a few were locals who were still celebrating the Day of the Dead. At first, he didn't see anyone who looked suspicious. But as the last of the passengers boarded and jammed into the crowd, one man caught his eye: a Filipino, bald, heavy set, wearing a leather jacket. The weather was hot, even for Kincaid in his cargo shorts and polo shirt. There was only one reason to be wearing a jacket. He was concealing something, probably a weapon.

Kincaid walked toward the stern and stood among the stragglers who were still milling around, trying to find open seats. Now he was out of the Filipino's view. He watched as the man maneuvered to maintain a sightline between the two of them. Kincaid filtered out of sight again. Same thing. He was being stalked. The two men stood and stared at each other until the crew asked everyone to sit. He sat down in an aisle seat of the last row. The big Filipino sat on the opposite end of the same row. Kincaid waited until the boat left the dock and was well underway. Once on plane, the catamaran was swift and light. Kincaid reckoned its speed to be about twenty-five knots.

He moved to the cargo stacks and paused to make sure he was being followed. He was. He stepped behind the crates, pressed his back against them, and waited. The first thing that appeared around the corner was a knife. The man in the leather jacket was holding it in front of him, ready to strike. That was his first mistake. With his right hand, Kincaid grabbed the man's wrist and pressed down hard with his thumb. He struck the man's face with his left elbow as he twisted the wrist. The knife fell to the deck. Kincaid grabbed the man's upper arm and knelt. He pulled the arm onto his knee and pushed with all his strength. That, combined with the weight of his upper body, snapped the arm like a twig. The man screamed in pain, but the roar of the two big engines ensured that no one heard. As Kincaid picked up the knife, the Filipino stood and kicked at his head. That was his second mistake. Kincaid grabbed his foot and sprang upright, pushing him against the stern's railing. The assailant felt excruciating pain in his back and then felt his own knife pierce his chest and lungs. Kincaid shoved him over the railing and watched as the man tumbled through the ship's wake. He slipped into the aft washroom to clean the blood from his hands. Then, he rinsed the assailant's knife, folded it into his pocket, and went back to his seat.

When he arrived at the resort, Kincaid only wanted two things. He wanted a cool shower, and he wanted a drink. As he got out of the shower, he remembered that he had drunk all his scotch. He'd have to get a drink at the bar. He got dressed in a clean, olive-green T-shirt and the cargo shorts he'd been wearing all day. Both were government issue from some previous job. As he walked toward the clubhouse, he met a burly man in a yellow shirt. He may have been one of Belka's men. His shirt was imprinted with the word Security in black letters. "Good afternoon," he said as Kincaid passed.

He sauntered through the lobby, noticed that Lucia wasn't on duty, and felt a twinge of disappointment. He sat at the bar and ordered a bourbon on the rocks. The bartender, a slight young guy with a pin that read Mike, poured him a double. "It's happy hour." He smiled.

"Thanks. I see you've got security here now."

"Yeah. We had some trouble here the other night, but it's nothing to worry about, really."

"I'm not worried." Kincaid downed the bourbon in one swallow. "Hit me again."

Mike brought him another double in a fresh glass and took away the old one. "How long have you been with us?"

"A couple of nights."

"Okay, so you know about the incident, then?"

Kincaid wondered which incident Mike was referring to. "That's a safe assumption, yes."

Just then, Tejada appeared and sat on the stool next to him, a serious expression on his face. "Mr. Kincaid, I'd like to sincerely apologize for my behavior at our last meeting."

"Forget it."

"I'm under a lot of stress right now. All these killings are bad for business, you know? I'm sorry I was so abrasive."

"I don't really care for an apology. Apologies are for the apologist. It's not my job to make you feel better."

"At least let me buy you a drink."

"I never turn down a drink." Kincaid stared at the mirror behind the bar.

Tejada motioned for Mike to come over. "Put Mr. Kincaid's drinks on my tab, Mike."

As he retreated, Mike replied "Yes, sir."

Kincaid took a sip of his fresh drink. "So, what did you really want to talk to me about?"

"You're a hard man, Kincaid."

"These are hard times."

"Have you heard anything from the police?"

"No. I've been busy with other pursuits."

"I saw you get off the ferry. Did you have a good trip to

town?"

"Yeah, I had a good trip."

Tejada twisted on his barstool.

"Is there something else on your mind?"

"Actually, there is. I need to ask you for a favor."

"Ask me."

"It's about my niece."

Kincaid felt he knew what was coming, but he wasn't going to make it any easier for Tejada. "What about her?"

"Lucia is an impulsive young woman. I am her only living relative, and I feel responsible for her."

"And?"

"And given the events that have transpired since you've been here, and also the difference in your age and experience..."

"There's nothing for you to worry about, Tejada" he interrupted. "She's a charming girl, and that's it. I won't let anything happen to her."

"I knew you'd understand."

"Thanks for the drink. Now, if you'll excuse me." Kincaid finished his bourbon, stood up and left the bar.

As he crossed the lobby, he realized he had let his guard down too much lately. Given the circumstances, this wasn't the time to get complacent. He scanned the area for anyone or anything unusual and decided to use the side entrance for a change. Unpredictability was mandatory when under surveillance, and it was clear that someone was interested in him. When he got back to his room, he searched it for cameras or microphones. He was satisfied the place was secure but noticed a rubber wedge in the corner, the kind maids put under a door to hold it open while they cleaned. He slid it under his closed door. It wouldn't stop an intruder from forcing his way in, but it would slow him down, and that might be enough of an edge for Kincaid.

He took off his cargo shorts and went out to the veranda. The sun was bright. A light breeze filtered through rustling bamboo and palms, cooling his face. That's when he remembered he didn't have anything to drink. He had been so eager to escape Tejada that he'd forgotten to get a bottle to bring back to the room. As he phoned room service, it occurred to him that all his clothes had been worn at least once since he'd washed them. He hung up and dialed the concierge instead. "Could you please send over a bottle of bourbon and some ice? And pick up my laundry?"

"Right away, sir."

A few moments later, there was a knock at the door. He kicked the wedge away and opened the door slightly. It was Ricky with Jim Beam.

He took the bottle and said, "Just a minute." He stuffed all his clothes except what he was wearing through the opening. "Have these cleaned and returned to me as soon as possible, kid."

Ricky took the bundle. Kincaid stuck a five in his face. "Please."

"Yes, sir."

Kincaid sat on the veranda, sipping his drink and watching two windsurfers in the ocean beyond the breakwater. Closer in, there were a few swimmers. A slender woman, burnished by the sun, lounged on the beach. The languid whisper of the waves and the smell of bougainvillea on the gentle wind combined to lull him to sleep.

Chapter 17

HELLO, I MUST BE GOING

He was awakened by a voice calling his name. He looked over the wall to see Lucia standing in the landscaping. She was carrying a basket and waving. "Don't you answer your door?"

"Sorry, I didn't hear you. I think I dozed off." He didn't know how much time had passed, but the sun was setting over the horizon. He met Lucia at the door. "Please come in." She was tantalizing in tight white pants and a red sleeveless blouse that matched her lipstick and accentuated her dark skin.

"I hope I'm not intruding" she said. "I was at the cemetery today. All the families were celebrating, and I started thinking of you here all alone, so I brought you dinner."

"Really? Your mother is buried here in El Nido?"

"No, but it doesn't really matter. Any cemetery will do. My mother and father are always with me." She paused. "Anyway, are you hungry?"

"As a matter of fact, I'm starving."

She looked down at his boxers. "Don't you ever wear pants?"

He had forgotten he was in his underwear. "How embarrassing. I sent all my clothes out to be laundered." But he wasn't embarrassed. She laughed. It was a lilting laugh that said she wasn't embarrassed either. He peered into the basket. "What have you got there?"

"It's adobo chicken. I made it myself. It's an old family recipe."

"I'll bet it's delicious. It certainly smells spicy."

"Not too spicy. My mother taught me how to make it. I think I told you she was a chef. But adobo chicken is not a fancy dish. Everyone in the Philippines knows how to make it. Of course, hers was the best."

"Of course. The answer to the question 'who's the best cook in the world' is always Mom."

Lucia spooned the meat onto paper plates and warmed it in the microwave. There was also a bottle of white wine that Kincaid opened with his multi-tool. They sat at the table on the veranda and watched the last moments of the setting sun. The sky was streaked with purple and crimson as the brilliant orb settled into the sea. Lucia shrieked with delight. "Did you see it? The green flash! Did you see it?" She jumped out of her chair and grabbed his shoulder. "I've seen it only once before. It's so beautiful!" Her euphoria was amusing.

"Yes, I saw it" he replied. "It was pretty awesome."

Lucia stood with her hand on his broad shoulder and stared at the spot where the faint, green glow had shone for a brief moment just as the sun disappeared over the horizon. Her touch felt good, but Kincaid sensed that, for her at least, the contact was incidental and without intent. The moment passed. She sat back down opposite him.

"The adobo is tasty. Thank you."

She smiled. "I'm so glad you like it." She sipped her wine and gazed coyly over the rim of her glass. "You know everything about me, but you haven't told me anything about you."

"There's not much to tell." He meant there wasn't much he was going to tell her.

She put her hand on his bicep and pushed up his shirt sleeve. "I noticed your tattoo the other day. I like the sword, but I can't read the words."

"Ense pacem petimus. It's Latin and means 'by the sword we seek peace.'"

She was silent for a moment. "My uncle says you are a soldier for hire."

"I prefer security professional."

"How does one become a security professional?"

"I joined the army."

"As simple as that?"

"Simple as that."

"The way you handled those men that first night makes me think you're good at it."

"Good enough, I guess." He wanted to show her what else he was good at. "Enough about me. Is there a man in your life? I'm thinking there must be."

"I had a boyfriend, but he's not here anymore."

"Where is he?"

"He's in a cover band. There are lots of cover bands in Manila, so he went there. His band's ambition is to be good enough to go to the United States and play in Las Vegas. So far they have only been good enough to play on a cruise ship."

"You don't sound too sad about that."

"No, I guess I'm happy for him. He should follow his dream to go to Las Vegas. In my heart, I have said goodbye to him. There are many beautiful women in Las Vegas."

"You are a beautiful woman too, Lucia."

She blushed. "I'm glad you think so."

"I'm sure I'm not the only one."

"No, you're not." She smiled seductively.

He poured the last of the wine into their glasses, but Lucia picked up the empty plates and headed inside. He followed her. She tossed the plates into the trash and took her glass from him.

"To the green flash," she said as she raised the wine. "I'm glad I got to share it with my security professional."

He clinked his glass with hers and then drained it.

He stood there as she threw away the wine bottle and put the glasses back into her picnic basket. "I have to go now," she said. She sat the basket on the floor, sidled up to him, and put her palm against his chest. He leaned down, and she kissed him. "I really have to go," she sighed. She grabbed the basket and moved swiftly to the door. A moment later, she was gone.

Chapter 18

GUN RUNNERS

No sooner had Kincaid said goodbye to Lucia than the SAT phone rang. It was Alex.

"Hey, man, I got some info to share with you, and it's kinda interesting."

"Great, let's hear it."

"It turns out both of your guys are involved with gunrunning. That's the first thing, but I don't think they are working together. Is that consistent with your thinking?"

"Not necessarily."

"Okay. James Welde has been dealing arms for years, but he's still pretty small time. Several major players know who he is and even know who some of his clients are, but nobody knows where he sources his product. This is the part you'll be interested in. He's been selling to a splinter group of terrorists in the Philippines. Some guy by the name el-Fasil. That's all I could get on him. My sources get real tight lipped after that. Any of this mean anything to you?"

"Not really. Is this el-Fasil part of a group called Abu Sayyaf?"

"I don't think so. That's a serious outfit. This guy doesn't play with the big boys."

"That's interesting. What about Grey?"

"Grey's a different story. He was the ambassador to Vietnam for a few years, but then he got caught up in some sort of scandal. He's British, so it probably was a sex deal of some kind. Anyway, he's been soliciting some people to sell them rifles. Word is without much success. My guy thinks he may be connected to a black market operation in Hanoi, but I can't verify that."

"Wow, Alex. That's even more interesting than the stuff on Welde."

"How's that?"

"Grey was apparently kidnapped by terrorists here the other day. They killed his girlfriend in the process."

"Hmm. What do you make of that?"

"I don't know, but I'm going to find out."

"Just be careful, buddy. I know you tend to get in over your head. If you need help, call me. Okay?"

"Yeah, okay. You've already been a big help. Thanks." Kincaid clicked his phone off.

"You're welcome," Alex said to the dial tone.

Chapter 19

FLYING TO MANILA

K incaid woke with the sun. He removed the wedge from under the door and opened it to find his laundry folded and in a neat stack, tied with string, just outside the threshold. After a quick shower and shave, he dressed and microwaved a cup of instant coffee. It was just after seven, so he meandered down to the dock and sat until the ferry arrived to take him to El Nido for his rendezvous with Jillian. As he boarded, he noticed the yellow crime scene tape was still stretched across the entrance of Cottage 4, but no one was around.

She was waiting when he came down the passerelle. He smiled as he slid into the passenger seat of the rented Toyota. Jillian was radiant. She was wearing a white, embroidered top and a short, yellow skirt that accentuated the golden streaks in her hair.

"Good morning, beautiful."

"Good morning. I brought coffee." She handed him a paper cup. It's Illy, the favorite of the locals."

"It's very good. Just what I needed this morning."

"Did you sleep well last night?"

"Not particularly. My mind was focused on what we should do when we get to Manila."

"What's the plan then?"

"The first thing I want to do is find someone who may have seen your dad or at least his helicopter. Do you have any idea where he hangars it when he's in Manila?"

"No idea."

"If he's shipping boxes, it has to be either at the airport or at the docks, so that's where we start looking."

"We're going to be searching for a needle in a haystack," Jillian fretted.

"We'll find him." Kincaid tried to sound confident.

He was quiet for most of the six-hour drive to Puerto Princesa. Jillian thought he must have been formulating a plan. She had faith in him that he would know what to do. A man with his background must do this sort of thing all the time. What was the word…reconnaissance?

They arrived at the airport in Puerto Princesa, left the car in short-term parking, and checked in at the Cebu Pacific desk for the flight to Ninoy Aquino International Airport. They were right on time. After perusing their passports and running Jillian's American Express card, the agent said, "You are all set for Flight 636, departing at fifteen hundred hours from Gate 3." She handed Jillian the tickets.

Before going through security, Kincaid took the handcuff key he had in his pocket and put it in his mouth. The scanner missed it. He put it back in his pocket as they walked down the jetway. It was open seating, so they chose two seats over the left wing. "It's the safest place to sit," Jillian said.

Kincaid knew better. The safest place to sit, according to the research, was behind the trailing edge of the wing, but he didn't say anything. *Why add to her uneasiness at this point?* In a little over an hour, they'd be on the ground in Manila.

He eyed the handbag she slid under her seat. "Do you have a computer in that bag?"

"I have a tablet, but I don't know if this plane has Wi-Fi."

"Let's see."

She pulled her purse into her lap and dug out the tablet. She turned it on, and it connected immediately.

Kincaid said, "See if there is a heliport at Ninoy Aquino."

Jillian studied the screen for a few minutes before she replied, "It looks like the closest general aviation one is in Makati. It's ten miles away."

"Then we'll start there."

They landed in Manila just after four. They disembarked and found the exit for ground transportation. A line of taxis extended along the curb in front of the terminal. Kincaid opened the door of the nearest one and followed Jillian in. "We want to go to the Aurora Tower Heliport," she told the driver, a heavy-set Filipino with a neck tattoo of a naked woman.

"That's in Makati. An hour in this traffic."

"Let's make it thirty minutes," Kincaid said sternly. He knew how far it was and didn't have time to be jacked up by a dishonest taxi driver.

"I'll try, but I promise nothing."

The driver wasn't lying about the traffic. It was as bad as Kincaid had ever seen. Bumper to bumper with the more adventurous drivers jockeying for position at every inter-section. He was glad he wasn't driving; he was nervous just watching. He turned to Jillian. "Do you happen to know the tail number of your dad's chopper?"

"Tail number?"

"Yeah, the number painted on the side." He already knew she didn't.

"I don't have the slightest idea." She thought for a minute. "I think I have a picture of him with it in the background." She took out her phone and scrolled through her photos. "Here it is." She handed the phone to Kincaid. A man wearing aviator sunglasses and a toothy grin was standing in front of a Eurocopter EC 130. It was green with a black stripe down the side of the fuselage and black letters and numerals on the boom. The first characters were RP-C. The man's head was blocking the next numbers, but the last two were 88.

"He's standing in front of the number."

Jillian was looking over his shoulder. "We can see most of it."

"Not really. RP is the country designator. Every aircraft in the Philippines uses that prefix. We have a C, then there should be two or three numbers, followed by 88. Maybe there won't be a lot of green helos with eights for the last two digits."

Thirty-five minutes later, they passed a car park with ten-foot lettering that read Park'n'Fly.

"Pull over right here," Kincaid said.

"Sir, this is not the Triangle Tower," the cabbie protested.

"This is where we want out."

The taxi stopped in front of the building adjacent to the car park. "Here we are."

Jillian paid the fare, and they got out. "This doesn't look right to me," she said.

A revolving door led to the lobby. They used it and crossed to the other side of the building where double glass doors led out to a long expanse of tarmac. Coastal Air was printed backwards across the right door.

"I guess we used the wrong entrance," Kincaid quipped.

There was a small, red circle within a larger circle, painted in white, on the tarmac directly in front of the doors. The outside circle was thirty meters in diameter. Across the tarmac was a long row of hangars, all painted red. Most of the hangar doors were open. "Let's start looking."

They worked their way along the row, checking the open ones first. There were several choppers in the hangars but no green ones. When they reached the far end, they started back up the line. Kincaid stopped at the first closed hangar door and tried the pedestrian door next to it. The small door was unlocked. He stuck his head in. No luck. At the next unit, he did the same thing. There wasn't much light, but he could make out a green Eurocopter with a wide, black stripe the length of the fuselage. The number on the boom was RP-C6W88. This was it. He had just started in when they were interrupted. A big man in brown coveralls came up from behind Kincaid.

"What are you folks doing snooping around here?" His accent said he was an American. Probably from Michigan or Indiana. Somewhere in the middle of the country. The white patch on his left breast said his name was Carl.

"Oh, hi, Carl," Kincaid said easily. "We were supposed to meet someone here. I guess we're early."

Carl wasn't convinced. "Who are you meeting?"

"Mr. Welde, of course. Jillian here is his daughter, and I'm a friend of the family. This is his 'copter, right?"

"I'm not sure. I don't know everybody here yet."

"So, you're new here?"

"Kinda."

"That explains it then." Kincaid was doing a good job of putting Carl on the defensive. "Can you check for us? We don't want to be in the wrong hangar."

"Yeah, I can check. You two come with me."

"Jillian, you go with him. My knee is giving me trouble again. I don't think I can walk down there and all the way back."

Jillian smiled her most seductive smile at Carl. "He was wounded in Afghanistan. He's a Ranger."

Carl seemed impressed. "Cool."

He and Jillian headed for the office, and Kincaid went back into the hangar. The chopper was unlocked. No surprise there. The doors on helicopters were flimsy affairs, more to keep the wind out than anything else. Nobody used the locks. There were no rear seats. Nothing was in the aft section of the cabin at all. He crawled into the left seat in the cockpit. Avionics occupied all the space on the dash. He looked in the door pocket. A flight manual and a sectional chart. An island on the map had been circled in ink: Siquijor Island. The return address on the envelope at Welde's house. Kincaid folded the chart and stuffed it into his pocket. He got out and tried to open the external luggage compartment, but it was locked. He started to climb back into the cockpit to look for a key, but at that moment, the hangar was flooded with light. Carl had flung the door open and hit the lights. Jillian stood behind him with a serious look on her face.

"My boss says you need to leave. Now."

"What about Mr. Welde? He'll be along in a minute, and you'll have to tell him you threw us out."

"Let me worry about that. Take your girlfriend and get off this property, or I'll have to get rough."

Carl may have thought he was able, but whether he was willing was an open question, especially when he added, "Nothing personal."

"Okay, Carl. We'll wait out on the street. Maybe we can catch him out there."

They went back the way they came and hailed a cab. The cabbie was a little, skinny man with a big, gold tooth right in the front of a wide smile. "Where to, boss?"

"We need a good hotel. Where do you recommend?"

"I know just the place."

A few minutes later, they were standing at the front desk of a small boutique hotel. "Should we get two rooms?" Kincaid was tentative.

"I think so."

He turned to the desk clerk. "We need two adjoining rooms on an upper floor."

"Certainly, sir." The woman smiled.

Jillian handed her American Express card and passport to the clerk who ran the card and slid two key cards back to her. After they had settled in, they sat at the table in Kincaid's room to discuss their situation. Kincaid showed Jillian the map he found in her father's chopper. "He has obviously flown to this spot at some point." He pointed to the island. "This is Siquijor Island, and see, he has circled it and written a set of coordinates beside it."

"Do you think that's where he is?"

"No, but I think he's been there, maybe more than once. We need to check it out. It's all we have to go on. Maybe there's someone there who can tell us where he is or what's happened to him." Kincaid realized he had said the wrong thing.

"You think something bad has happened to him, don't you? That we'll never find him alive?"

"I honestly don't know, Jillian. I'd say it doesn't look good right now. You haven't heard from him in over a week, and his helicopter is sitting in a hangar in Manila. What do you think?"

"I don't want to think about that. I just want to keep looking. I'm trying to stay positive, and you aren't helping much right now."

Let's talk about something else. Are you hungry? We haven't eaten all day, and I'm starved."

They took the elevator back down to a little café they had noticed just off the lobby. After the waitress took their order and brought coffee, Kincaid picked up the conversation where he had left off. "Let's plan on leaving the first thing in the morning, and we'll go to that island to see what we can find out there. After that, we'll fly back to El Nido. I want to talk to Marco at the plant again. He knows more than he's telling us."

"That sounds good, I guess. I can't think what else to do."

When the last of dinner had been devoured, they crossed the marble floor of the lobby to the elevator. Kincaid suddenly remembered something. "I need to see if they sell toothbrushes in here." There was a counter in a corner room where snacks and sundries were on display. He went in and picked up a toothbrush, a spray can of deodorant, and a tube of toothpaste. He carried everything to the cash register where a kid was standing, punching the keypad of his cell phone. "I hate to interrupt your game, son, but I want to pay for this stuff."

The boy kept staring at his phone. "Ayos lang."

Kincaid had no idea what he said, but figured it meant he was busy. He slapped a twenty down on the counter, gathered his items, and walked out. The elevator took them to the fourth floor where they got off, turned left, and went to their respective doors. He watched Jillian slide her key card and heard the click of her lock before opening his own door. He went into the bathroom and brushed his teeth. He was about to switch on the television when she knocked on the door that connected their rooms. He opened it.

Jillian was holding a brochure she had picked up in the lobby. "It's still early" she said. "Why don't we go out and see the sights?"

"Why not? We've got nothing better to do."

Chapter 20

NEGOTIATIONS

Six hundred kilometers south, a white flatbed truck turned left onto a narrow dirt road. It rolled through the underbrush past a lone sentinel armed with a radio and a rifle. The soldier keyed the mic and spoke softly into his radio. "The delivery is on its way."

The big truck was loaded with lumber, mostly recycled wood salvaged from an old plantation house, long since forgotten and abandoned by all except the inexorable jungle. The two men in the cab had been contracted to deliver building materials to the camp of the Philippine Islamic Separatist Front by one of its captains known to them only as Bakar. The road grew narrower, and the engine labored and roared as the vehicle's wheels spun and struggled over rocks and the roots of ancient trees that had scabbed the jungle floor in their search for sustenance. In the environs of the rainforest, even the trees, like every other living thing, vied for survival.

About three kilometers down the road, the driver turned right through a stand of pine trees. Finally, they arrived at a broad clearing where they saw a man standing and waiting for them. They recognized him immediately. Bakar was known by the red bandana he always wore tied around his head. He waved the two-ton truck to the right and directed them to park parallel to a deep ditch that was at the edge of the encampment. The driver and his partner scrambled down from the cab.

"Did you bring tin for the roof?" Bakar asked.

"Yes, sir. We brought nails and hammers too. Everything you need, just as you ordered."

"Good. I'll have some of my men help you unload."

Bakar strode smartly across the clearing past the smoldering ashes of the morning's fires. Plumes of blue smoke wafted upward, their earthy aroma blending with the fragrance of the jungle canopy. The ground was damp from last night's rain.

"Permission to enter." He paused at the door of el-Fasil's tent.

"Come in, Bakar."

"The material has arrived for the storage shed. It is being unloaded now."

"Excellent. And what of Reyes? Is there any word from him?"

"Nothing so far."

"He should have been here yesterday. It was a simple task. Kill the American. I didn't think that would be a problem for Reyes. He is the best at what he does."

"That is true, but this American, Kincaid, has a reputation. We have been able to find out some things about him. He was a Special Forces operative for the United States in Iraq and Afghanistan. Now he works as a mercenary. Apparently, an accomplished one."

"Yes, I can see that. He has killed three or, maybe four of my men. We cannot afford to lose any more. He must be eliminated immediately."

"I agree, of course."

"The question is, who is he working for?"

"We don't know that yet." Bakar watched as el-Fasil paced the floor.

"What do you think, Bakar? Has this Kincaid killed Reyes?"

"I don't know, sir, but if he doesn't return, I will take care of the American myself."

el-Fasil was wearing a stony stare. "See to it. I don't want any more excuses. We must have results."

"I will not fail you, sir. I swear on my life."

"Good." el-Fasil seemed satisfied. He changed the subject. "What of our friend, the ambassador?

"He is resting in the main shelter, but I'm afraid he is not happy."

"He is not meant to be happy. Something is not right with this man. I don't believe he is being truthful with us."

"If you will permit me, sir, I'm sure I can get the truth from him."

el-Fasil grinned. "Not yet, Bakar. Bring him to me."

Bakar turned and exited the tent. He checked the progress of the men unloading the truck. It was slow going as they labored in the heat and humidity, their sweat-soaked shirts clinging to their skin, but they were keeping a steady pace.

The shelter was a crude construct dug into the side of a small hill. Large timbers formed a frame. On three sides, smaller timbers were wedged between the dirt walls and the frame to prevent a cave-in. The front of the shelter was open. The roof was a green tarp laid over with leafy branches, palm fronds, and vines. The result was a primitive, well-camouflaged structure that served as a barracks for several men. Its only inhabitant presently was Earl Grey, former ambassador to the Republic of Vietnam. He was lying at the back end of the shelter, chained to one of its large posts.

"Get up, Grey," Bakar ordered. "We want to talk to you."

The ambassador said nothing but struggled to his feet. Bakar unlocked the handcuffs that connected him to the heavy chain. Both men were silent as they walked to the command tent.

el-Fasil greeted them with a smile. "Hello, Ambassador. I hope you had a pleasant night."

"Sir, I must again protest this barbaric treatment. I will not be chained up like a wild animal in the company of your most uncivilized soldiers." He was covered in sweat and dirt. He scratched desperately at red, swollen ant bites.

el-Fasil replied smoothly, "It is only temporary, Mr. Grey, until we have completed our transaction. I am only thinking of your safety. I can't have you wandering around in the jungle. You might fall prey to a wild animal or, worse yet, be spotted by the authorities who are undoubtedly searching for you as we speak. I'm sure you understand."

The ambassador's face was crimson, his eyes glared. "No, I don't understand. I'm here to help you, and in return, you treat me as a hostage. You have nothing to gain by killing me. I am your only hope of getting those rifles."

Bakar interrupted. "Then let us talk business. Maybe I can convince the general to not chop off your head when you deliver the five hundred rifles to us."

"This is preposterous. I came here to deal with you in good faith. The so-called kidnapping was, according to you, staged only to give me cover. Instead, you killed an innocent young woman, and now you're threatening my life unless I give you the arms. What kind of men are you anyway?"

Bakar grabbed Grey by the collar and raised his fist to strike him in the face.

"Stop it!" el-Fasil barked. "Leave us. I will speak to the ambassador privately."

Bakar looked puzzled and angry, but he released Grey, turned on his heel, and stormed out of the tent.

When they were alone, el-Fasil motioned for Grey to sit. He collapsed into a canvas camp chair across the table from his host, who spoke softly and deliberately. "Islam is the oldest religion in the Philippines. We have been here for hundreds of years, yet we are the minority in our own country. The Americans and other Westerners brought Christianity and Catholicism to our islands. In the name of religion and through coercion and intimidation, they eventually came to dominate the Muslims. Have you ever heard of Jolo Island, Mr. Grey?"

The ambassador shook his head.

"The Americans slaughtered a thousand Moro people there for the crime of being Muslims, and yet this country has been allied with the United States for a hundred years. My grandfather fought alongside the Americans during the last world war. What did he gain for his bravery and loyalty? Nothing. Less than nothing. They took his land, and by doing that, they took his soul.

"The Philippine government was corrupted by the United States when it built its military bases here. I took up arms against the land-grabbing Catholics after they raped my mother and killed my father." His voice was getting louder and higher pitched as he recalled the violence against his family. "They cut my father's ears off as trophies for their walls. I trained in the jungle camps and have been fighting not only for revenge but also our rights ever since.

I am not an unreasonable man, Mr. Grey. I only want what every man wants. Peace and the privilege to live the life I choose and to serve my god, Allah."

He stood, and his voice softened. "Yes, I am a peaceful man. A sophisticated man who finds no pleasure in taking a life. I regret that I cannot say the same for some of my men. Bakar, for example, takes great delight in killing. He would like nothing more than to behead you with his bolo knife. This is why you must deliver the guns to us right away. I will not be able to dissuade him much longer."

Grey was unmoved by el-Fasil's speech and emboldened by his own outrage. "We had an agreement, sir."

"No. You made an offer, and now you have my counter-offer. We have heard nothing from your friends. Why not?"

"I told you before. They are not my friends. They are business partners. They understand cash, nothing else. That is the deal."

"My deal was with James Welde. Where is he, with my money and my rifles, and why am I now talking to you?"

"Welde has given me the authority to speak for him. He regrets that he can't be here himself, but we will not give in to threats."

el-Fasil's face tightened, and his eyes narrowed. His tone was low and menacing. "You are a fool, Mr. Grey. Yes, a deal was made. Money changed hands, and yet I have agreed to accept the American rifles instead of the AK-47s. I have been more than reasonable, but my patience is wearing thin. Now you will deliver the guns to me, and perhaps I can persuade my captain to let you live. I trust you will find that a very generous offer." His demeanor darkened. "That is the new deal," he shouted, pounding the table to punctuate his words.

Fear swept through Grey's body in icy waves. He could say nothing.

"I will give you some time to consider, but I must warn you, don't take too long." He clapped his hands sharply, and Bakar appeared at the door of the tent. He had obviously been listening from outside and was now grinning broadly.

"Take him back now," el-Fasil ordered. He turned his back and said nothing more.

Bakar unholstered his pistol and stuck it in the Englishman's ribs. He pushed him out the door and kept the gun in his back until they reached the shelter. He clapped one handcuff around his prisoner's wrist, the other to the heavy chain, and made sure they were both locked.

"You won't get away with this!" Grey screamed. "You need me alive. I'm not fool enough to fall for this, you'll see."

Bakar said nothing as he walked away. He went back to check on the truck. The flatbed was almost empty. The lumber was arranged in stacks according to size. The tin for the roof was in a stack of its own. There were several hammers and two boxes of nails on top of the tin. The printing on the boxes said there were a thousand nails in each one. He yelled sharply, "Hurry it up. We haven't got all day."

The two men were hurrying as fast as they could. They were anxious to finish and collect their money. It had taken them two days to demolish the old house and sort out enough good lumber to fill the truck. It had been hard work, but it would be worth it. Each of them had a family to feed, and good-paying jobs were scarce. Bakar sat down on one of the stacks and watched as they finished. "Excellent," he said. He got to his feet and made sure he was positioned where Grey could see him. "Come around to the front of the truck, and I'll pay you."

The two men scrambled around the truck and stood side by side. Their backs were to the open ditch. Bakar pretended to go into his pocket but pulled out his pistol instead.

"I'm sorry, boys, but I can't let you go back and tell anyone how to find us." His eyes were black and stony like the eyes of a shark about to attack. Emotionless.

The man who had driven the truck was beginning to panic. His face was ashen, and his hands twitched. His voice trembled like that of a child in extremely cold weather. "You can trust us. No one even knows we're here I swear."

"Good. Then no one will ever know what happened to you."

"Please," the driver begged, "we aren't going…"

But he never finished his sentence. Bakar shot him in the middle of the forehead. He tumbled backward into the ditch. The second man turned to run, but Bakar's second bullet caught the side of his head just behind the ear. He ordered the men who had helped unload the truck to push the body in with the driver and to cover them with dirt.

"I don't want them stinking up my camp."

Chapter 21

INTRAMUROS

"The Philippine Islands were named for Spanish King Phillipe II, and the Spanish occupied them for 350 years. Subsequently dominated by the Chinese and briefly by America, the Philippines truly became a land of contrasts. Manila has a population of over fifteen million people and is actually comprised of four smaller, interconnected cities," Jillian read from her brochure. "We are in the most modern section, Makati, right now. I think we should go to the Intramuros. It's in the city center and is the historic part of Manila."

"Sounds good. I like history," said Kincaid.

They took a cab, passing from modern splendor through abject poverty and into the old city that is the Asia most Westerners think of when they think of Manila. The cabbie let them out near the walled fortress that was built by the Spaniards in the sixteenth century and now preserved by the Filipinos as a historic district. They strolled among ancient ruins and monuments from World War II to a lush garden in the center of the Intramuros.

"It's amazing that so much beauty can exist alongside the artifacts of war," Jillian said as she gazed at a bullet-riddled wall.

"The United States bombed the Philippines during the last world war. I'm amazed that these walls are standing at all."

"War is so stupid," Jillian said.

"Thomas Hardy said, 'War makes rattling good history, but peace is poor reading.' And I told you, I like history."

"Sometimes I really don't get you, Kincaid."

"I think you've forgotten that I'm a soldier. I'm comfortable with war."

She just looked at him. She had no answer to a statement so foreign to her sensibilities.

Kincaid suggested they explore more of the city.

"Yes, let's. I'd like to check out the market," Jillian said.

The streets were alive with vendors, tourists, and children. Pedicabs, scooters, and horse-drawn carts added to the gallimaufry. The colors, sounds, and smells were intoxicating as the two explored the shops and the market of the city center.

"I want to buy you a shirt," Jillian said.

"I like the shirt I'm wearing."

"It's nice, but I suspect it will have lost its charm by morning."

"You may have a point." In addition to a toothbrush, Kincaid had neglected to bring a change of clothes.

Jillian thumbed through a stack of shirts and picked out a blue, linen guayabera. "What size are you, extra-large?"

"Yeah, good guess."

"How much for this shirt?" she asked the merchant.

The woman who owned the little shop replied, "Eighty-five dollars US."

"That is way too much. I am thinking forty dollars."

"Sixty," the old Filipina said.

"Okay, let's split the difference. Fifty dollars."

"Because I like you, the shirt is yours," the woman said. "It will look nice on your handsome man." She smiled at Kincaid.

"Thank you," he said to them both. He took the bag, and they started down the street.

They hadn't gone far before Jillian exclaimed, "JolliBee! We have to go in here. JolliBee is a fast-food chain that is very popular in the Philippines." She ordered spaghetti with hot dogs, and Kincaid, who wasn't feeling particularly adventurous, tried the fried chicken and a cup of rice.

"What is this brown sauce?"

"No one really knows, but it's good. Try it."

He cautiously touched the spoon to his tongue. "This is tasty. I wasn't expecting big things."

Jillian was halfway through her spaghetti when she put down her plastic fork. The wistful expression on her face slowly turned to one of dismay.

"What's the matter, Jillian?"

"I was just remembering when my dad brought me here. I'm so worried about him. I keep telling myself that he's okay, but not knowing for sure is hard."

"We're going to find him. Try to think positive thoughts."

"I think I need a drink."

They found a bar, sat at a small, round table, and ordered martinis. The bar was modest in size and dimly lit with blue lights and a large mirrored ball that flung tiny dots of white light over the entire room. At the far end of the bar was a narrow stage where a spotlight was focused on two exotic dancers. They were topless and wearing tiny bikini bottoms.

Jillian squirmed uncomfortably and shielded her eyes with her hand. "I didn't realize this was a strip club." She turned in her seat to face Kincaid. "At least you get to see some beautiful girls."

"Uh. I don't think so. Those are not girls. They're boys." He chuckled.

"No way! They have breasts. And nice ones at that."

Kincaid said, "You don't get out much, do you? They're called ladyboys. All silicone and duct tape."

"I think I'm ready for another martini."

Before they headed back to their hotel, they'd had several martinis. Jillian was a little woozy by the time they reached the street. "Let's take a jeepney back," Kincaid suggested.

They boarded a vehicle that looked like a jeep in the front and a bus in the back. It had no glass in the windows and was painted in several bright colors that featured lots of primitive artwork on all sides. There were few riders, so they picked two seats near the front. The driver appeared to be all of seventeen. Kincaid tried not to think about that. He knew Jillian would not be able to walk very far, and this was at least as safe as wandering the streets with an intoxicated woman.

By the time she had fumbled through her purse and found her room key, she had regained most of her composure. Kincaid followed her in and helped her onto the bed. She sank into the pillows and closed her eyes. He took off her shoes. "Is this the part where you undress me?" she slurred.

"Only if you'd like me to." He sat down next to her on the bed.

She sat up and started unbuttoning her blouse. When it was off and lying on the floor, she twisted around so that her back was to him. "Unfasten me?"

He unhooked her bra and held it while she slipped her arms out. Then she turned back to face him. Her firm breasts were perfect. Not small but not too big. She leaned in and pressed them hard against his chest. Her warm, moist lips met his, gently at first and then firmer. Her tongue teased and darted, then retreated, inviting him in. Kincaid had one hand on her cheek and the other on the small of her back. There was a moment of hesitation. Ethics wouldn't allow him to take advantage of an inebriate, no matter how tempting. And Jillian was nothing if she wasn't tempting. She trembled slightly as her hips wiggled the tight skirt up her thighs. She put her hand on his and moved it down, aching for his touch.

"Are you sure about his?" he whispered.

She said nothing but pressed her feet into the bed, rising to meet his timorous hand. He realized she wasn't wearing underwear when his fingers found her center, now warm and moist with desire. She tore hungrily at his clothes, silently imploring him to abandon them. With his one free hand and her help, he managed to unfasten his belt and shed his pants.

"Leave your shirt on," she gasped. "I don't want you to stop what you're doing."

But he did stop long enough to pull his shirt over his head. She used the moment to kick off her skirt. Kincaid lowered his head and used his tongue to pick up where his fingers had left off. Jillian squirmed and moaned with delight until she could stand it no longer. "Come up here" she panted, pulling him onto her. His body was firm and heavy, but she welcomed the weight. "I want you inside me," she whispered.

———

THE SUN SLITHERED THROUGH THE GAP OF THE HOTEL

curtains and streamed over Kincaid's face. He woke with Jillian burrowed into his side and her leg draped over his. She was beautiful in the golden glow of morning. Her hair cascaded over his left arm and onto her pillow. He hated to wake her, to break the concupiscent spell they had shared last night, but he was hungry for breakfast, and there was work to be done. Today they would travel to Siquijor Island to see if they could find any clues to the whereabouts of one James Welde. He had left a map of that area in the cockpit of his helicopter. *That must mean something.*

He gently slid her leg off his and nudged her awake. She opened her eyes and smiled at him. "Good morning," she whispered. "I was almost afraid you'd be gone when I woke up."

"Why would you think that?"

"I know how men are, typically."

"Well, honey, you'll find I'm not your typical male."

"Yeah, I am finding that out." She punched him playfully in the ribs. He laughed and pushed her face into the pillow. She wrestled free and tried tickling him but to no effect.

"Two can play that game." He dug his fingers into her side. She squealed and giggled uncontrollably, flailing around on the bed.

"Stop, stop, please stop," she pleaded breathlessly. He did stop and she climbed on him and sat with him between her legs. "Let's just talk about the first thing that pops up," she teased. She didn't have to wait long. She moved slowly at first, up and down, then side to side. She repeated the motion over and over, gradually increasing her speed until neither of them could hold back any longer. "Yes, yes," she shouted. Kincaid laughed a laugh of release and sublimation. Jillian collapsed on his chest. They lay there for several long minutes before either of them had the strength or the will to move.

"We have to get up and get going," he said, looking at his watch. "It's almost eight o'clock."

"I'm going to take a shower." She got up and walked naked toward the bathroom. She stopped at the door and looked back at him. "Don't try to come with me," she called.

Kincaid ignored her. He had taken the map out of his pants pocket and was unfolding it.

"I'm warning you for the last time, don't even think about coming with me to the shower."

"If I come in there, we'll never get out of here." He watched her as she disappeared into the bathroom. "That's one fantastic ass," he called after her.

The map he'd found in Welde's chopper was a Sectional Aeronautical Chart: a map with visual checkpoints such as railroads, towers, roads, etc. that enabled a pilot to pinpoint locations visually in flight. Siquijor Island had been circled on this one, and a pair of coordinates had been written in pencil inside the circle. Kincaid drew two straight lines along the coordinates and studied the point at which they intersected. It was in an area of heavy vegetation near a small body of water. That's where they needed to go.

Jillian eventually emerged, shrouded in a cloud of steam with a white towel wrapped around her head. He stepped around her and into the shower. "If you don't put some clothes on, I'm going to have to take a cold one," he complained. By the time he'd finished, Jillian was dressed in white shorts and a pink tank top. She watched him dry off and put on his shorts and the new shirt she'd bought him at the market. She stuffed his T-shirt into her bag along with her clothes from yesterday.

"The lady at the market was right. You are a handsome man."

Chapter 22

SIQUIJOR ISLAND

They ducked into the dining room and grabbed a quick bite from the free buffet before catching a cab to the waterfront. "We want the ferry to Siquijor Island," Kincaid told the driver. A few minutes later, they were at the port. The agent at the ferry office told them the next trip started in ten minutes. Two hundred and fifty pesos bought two seats for the ninety-minute ride. Once on the island, they rented scooters and set off.

"I hope you know where we are going," Jillian shouted over the buzz of the engines.

"Map reading is one of my specialties," Kincaid yelled back.

A few kilometers out of town, the pavement ended. There was a shack where a girl of about twelve was selling fruit and water. They purchased a couple of bottles of the water and headed down a narrow sandy trail. The trail got narrower and rougher as it went deeper into the jungle. Kincaid led the way. Every so often he would stop, consult the sectional, and check the coordinates on his SAT phone. "We're almost there," he said each time.

After they had gone a few kilometers seeing nothing but jungle, they passed a white frame house with a large front porch. The trail was nothing more than a path now, and Jillian's instincts were begging her to turn around. "Are you sure you know where we are?"

Kincaid didn't answer. A few hundred meters past the house was a large clearing. Three crude huts were positioned around a deep, blue pond. A long block building stood thirty meters from the pond, and beyond that was an empty field where an orange windsock fluttered from a tall pole.

"We're here." Kincaid parked his scooter in front of the building. A large steel door set into the block wall was locked with two large padlocks. They walked around the entire structure. There were no windows. It looked to Jillian like they had come a long way for nothing.

They heard it before they saw it. A green ATV was approaching from the direction of the house. It was moving quickly and heading straight for them. Then it was there. It was driven by a woman with a shotgun. She stopped and pointed the gun at Kincaid. He wished he could have brought his pistol with him.

The woman cut the engine and climbed off the vehicle, keeping the shotgun trained on him. If she pulled the trigger, he would be a bloodstain on the wall behind him. "What are you people doing here?" she demanded. She was American and could probably be quite attractive when she wanted to. Right now, she seemed to want to look intimidating. She was doing a good job.

"We were just out on an explore, and I guess we got a little lost," Jillian said.

The woman stared at Jillian as if she had just seen Elvis. Her eyes brightened, and her mouth spread into a wide grin. "You're Jillian Welde."

"How did you know that?"

"I've seen pictures of you at your daddy's house."

"You know my father? Is he here?" Excitement flashed across Jillian's face. Her heart beat faster in her chest. *This must be the woman the neighbors had seen with him at his house.*

"Of course, I know him. He's a real good friend of mine."

"Is he here?" Jillian repeated.

The woman looked at the ground. "No. I haven't seen him in over a week. I'm not sure where he is."

The words doused Jillian's elation like cold water on an abandoned campfire.

"Where do you think he is, ma'am? You must have some idea." Kincaid said.

"Not really. At least not for sure. He said he was going out of the country for a few days."

"Out of the country? Do you mean like Taiwan, Singapore, or where?"

"He didn't say. I know he goes to London sometimes."

"London? That's quite a trip."

The woman bit her lower lip as if she had said more than she meant to. "He was supposed to be back by now. He was excited to see you, Jillian."

Jillian said nothing. Kincaid spoke again. "We've been looking for him ourselves, ma'am. We found this place with a map from his helicopter."

"Gloria."

"Ma'am?"

"My name is Gloria. Gloria Chatham."

"Nice to meet you, Gloria. I'm Jillian's friend. Call me Kincaid. Would you mind putting that shotgun down? No offense."

"Oh, sorry. Habit. We don't like people snooping around here."

"Then I don't suppose you'd tell me what this place is."

"James won't mind. Jillian is his daughter, after all. That's my house up yonder. I heard you go by. This is a waypoint where he warehouses stock sometimes before he ships it out to his clients."

"What kind of stock?"

"Computer parts. You know, that's his business. He makes computer parts."

"And he flies them in and out of here in his chopper?"

"That's right. Helo is about the only way to get around the Philippines if you're in business. There are over seven thousand islands in this archipelago."

"Do you think it would be okay if we had a look inside the warehouse?"

"What for?" Gloria's lips tightened and her eyes narrowed.

"Maybe there's some clue in there, something you might have overlooked."

Jillian followed his lead. "I'm sure Dad would want us to check it out if he is in trouble," she said. "Kincaid is trained in matters like these. I trust him."

Gloria hesitated but she thought Jillian made sense. "I guess it's okay." She took a key ring out of her pocket and unlocked the padlocks.

Inside, the heat was stifling. There were no lights. Kincaid could only see the concrete floor as far as the sunlight streamed through the door. Gloria took a lantern from a hook on the wall, switched it on, and handed it to Kincaid. There was just one room. It was empty except for a wooden crate standing in a corner. He went over to it and lifted the lid. There were several sheets of grease-proof paper and a faint odor that smelled a little like marzipan. It was the same smell he'd detected in the crates at Welde's factory. There had definitely been plastic explosive in this box at some point. C4, or its British cousin PE4, is usually manufactured in small blocks and wrapped in grease-proof paper.

He looked at Gloria. Her face was only partially lit by the lantern, so he couldn't read her expression. *Does she really believe Welde is flying computer parts in and out of her backyard, or is she complicit in the gunrunning operation?* He had to believe she knew what was going on, especially if she was an intimate friend who spent time at his beach house. Jillian was having similar thoughts but said nothing. Kincaid decided it was pointless to pursue the issue. "Nothing here," he said, slamming the lid shut. They walked the perimeter of the room. There were broad scratches on the floor, probably made by heavy crates being dragged in and out, but that was all there was to see. The two women followed him out the door and into the bright sunlight. He stood for a moment and waited for his eyes to adjust.

"It was nice to meet you, Gloria," Kincaid said.

"You, too. Try not to worry too much, honey. Your daddy can take care of himself. He'll be back soon, I'm sure."

None of them were convinced, but these were the things people said when they were fearful. Jillian tried to hold back her tears but a couple of them escaped around the corner of her eye. "I'm sure you're right." Her voice quivered. "I'm so glad we met." She stepped into Gloria's arms, and the women hugged warmly.

Kincaid interrupted. "If I leave you my number, would you call me when you hear from him?"

Gloria motioned at the dense jungle surrounding the clearing. "Are you kidding? You think I get phone service out here?"

He shrugged. "Never hurts to ask. Let me give you my number anyway, just in case something comes up and you can get to a phone."

"Okay, but I don't think I'll need it."

Jillian produced a scrap of paper and a pen from her purse. Kincaid wrote his name and number on it and handed it to Gloria. "Just in case," he repeated.

They said their goodbyes, and Kincaid started his scooter. Jillian followed as they rode past Gloria's house and up the path. After they had gone a half mile, he pulled over to the side of the trail. Jillian stopped beside him. "I know you're feeling discouraged right now," he said, "but at least we know he hasn't been in a plane crash. His helo is in Manila, and we know he flew commercial, so that's one less thing we have to worry about." He was right, but his words offered scant solace. The fact remained that her father was way overdue to return home and his whereabouts remained a mystery.

"Yeah," she said over the hum of the motors, "that's one less thing." She twisted the throttle on her handlebars, and the little scooter sped off toward the main road.

It was the middle of the afternoon, and they still had to catch a ferry, a cab, and a plane to get back to the rental car for the six-hour drive back to El Nido. They stopped along the road for roasted chicken on a stick that a black man was selling from a rusty barrel that he had cut in half to create a makeshift cooker. It was lying on its side, and a piece of a shopping cart served as the grill over a smoky wood fire. It was the best chicken Kincaid had ever tasted.

By six o'clock, they were on the plane winging their way to Puerto Princesa. "I wish we'd gone back to that hangar to see what they know about your dad's business," he said.

"You really think he's in the arms business, don't you?"

"I know he is, Jillian. We've seen the evidence. And Gloria knows it too. I think she's a part of his operation."

"I don't know how you can be sure. All we have found are some empty crates. They could be used to pack computers as easily as guns."

"Time will tell."

The flight attendant came by with the drink cart and served them two glasses of wine. By the time Kincaid had finished his, Jillian had fallen asleep against her window. It was after eight o'clock when they retrieved the Toyota from short-term parking. "Can you drive home?" Jillian asked. Her eyes told him she was much too tired to take the wheel.

"Sure, doll. Why don't you get some sleep? I'll get you there."

"I think maybe I will." Then she added, "It's going to be way too late to catch the ferry to Oceania by the time we get back. Will you stay with me tonight?"

"It'll be a pleasure." He smiled.

Chapter 23

4 NOVEMBER

It was two o'clock in the morning when Kincaid drove through the gate and into the sandy driveway of the Welde beach house. Jillian was asleep in the back seat. He opened the door and gently shook her awake.

"Jillian, we're home."

She sat upright and rubbed her eyes. "What time is it?"

"Just past two. You slept most of the way home."

They stumbled up the concrete stairs, and she unlocked the door. "You want some breakfast?"

"No thanks. I'm dead tired. I just need some sleep." He yawned as he shuffled into the hallway toward the guest bedroom.

She said, "I'm wide awake now. You go ahead. I'm going to make myself an egg or something."

Kincaid grunted in acknowledgment as he took off his clothes and fell into the bed. When he awoke, the mid-morning sun was streaming through the open window and puddling on his ivory sheets. The gauzy curtains danced on a gentle breeze fresh from its journey across the cobalt sea. He could hear the waves rushing to the beach and the hiss of their retreat.

He pulled on his shorts and padded to the kitchen. Jillian

had made a pot of coffee, but she was not there. He took a cup from the cupboard, filled it with the steaming, black elixir, and went into the living room. No Jillian. Through the windows, he saw her splashing along the edge of the water. She bent down, picked something up, and started walking again. She was gathering seashells. A few delicate, white clouds dotted the sky like errant brushstrokes on a canvas almost as blue as the water.

Kincaid went outside and sat on the deck, his legs dangling over the side. He watched the lithe young woman, her honey-blond hair flitting about her face on the silken breeze. Occasionally, she made a vain attempt to hook it behind her ears. He was struck by the beauty of the scene. It was almost enough to make him forget the list of things he needed to do today. After a few minutes, he went down the stairs and across the sand to her. "Good morning, lady," he called over the delicate percussion of the surf.

"Good morning yourself." She smiled back. "Did you sleep well?"

"Like a babe in arms." His feet sank into deepening holes as he stood in the lacy waves. His ankles were alternately pushed and pulled by their motion as they advanced and retreated across the shifting, gray sand. He could taste the salt through his nose.

"Would you like me to make you breakfast? I've already had mine."

"No thanks. I need to make a trip to town. Do you think that old jeep in the garage runs?"

"I don't know, but why don't we drive the car?"

"My plan is to go alone. You need to stay here in case your dad returns today. I'd hate for you to be out looking for him only to find out he's back here."

"That's a good point, but where are you going?"

"I want to go back to the plant and talk to Marco again. He knows more than he's told us. Then I'm going to the police and file a missing person report. We need to get them involved if we can. Lastly, I want to get my things from the resort. If you don't object, I think it best if I stay here with you until this is all over."

"I don't object at all. I think that would be fine."

"Good. Then I'm going to go check out the jeep."

She watched him walk back toward the house. He was a strong, fit man. Not big with bulging muscles but rather, lean and athletic. More than anything, he was tenacious. A man who inspired trust. She felt safe with him.

Kincaid walked around the jeep. It was a more fitting vehicle for a soldier, and he liked it. The tires seemed okay. There were a few loose tools in the back: a lug wrench and jack, a rusty machete, and a couple of wrenches. He climbed into the driver's seat. The gas gauge registered half full. He turned the key. The starter motor hesitated for a moment and then labored against the torque of the engine. It turned over slowly but suddenly burst to life. Apparently, there was just enough juice in the battery to start the jeep once. Kincaid breathed a sigh of relief. The drive into town would probably be enough to recharge it. He left the engine running and went back into the house. He took a quick shower and got dressed. By then, Jillian was inside, waiting in the living room. She was holding a sandwich.

"Just in case you get hungry." she said. "It's ham and cheese."

"My favorite."

As he took the sandwich, she pecked him on the cheek. "Be careful, Kincaid. Stay safe."

"I always do," he replied. "Close the gate behind me,

and make sure it's locked. Don't let anyone in, and keep the doors locked until I get back. I shouldn't be too long."

"Be back before dark?"

He could hear the concern in her voice. "Don't worry. I'll be back way before then."

Chapter 24

SOME ANSWERS

He drove the jeep through the gate and watched in his mirror until he was sure it was closed. He turned north and headed into El Nido.

His first stop was the police station. He parked the jeep and went through the chain-link fence and then the front door. The same uniformed officer he'd seen the last time he was there was occupying the same desk as before. Cutro was at a desk to the left and behind the cop. "May I help you, sir?" the officer said.

"I'm here to see Cutro."

By this time, Cutro had left his desk and was walking toward Kincaid. "Look what the dog dragged in," he joked.

"Hello, Sergeant." Kincaid towered over the policeman as they shook hands. "Any news about the murder?"

"Which one?" Cutro replied. There was a hint of resignation in his voice.

"Any of them."

"Not to speak of. Are you here with news for me?"

"No. Actually, I'm here to file a missing person report."

"Really? Who's missing?"

"His name is James Welde. His daughter was in here but was told to wait a few days. Apparently, you guys don't start looking for someone until all hope of finding them is lost."

"C'mon, Kincaid. Half the time someone is reported missing, they're just on a drunk someplace. We don't have the manpower to go on a wild goose chase every time a guy goes on a bender. You say James Welde is missing?"

"That's right."

"How long has he been gone?"

"I'm not sure. His daughter came to visit, and he wasn't home. We've been looking for a few days without any luck."

"James Welde owns that computer business, right?"

"That's him."

"We've had a little interest in him ourselves. We suspect he might be using that business as a cover for illicit activity of some sort. I don't suppose you know anything about that?"

"Hey, I've been told to stay out of your business. I'm just helping a woman find her father, that's all."

"That would be the woman I saw you with the last time you were here? She's a looker."

"That's her. Jillian Welde. She just flew in from the States, and she's plenty worried about her dad."

"She should be. A guy like that could be anywhere. He flies his own helicopter and mixes with a questionable crowd. Hell, he might even be dead."

"Yeah, he might be. Can you help us or not?"

"I'll put somebody on it. We'll ask around. You've got me interested now, but don't wait by the phone. Like I said, we have our hands full already, and I'm short on manpower."

"Okay, Cutro. Thanks." He started toward the door.

"Oh, Kincaid, one more thing. I'd watch my back if I were you. You've already pissed some people off."

"That's what you keep telling me."

As soon as he was out the door, the cop at the front desk picked up the phone.

Kincaid climbed into the jeep and held his breath as he turned the ignition switch. The engine started right up. He exhaled heavily. The drive into town had charged the battery.

He found Welde's factory and drove through the gate. As far as he could tell, the same cars were parked in the lot as before. As he approached the door, he saw a surveillance camera overhead that he hadn't noticed when he was there with Jillian. He pressed the buzzer, and Marco answered.

"Hello, Marco. It's Kincaid."

"We are not accepting visitors right now."

"Open up. I want to talk to you about your boss."

"Get lost, man. I have nothing else to say to you."

Kincaid was getting impatient. "Open the door, Marco. If you don't, I'll bring the police out here. I have enough on you to get a search warrant. I think you'd rather talk to me."

The buzzer sounded, and he pulled the door open. Marco was coming down the stairs from the office. "What do you want?" His face was taut with tension, betraying his act of defiance.

"I want to see in your storage rooms."

"There's nothing in there, just like last time."

"Open the doors, Marco. I'd hate to embarrass you in front of all these women."

Marco reluctantly open the first door. The room was empty. He opened the second one. The folded cardboard boxes were still there in neat stacks. The third room was empty except for more boxes and the two crates that he found when Jillian brought him here. Marco had told the truth.

Kincaid clapped him on the shoulder. "You weren't lying, Marco. That's good. Now let's go up to your office."

"What for? What do you want from me?"

"I need some information, that's all. Then I'll be on my way."

"You can ask me here. My girls don't speak English. Besides, I can't tell you nothing."

"No, let's go up. I doubt you want your employees to hear what I have to say."

"Can't you hear, you son of a bitch? I said they don't speak English." He was almost shouting now, out of frustration and more than a little fear. He didn't want to be alone in a room with Kincaid and no witnesses.

Kincaid was silent, but his stare sent chills up Marco's spine. It seemed to him to be the cold, hard look of a man who had taken many lives. Marco turned and headed back upstairs. Kincaid followed him. When the door was closed, Marco faced him.

"I want you to tell me everything you know about Welde and your operation here," Kincaid said.

"I'm not telling you shit, man."

"Okay. Let me tell you what I know. This factory is a front for a gunrunning operation. Welde picks up the arms and munitions in Manila and flies them in his helicopter to an intermediate location on Siquijor Island. From there, they go out to the buyer, or he brings them here, and you store them in those rooms downstairs. He's probably been selling AKs to a guy named el-Fasil. All the while, your sweet little ladies are soldering motherboards out front and collecting fifty cents an hour. How am I doing so far?"

Marco looked thunderstruck, so Kincaid pressed on. "Your boss has gone missing somewhere out of the country. My guess is he stepped on somebody's toes and they've eliminated him. If I'm right, that means you're next, Marco. So, the question is who would want him out of the way."

"I don't know, mister. That's the truth." Marco moved and took a position behind the desk.

"When was the last time you spoke to him?"

"Why should I tell you anything?"

"Because if you don't, I'm going to make the rest of your day very unpleasant."

Marco made a move to open the desk drawer. Kincaid grabbed Marco's arm with his left hand and his fingers with the right. The smaller man struggled to free himself, but Kincaid bent his fingers back. The pain was so intense that Marco stopped resisting, and Kincaid relaxed his grip on his fingers.

"You shouldn't try to go for a weapon, Marco. I'll only feed it to you one bullet at a time. Now are you going to answer my questions, or would you rather I beat it out of you?"

Marco could see he had no choice but to cooperate. "What was the question?"

"When was the last time you talked to Welde?"

Marco was sweating and his heart was pounding in his chest, but he said nothing. *Who is this guy, and why is he here?*

"The questions are going to get much tougher, so you might as well start answering the easy ones."

"He called me a few days ago."

"Exactly when was it, Marco?"

"I'm not sure. A week, ten days, maybe two weeks. I can't remember."

"You're trying my patience, pal. Where was he?"

"He didn't say."

Kincaid let go of all Marco's fingers except the little one. He put his thumb against its knuckle and squeezed. It snapped like a twig. Marco screamed and tears welled up in his eyes.

"Where was he?" Kincaid gripped Marco's fourth finger tightly.

"I swear to God I don't know. Please, mister, I don't know, on my mother's life. He didn't say."

"I believe you. Let's try another. What did he say? And don't say you don't know. I'm getting tired of this game already."

Marco thought his attacker was weakening. Maybe he didn't have the stomach to keep going. "I can't tell you that. Sorry."

Kincaid broke the finger. Marco screamed so loud that the women downstairs stopped working to listen. They were afraid of what was going on in the office. Marco was crying now; veins were pulsing in his neck. Kincaid grasped the middle finger. "I'll bet this one will hurt," he said calmly.

"Okay, okay. I'll tell you. Please don't break it," Marco begged.

"What did he say, Marco?"

"He said that I should expect a shipment in a few days."

"What's a few days?"

"I don't know. A few days, that's all he said. Please, please believe me, that's all he said. A big shipment was coming, and I should prepare for it. I'm begging you, please let me go."

Kincaid snapped Marco's middle finger. The pain was so intense he almost passed out. Kincaid let go of his arm and shoved him to the floor. "That was for causing me trouble and so you don't forget. Next time I won't be so gentle." He left the plant manager writhing on the floor and crying.

The workers, huddled at the far end of the room, watched as he descended the stairs. "Magandang hapon, ladies," he said as he went out the door. He smiled to himself. He had learned how to say "good afternoon" but had no idea how to say "ladies" in Tagalog. *They probably speak Spanish anyway.*

He headed the jeep back toward town and the docks. He checked his watch. If he figured it right, there should be a ferry back to Oceania within the hour. He figured right. When he arrived at the boat, the last of the passengers were shuffling aboard. He parked the jeep, took the key from the ignition, and hurried up the passerelle. He settled into a seat beside the starboard railing. This was a smaller craft than the catamaran he was accustomed to and much slower. He gazed out over the sea that stretched lazily to the horizon. Bright blue here and emerald-green there and yet the clearest water he had ever seen. It seemed almost surreal. Kincaid took a deep breath of salt air and thought about what he had learned so far.

Marco had confirmed his postulate. James Welde was, indeed, trafficking arms. Probably in small quantities. His Eurocopter could carry maybe five hundred kilos comfortably. Not a lot of guns and ammunition but enough to supply a modest force. He was using Gloria Chatham's warehouse and his own plant to store them until they could be sold to the locals and, most likely, to interests in other parts of the world. There wouldn't be enough demand locally to live the life he was leading. He was a person of interest to the El Nido police, and he was alive as of approximately ten days ago. *Not bad for a day's work.*

Chapter 25

19 OCTOBER

James Welde was a self-made man and proud of it. He rose from being an airman at Clark Air Force Base to being a successful entrepreneur. He had started small, smuggling pistols off the base and selling them to local thugs. As time went on, he made contacts that would enable him to procure more sophisticated weapons and solidify other contacts willing to purchase them. It was a spectacularly lucrative undertaking, and by the time he was honorably discharged, he was in a position to buy a company to cover for his real business. In the Philippines, there was a workforce that already had the skills necessary to fabricate computer components. He gave them jobs and saw it as a noble undertaking—empowering people to finance a better way of life, support their children, and maintain their dignity. Welde Technologies was good for everyone.

At least, that's how he rationalized his illicit endeavors. And when an official at the base discovered weapons were being sold to Welde, plastic explosives wired to the ignition of that man's car made sure that he didn't interfere with Welde's enterprise. An enterprise that supplied instruments of war to forces, initially in the Middle East and, most recently, Africa. An enterprise that aided in the destruction of property and human life but also sponsored the lifestyle and the respect that Welde coveted. By the time his source of American arms inevitably dried up, he had cultivated contacts in Russia, Great Britain, and Egypt that were able to supply him with AK-47s and PE4 that he, in turn, could sell to insurgents and terrorists the world over. He had a house on the beach, his own helicopter, a thriving business, a devoted girlfriend, and two beautiful daughters. He wore a Rolex and drove a Mercedes-Benz.

Lately, Welde had been purchasing inventory from an Egyptian arms dealer. A manufacturer in Egypt had acquired the Russian tooling necessary to build a gun almost identical to the original Kalashnikov rifle. They were producing a semi-automatic model for export to the United States. Welde's source was a secondary factory that converted the semi-automatic rifle to fully automatic. Since he was buying in bulk, he quadrupled his money on each one, and he sold them by the hundreds. The weapons would come in to a remote airfield in the Philippines by transport plane. Welde then flew them to his warehouse on Siquijor Island and stored them there until he sold them. Sometimes he helicoptered them to El Nido for distribution to his local clients, and sometimes he shipped them right back out again for overseas sales. Lots of wars and lots of terrorism lately meant the demand for AK-47s was high. After all, AKs were the most popular weapon of "freedom fighters" everywhere. He got his ammo and plastic explosive from the same vendor. British-made PE4 was not as popular as the American C4, but it was essentially the same, and the suicide bombers who employed it never knew the difference. Business was good. Life was good. Until it wasn't.

It was his largest purchase to date—two thousand rifles, one hundred thousand rounds of ammunition, and five hundred pounds of PE4. They were to arrive directly from Egypt in a C-47 transport, essentially a Douglas DC3 built for the military during WW II. The plane was old and slow, but the cool thing was it would be his. It was part of the deal, and it would mean that after this initial investment, his profit margin would increase exponentially. There was some risk in this transaction, Welde knew that. To make the nine-thousand-mile trip, his shipment would need to refuel six times with stops in Saudi Arabia, Iran, Pakistan, India, Myanmar, and Vietnam before arriving in the Philippines. But Welde was used to risk. The bigger the risk, the bigger the reward. Besides, he knew who to bribe and who needed to be paid off in each of those countries to ensure his cargo wouldn't be scrutinized too closely. He had forged all the necessary paperwork including end-user certificates. He had leased warehouse space near his airstrip and trucks to move the munitions there from the plane when they arrived. He'd hired drivers who he knew could be trusted. They could be trusted because they were told they were transporting farm implements. They didn't ask any questions.

Welde was excited. It was the beginning of the next phase of his business. He was moving up in the world. He wired half the money to the seller and flew his helicopter to the rendezvous point to await the arrival of his new plane. He waited and then he waited some more. Five hours dragged by, then six. Six agonizing hours before he got the call.

Something had gone wrong. Two F1s of the Iranian Air Force intercepted the plane over Bandar Abbas. His pilots were instructed to follow the Iranians to the airport and land there. The pilot of the C-47 apprised Welde of the situation by phone while they were still in the air. That was the last he heard from them. They weren't coming to Manila. Not tonight. Probably not ever. He had lost a small fortune.

Welde was devastated. It was money he couldn't afford to lose. There was payroll to be made, mortgage payments on his house, business loans and lease payments on the factory, the car, and the helicopter. And alimony payments. He hated sending money to his ex-wife. *Why didn't she ever remarry?* Welde was sure she remained single out of spite, to punish him for neglecting her to pursue his business. She could have stayed with him. He didn't want a divorce, and she chose to go back to America, but still he had to pay. *How could that be fair?*

Where, exactly, was his airplane loaded with smuggled arms? Would the Iranians be able to trace them to him? Could INTERPOL be involved? What was his exposure? The pressures weighed on him. He had to find answers to his questions, and he had to recoup his losses. Quickly.

Maneuvering over the city of Makati, he spotted the familiar Park'n'Fly sign on the side of the car park first. Then the hangars on the other side of the street. He checked the windsock. A stiff breeze right to left. It was going to take a little luck to stick this landing. He maneuvered the chopper carefully between the row of hangars and the adjacent building. There it was, the big, white circle. He eased in and hovered for a moment, making slight adjustments in the craft's position and attitude. The undersized rubber wheels settled to the tarmac precisely on the small, red inner circle.

"Am I lucky or just good?" Welde smiled. He told himself the landing had been all skill, and no air force pilot could have done better. As he rolled the chopper into its hangar, his mind raced through the list of contacts he kept in his head. Someone had to know what had happened to his shipment. And someone had to know where he could get more guns. He had made promises to his clients. They expected their arms. Most of them had already given him deposits, which he used to pay for the missing plane and its lethal cargo. He would have to stall them until he could restock.

But James Welde was nothing if not lucky. He drove his leased Mercedes to his favorite hotel in Manila. As soon as he got to his room, he was on the phone. He dialed his contacts in each country along the flight's intended route. No one had seen the plane in Pakistan, India, or Myanmar. Then he called his contact in Vietnam, a man he knew only as Trang. Trang had not seen or heard anything of Welde's shipment either. That told him the plane never made it out of Iran.

Trang did have other information that might be of interest. "I'm sorry to hear of your troubles, James, but I'm glad you called. I've been trying to reach you."

"If it's good news, I'm all ears. Otherwise, I don't want to hear it."

"There are rumors that an Englishman is trying to sell some American M16s. My source tells me that there is a huge number of the rifles in Ho Chi Minh City that only a few people know about."

"Can you put me in touch with these people, and can we get our hands on the guns before someone else does?"

"You know how business is done here. The money talks, and the first, best offer wins."

"I can get the money. And I want all the M16s they have." The truth was he wasn't sure he could get the financing to swing a big deal right now. The cash outlay for the lost ship-ment had nearly bankrupted him and undoubtedly would have a deleterious effect on his credit. There was no reason to believe he could recoup his money if the shipment was truly confiscated by the Iranians.

"All they have?"

"Let's say up to a thousand, if the price is right."

"Okay, boss, but you'd better bring a lot of cash."

"Just get me in, Trang. I'll make the deal."

"What's my end?"

"I think a dollar a rifle should make you happy."

"Five would make me ecstatic."

"Let's go for 'thrilled'. Two bucks."

"Three, and I'll settle for euphoric."

"Fine. Three dollars US."

"I'm on it."

Chapter 26

TWO HUNDRED
THOUSAND DOLLARS

elde left the car in long-term parking, as he always did, and caught the 7:00 a.m. nonstop flight to El-Nido. The most expensive but by far the fastest way home. He called his girlfriend to pick him up at the airport.

She was younger than him, but then Welde had always been attracted to younger women. Maybe she was too young. After all, he had met her through his daughter, but her incandescent smile, nubile figure, and vivacious personality proved irresistible, and he had unabashedly responded to her flirtations. Unfortunately for him, nothing developed between them. That is, until about two months ago when she showed up at his house and said, "I feel like doing something promiscuous."

This morning, she was behind the wheel of her yellow Datsun 240Z, the wind blowing her hair across her face as they motored out of town.

"I missed you," she said. "Did you miss me?"

He stared at the muscles of her honey-brown legs flexing as she shifted gears. "Of course."

"Did your business go well?"

"Yeah, it went well," he lied. She didn't need to know the truth and probably didn't care anyway. As far as he knew, she had no idea that the computer business was a cover for his arms deals. The roar of the wind and the tires on the highway made conversation difficult, so they didn't talk much until they reached the house around noon.

"Let's go sit on the beach," she said.

"You go. I need to make some calls." He picked up the phone and dialed his office.

"Welde Technologies."

"Hello, Marco. It's me."

"How did it go?"

She stuck her hand between his legs from behind and gently squeezed.

"Don't do that," he yelped.

"What?"

"Not you, Marco." He put his hand over the phone and turned to face her. "I thought you were going down to the beach. I'm busy."

She smiled broadly, revealing bright, white teeth. "Okay, I'm going."

Welde returned the phone to his mouth. "It's bad, Marco. The plane was intercepted somewhere over Iran. We don't know where it is now or the disposition of the cargo."

"No way! What about the pilots?"

"Nothing."

"What are you going to do?"

"There's not much I can do except wait and see if I have any exposure. The arms are gone. I'm sure of that."

His girlfriend emerged from the bedroom carrying a towel and wearing only a red bra and matching silk panties.

"See you later," she called as she went out the door.

He followed her with his eyes. "What's going on at the plant?"

"Everything is fine on this end. We have orders, and the girls are working on them. That's about it."

"No one has been there looking for me?"

"No, boss. It's business as usual around here."

Welde was relieved. At least the authorities weren't breathing down his neck. Yet.

His next call was to his Egyptian contact. He figured it would do no good, but it was worth a shot.

"Tarek, where's my airplane?" he barked.

"What do you mean? It isn't there?"

"No, it isn't. The last I heard from them they were being forced down somewhere over Iran."

"Then, you know much more than I do, Mr. Welde."

"I know you have my money, and I have nothing."

"I understand, but you are aware, I'm sure, that our transaction was for the merchandise as is, where is. As soon as the aircraft left the hangar, it became your responsibility."

The thought had entered Welde's mind that maybe his loss was the result of a scheme between the Egyptian and the Iranians. It was a possibility. "How do I know you don't have my plane right now?"

"You are going to have to trust me, Mr. Welde. I am saddened that this misfortune has befallen you, but beyond my sympathies, there is nothing I can offer. I am sorry."

"Let's say, for the sake of discussion, that the Iranians have the merchandise. What are the chances of getting it back from them?"

"You already know the answer to that."

It was no use. There was nothing left to say. He had

been foolish to make the deal in the first place. He was well and truly screwed. "Okay, fine, Tarek. But lose my number. And if INTERPOL comes calling, I'll make sure they don't overlook you."

"Ah, Mr. Welde, there is no need for threats."

He made a couple of calls to people who had financed him before. He needed capital if he was going to make the deal with the Vietnamese. And he needed that deal. If he could get the M16s for the right price, he could make up for some of his losses. His first call yielded a flat "no," and the second moneyman wouldn't even take his call. Could the news have gotten around already?

His last hope was in London. Some people there had been helpful a couple of years ago. Maybe they would be receptive to another business proposition from him now.

Financing for an enterprise like Welde's could not be obtained through traditional channels. A commercial bank was out of the question, but there were people with venture capital who were happy to lend money if the potential return was substantially higher than the risk. He took a deep breath and punched in the number.

"Sasher Global Investments."

"Bruce Sasher, please. This is James Welde calling."

"With?"

"Welde Technologies."

"Just a moment, sir." The secretary put him on a brief hold.

"James Welde. To what do I owe the pleasure?"

"Just thought I'd call to see how you were doing."

"I'm sure. What's the real reason?"

"Okay, I'll get right to the point. I have a lucrative deal going, and I need a backer."

"That's surprising. I've heard that you're doing quite well

these days."

Good. He doesn't know about the Egyptian thing yet. "I am, but I've had a slight setback."

"Really? What kind of setback?"

"I don't want to bore you with the details. Let's just say I was a victim of the Middle East problem."

"I'm sorry to hear that, James. But I would expect that your line of work must be a little dicey these days, especially in the Middle East. Why would I want to put my money at risk over there after you've already experienced a setback?"

"This deal doesn't involve the Arabs at all. That's the beauty of it."

"What does it involve, exactly?"

Welde didn't want to say exactly what he was up to. "I need inventory for clients that I already have lined up, and my source is actually in Vietnam."

Sasher sat up in his chair. "Vietnam, you say?"

"Yeah, go figure. I fell into a big deal over there. We can make a lot of money."

"Tell me how much I can lose before you tell me how much I can make."

"I need two hundred thousand."

There was a long silence before his potential investor replied. "That's a lot of cash, James."

Welde didn't want to focus on the front end. "The back end will double your money in thirty days. Where can you get a better return?"

"I must say I am intrigued. Where are you now?"

"I'm at home. The Philippines."

"I'll need to discuss it with my partners. It sounds risky, but maybe they can be persuaded."

"I'm good for it. You know that."

"Sure, I know that. Tell you what, why don't you come to London? You can lay it all out for us, and if you pitch it right, I think we can work something out. That is, if this is as good as you say."

"Great. I can be there in a couple of days. And it's good, believe me."

"Ring me when you get here."

"I'll do that. Thanks."

"Goodbye."

As soon as he hung up, Sasher made a call of his own.

"Grey here."

"Ambassador, Bruce Sasher. We may have a problem."

"What kind of problem?"

"The fellow you're trying to squeeze out in the Philippines just rang me up to ask if I'd bankroll a deal for some merchandise in Vietnam."

"Welde?"

"James Welde, yes. I've done business with him before. I have no idea how he knows about our merchandise."

"Actually, my associate, Trang, told him about it. He thinks we can use him to expand our business into other markets."

"Not a bad idea, Ambassador. The fucking guy has contacts all over the place."

"I've heard. I've also heard he's in desperate straits right now. What did you tell him?"

"He's coming here in a few days to make his proposal. This has the potential to be a very profitable deal for us. We lend him the money to buy our merchandise. We make a profit on both ends. What do you think?"

"I only know him by reputation. Do you think he's for real?"

"He always has been."

Chapter 27

EVERYTHING WORKS OUT FOR ME

J ust outside El Nido, Welde hung up the phone, grabbed a bottle of chardonnay from the fridge, plucked two glasses from the rack hanging over his counter, and headed out the door. A warm wind was blowing in across the beach. From the top of the stairs, he could see her. She had dragged a lounge chair down to the ocean's edge and was sitting with her toes in the water. Her bra was hanging from the back of her chair. His mood was brightening more each minute. He went down the stairs and approached her from behind.

"I know you're back there," she called without turning around.

"I come bearing refreshment."

She giggled. "How did you know I was thirsty?"

He poured the chilled wine into the glasses. "A toast," he said grandly. They clinked their drinks together. She took a sip before asking, "What are we celebrating?"

"You mean besides your beauty?" he said. Beads of sweat were glistening on her tanned chest. Some had lost their grip and rolled down her petite breast to drip from a pert, brown nipple. She felt his eyes on her body. She was without shame or false modesty. She wanted to excite him, and she knew she could anytime she pleased.

"Yes, besides that."

"I just got off the phone, and I have a big deal in the works."

"Another deal. It's always the same story with you. What kind of deal?"

"A business deal but a very profitable one. Anyway, I have to go to England for a couple of days. Do you want to go with me?"

"I don't know if I can get out of work right now." She could see the disappointment on his face. She hooked her thumb under the waistband of her panties and tugged them down slightly on one side. "Of course, I want to, but I don't even have a passport."

"That's not a problem. I have a guy who can get you a passport tomorrow. All I need is a photo."

"Is that legal?"

"The point is it will get you into England and back. That's all that matters."

She wrinkled her nose. "I guess."

Welde took a long, bracing drink from his glass. "Then it's settled. Tell your boss you need off and that's it. What can he do?"

"He could tell me not to come back."

"No man would ever tell you that." He bent over, scooped her up, and started across the sand back to his house. She laughed and waved at the woman who was staring at them from the patio next door.

The next morning, Welde started preparations for the trip to London. The first thing he did was to contact

Trang. "Trang, did you make the connection to purchase those M16s?"

"I got some information. You can have at least a thousand of them, still packed in grease paper and crated. Two hundred dollars each, FOB Bien Hoa."

"That's way too much. And where is Bien Hoa?"

"Just outside Ho Chi Minh City. Saigon to you. It's about thirty kilometers from there. It has one airport capable of landing cargo planes. Concerning the price, they say they have other buyers. That they are doing you a favor to let you have them."

"That's bullshit, Trang. If they had other buyers, they'd just sell to them. Why are they doing me a favor?"

"Actually, they're doing the favor for me."

"Yeah, and you're doing me a favor. Real heartwarming. This is business, so cut the crap."

"I don't know what to tell you."

"Don't tell me anything. Tell them I'll take three thousand guns, but I want them for fifty dollars US, all cash."

"That's too low, James. Even if they have that many rifles, they won't go for that deal."

"Yes, they will. Explain to them that I've got to arrange shipping and pay off the right people. Then there's your cut. I have to make a little something too. It's all found money to them."

"I can't negotiate for you, but maybe I can set you up with a meeting. There's a guy."

"Well, of course there's a guy. There's always a guy. Who is he?"

"He's British, and he wants to be in the business, but he's pretty green."

"Sounds like a man I can do a deal with. What's his name?"

"His name is Grey. He's the ex-ambassador to Vietnam, and he lives in London."

"That's perfect. I'm going to London this week anyway. Make it happen, Trang."

"I'll see what I can do."

Next, Welde made reservations for two on a nonstop to London and then called the plant.

"Welde Technologies."

"Marco, it's James. I'm going out of town for a couple of days. We're flying to London to make a deal. Get ready for a shipment. A big shipment. You need to get a truck ready and hire some men to load and unload it. We'll store the items temporarily until I can move them. Got it?"

"Yeah, boss. No problem, but I need to tell you something."

"Like what?"

"A couple of guys came around looking for you. They smelled like cops."

"What did you tell them?"

"I told them you were out, and I didn't know when you'd be back."

"That was it?"

"Not exactly. They said they'd be back with a warrant."

"A warrant? For what?"

"They didn't say, but they definitely meant business."

"Don't worry about it, Marco. They aren't going to find anything there except circuit boards. Right?"

"That's right, boss. We're clean."

"Screw them. There's no law against making parts for computers, and that's all we're doing, right?"

"That's it. Just making computer parts."

"Okay. Stick to your story. Let 'em look around all they want. I'll see you in a few days."

But Welde was worried. *Who's looking for me? Must be INTERPOL. They know about the plane and the munitions, and they've traced it to me, or else the pilots gave me up.*

That would be even worse. He could probably talk his way out of trouble if he wasn't specifically implicated by witnesses. Plausible deniability. But if the crew had fingered him, it would be a different story. If he was lucky, the Iranians had killed them trying to flee, but he couldn't spend time thinking about that now. This new deal had to work. He'd make it work and handle the police later.

He dialed his printer in El Nido. "It's Welde."

"Ah, Mr. Welde. I haven't heard from you in a while. What can I do for you?"

"I need a couple of passports. Right away."

"Hold please. I need to go into my office."

Welde waited.

"Sorry, Mr. Welde, I have to have more privacy to speak about passports."

"Sure, I understand."

"Now, tell me exactly what we are talking about."

"I need two passports. The names are John Weldon and Linda Weldon. You have my vitals. Make hers five feet eight inches, one hundred ten pounds. She's Filipina and twenty-seven years old. I'll send you her photo. Courier them to me no later than Thursday."

"I can do that, Mr. Welde. Thank you. I'll call you when they are ready."

Welde clicked off. He needed to contact Allison, who was at school in England. He figured he'd stay with her while he was there. She never answered her phone, so he texted her.

Allison, I'm coming to London, and I'm going to stay with you for a few days.

I'd rather you didn't.

Why?

You know why. I don't care to be alone with you.

Sweetheart, that's all behind us now. I've apologized a hundred times, and I promised you.

Please don't call me sweetheart. It's degrading.

Okay, I'm sorry. I'm bringing a woman with me, so you don't have to worry.

When are you coming?

Friday.

I forgot to tell you. I'm going to France with a group from school. We're leaving tomorrow.

Tell them something came up.

No.

If you won't be there, at least let me use the apartment.

For how long?

My business will only take a couple of days, but I thought we might spend some time together. We could at least have dinner.

It's not going to happen.

I could get a hotel, I suppose. I just thought that

my daughter might…

Fine. I'll leave a key with my landlady. She lives next door in 4C.

That works. Have a nice trip. Maybe we can get together next time.

There was no response. Welde didn't believe her story about going to France for a minute. It hurt to know that his daughter wanted nothing to do with him, but all he really needed was the apartment anyway. Hotel registers and credit card transactions were best avoided when people were looking for you. Besides, he was going to have to watch his expenses if he was to make any money on this deal.

On Wednesday, Welde heard from a woman purporting to be the assistant to one Ambassador Earl Grey, one-time British emissary to the Republic of Vietnam. Welde informed her that he would be in London on Saturday and would be honored to meet the ambassador then. "We'll be in touch," she said and hung up. He stored the number in his phone.

Friday came and brought his girlfriend to the house. They were on their way to the airport. She didn't take her eyes off the road but held the car steady around a sharp curve as she asked, "Isn't Jillian supposed to be coming to visit next week?"

"We'll be back before then. I'm looking forward to seeing her."

"It seems like all this is happening so fast."

"It's all part of the plan, sweetheart." He pushed his feet against the floorboard and pressed his back into the leather seat.

"I just hope everything goes according to your plan."

"It will. I'm a lucky guy." He smiled broadly at her. "Everything works out for me. Don't worry about that."

Chapter 28

LONDON

I t was just after 9:00 p.m., London Time, Friday 21 October, when they landed at Gatwick Airport. From there, they took a train, the subway (which the locals referred to as The Tube), and finally a cab to Allison's apartment. The cabbie wheeled past a wrought-iron gate into a cobblestone motor court where several cars were parked. The building was a four-story brick structure painted brilliant white. There were six front-facing apartments on each floor, and each of the twenty-four apartments had a set of bay windows with an excellent view of a lush, immaculately maintained park across the street.

It was a clear but cool evening, and she shivered in the chilly fall air as she waited for Welde to pay the cab fare. The cabbie pulled their luggage from the trunk and held the heavy glass door for them as they entered the lobby. They took the lift to the fourth floor, and Welde found apartment 4C. His knock was answered by a prim lady of about seventy. She was wearing a robe and appeared to have been sleeping.

"Hello, I'm James Welde, Allison Welde's father. I'm sorry to bother you at this hour, but we just flew in from the Philippines. Allison told me you were holding a key to her apartment for me."

"Oh yes," she said in proper Geordie English. "I'm Mrs. Comstock. It's very nice to meet you. Just a moment, and I'll fetch the key."

"It's a pleasure to meet you, ma'am. Thank you."

She was back in a few seconds with a brass door key. "Here you are. Will you be staying long, Mr. Welde?"

"Just a couple of days."

She eyed the young woman standing down the hall disapprovingly. "Well, I hope you will enjoy yourself."

"Thank you. I'm sure we will, Mrs. Comstock."

The landlady smirked and shut the door abruptly.

Allison's apartment was expansive with high, white ceilings and a well-aged, wood plank floor. It couldn't have been built later than the forties. The walls were pale green. A tarnished silver and crystal chandelier hung in the foyer. Despite its generous dimensions, the furnishings lent a cozy, comfortable feel to the public space. There was a brocade sofa draped with a shawl, and two matching wing-back chairs grouped around an English coffee table facing a welcoming fireplace. Tall oak bookshelves stood against two walls. They held classics and some novels but mostly texts and journals relating to the field of psychology. There were volumes by Skinner, Piaget, and the one she had heard of, Freud. The bay window area was defined by a well-worn Persian rug of faded reds and blues. The window itself afforded what she was certain would be a spectacular view of the park. Standing sentinel in the exact center of the rug was a polished brass telescope.

The young woman sat her suitcase down beside the fireplace. "This is beautiful," she exclaimed, rubbing her bare arms with the palms of her hands. "But it's cold in here. Can we have a fire in the fireplace?"

"Certainly." He turned a dial on the wall, and a bright, yellow-and-blue flame burst between the faux wood logs.

"Oh, it's gas. How clever!" She stood closer and held her hands out to meet the wave of warm air emanating from the hearth.

Welde wasn't paying attention but was checking his email. There was a message from Trang. The ambassador had agreed to a meeting on Saturday, two o'clock, at a place called Wolper's. This was almost too perfect. A diplomat who wanted to make a quick killing on stolen arms. His greed would make him an easy mark.

"Put your things in the bedroom. I need to make a phone call," Welde said without looking up. He punched in a number that he had saved to his phone.

"Sasher residence."

"Hello. This is James Welde calling for Mr. Sasher."

"One moment, please. I'll see if he's in."

Welde knew what she really meant was "I'll see if he wants to speak to you." *He'd better. I travelled nineteen hours to get here.*

Sasher came on. "James, I see you made it. Although it's frightfully late."

"Yeah, I made it. Sorry if I woke you. I'd forgotten how long the flight is or I might not have come," he joked.

"Yes, well, I imagine you'd like to get some rest before we meet then."

"Yeah. Jet lag, you know. I was thinking I could be there first thing Sunday morning."

"We don't usually meet on Sunday, but I suppose..."

"Let's do it tonight then. I can rest when I'm dead." Welde had hoped to put Sasher off until he met with Grey. He would be going in blind unless he knew the deal he was going to make with the ambassador. He'd have to improvise.

"I'm afraid tonight is quite out of the question, James. And Saturday afternoon we have the football matches. I can probably arrange something in the morning."

"Tomorrow morning is going to be difficult for me, Sasher. I know myself. Once I go to sleep, my body is going to quit on me. And I have family obligations in the afternoon."

"I understand. Let me make a few calls. I'm sure they won't mind coming in on Sunday, given the circumstances. We're curious to hear your proposal."

Welde was relieved. Great. What time can I come by on Sunday?"

"How about one o'clock?"

"One will be fine."

"Do you have the address?"

"Yes, unless it's changed since I was last there."

"No. It's still the same. Incidentally, where are you staying?"

"I'm at my daughter's apartment on West Carriage Drive. I think you might have been here before."

"Ah yes. Allison, isn't it? She has the splendid view of the park if I recall correctly."

"That's right."

"All right then, we'll see you Sunday at one."

He hung up.

Chapter 29

A DEAL

Welde's cab wheeled down West Carriage Drive onto Cumberland Gate and Park Lane before arriving at a large Gregorian building that housed Wolper's, a London dining tradition since the turn of the century. He checked his watch. The restaurant was only a few miles from his daughter's apartment, but traffic was heavy, and he had slept in. Now he was late. He paid the cabbie, bounded up the limestone stairs, and pushed through the double glass doors. He was met by a maître d' in black tie.

"Good afternoon, sir. Do you have a reservation?"

"Hello. I'm meeting someone. I don't know if he has arrived yet."

"That would be?"

"A Mister Earl Grey." Welde panted. He straightened his tie and tried to catch his breath.

"Of course, the ambassador. Yes sir, he is waiting for you. The ambassador is never late." The sarcasm in the man's voice was not lost on Welde. "This way, sir."

The maître d' took a menu from his desk and led the way through a maze of antique mahogany tables draped over with starched white tablecloths. The domed ceiling soared high overhead, and lush potted ferns stood on a gray and black tile floor laid out in a checkerboard pattern. In the far corner of the room sat Ambassador Earl Grey. He was perusing his menu and paid no attention to the men as they approached his table from his left.

"Ambassador Grey, your guest has arrived." He pulled out the chair opposite Grey and Welde started to sit. Grey stood and offered his hand. Welde shook it.

"It's a pleasure to meet you, sir."

"Nonsense. The pleasure is mine. Thank you for meeting me here." The old man went back to his menu as the waiter appeared.

"Would the gentleman like a cocktail to begin?" he asked.

"I'll have what the ambassador is having."

"A dry vodka martini with a twist. Yes, sir." The waiter hurried away.

"I recommend the brook trout if you like fish," Grey said without looking up. "It's flown in fresh every morning from the highlands, and it's the house specialty."

"Sounds good."

Welde stared across the room through great leaded windows at a cobblestone courtyard punctuated by an imposing marble fountain. A nude Aphrodite held a bronze pot overflowing with water that splashed into an immense pond. The faint sound of the fountain through the windows mingled with the hushed conversation and clattering china that echoed throughout the room. The waiter returned with the martini.

Grey handed over his menu. "We'll have the trout."

"Very good, sir. With the fingerling potatoes and carrots?"

"That'll be fine."

"Yes, sir. Trout for two." He took both menus and was gone.

"The service here is impeccable, and I'm sure you'll enjoy the food."

"I'm sure I will. Let's get down to business, shall we?"

"You asked for this meeting. What do you have on your mind?"

"I think you have been in touch with Mr. Trang. I would like to discuss the price to purchase some product from you."

"I'm sure Trang informed you of the price." The ambassador stared through narrowed eyes accented by bushy, gray brows.

"The price he quoted is full retail, sir. I'm in business to make a profit. Let me ask you this. How many units to you have in total?"

"I don't have *any,* but I can get as many as you want. That is not a problem, but I'm afraid the price is not negotiable."

Welde had anticipated Grey's answer and was ready with a proposal he hoped would intrigue the old man. "Everything is negotiable, Mr. Grey. Let's look at the problem a different way. Suppose we went partners on the whole deal. You supply product, and I'll sell it. We could split the profits."

The ambassador lowered his voice and looked directly into Welde's eyes. "Why would I want to take you on as a partner? What do you have to offer that I don't already have?"

"For one thing, I have established ties with clients. Customers eager to buy. And we're talking cash money. For another, I have transportation and warehouse facilities to hold the merchandise until it is sold."

The ambassador picked up his martini and held it at eye level. He inspected the clear liquid before swizzling the lemon twist around with his pinkie. Finally, he took a small sip and replied.

"You have my attention. One can never have enough cash customers. I don't need warehousing, but additional transportation could be useful. How about financing?"

"I have that too. Enough to buy a few thousand units."

"I was planning to move about five hundred."

"Then you need to think bigger. An enterprise like this won't pay off without a significant investment. I'm talking about numbers five or six times that, at least."

The ambassador slammed down his glass, splashing its contents onto the tablecloth. His right eye twitched involuntarily. "Mr. Welde, I'm sorry if I've wasted your time."

The waiter appeared with the food and sat the plates on the table. "May I get you gentlemen anything further? Perhaps another drink?"

"I'll have another martini, thank you," said Grey.

"Nothing for me," Welde said tersely. When the server was gone, he stared at Grey. "I don't mean to offend you, but I was told you have access to a large inventory. Five hundred units is small change. I'm a professional, and I've been doing this on a large scale for a long time. I want to do business with you, but only if we can make a lucrative deal. Lucrative for both of us."

"If you are so successful, why do you need me? The word is that you may have encountered some difficulty in the Middle East."

"Nothing that I can't handle. The reason I asked for this meeting, as I said, is you have product that I am interested in. You are a well-respected man. I think we'd make a good team."

The ambassador pushed the carrots around on his plate. A long moment passed. "Here's the thing, Mr. Welde. I am in the position to purchase these rifles, but I need the cash up front for them. The Asians, they have a mind for numbers, and they aren't keen on credit."

"As I said, I have the financing. I can come up with two hundred grand, but that money comes off the top when I move the merchandise. Then we split the profit."

"Very well. If you can deliver everything you claim you can, I can supply the inventory."

"What's your price per unit?"

"I'll have to renegotiate. If we're talking thousands of units instead of hundreds, I can assure you, you'll be quite happy."

Welde glanced furtively around the room and lowered his voice. "What about ammo?"

"Not a problem."

"Anything else? C4?"

"I think so. I'd have to look into that, I hadn't really…"

"Then we have a deal." Welde abruptly stood and stuck out his hand.

The ambassador looked him in the eye. "A fifty-fifty split?"

"That's right."

The ambassador nodded and took Welde's hand. "Deal," he replied simply.

"Give me a few days. I'll be in touch through Trang." Welde picked up his drink, gulped it down, turned on his heel, and crossed the room to the door.

Grey's martini arrived. "Where is your guest, sir?"

"I suppose he wasn't hungry after all."

When Welde arrived back at the apartment, he found her lying on the sofa with a large book. He read the title: *The Enigma of Human Behavior*. "I didn't realize you were into psychology."

"There are lots of things about me you don't know."

"For instance?"

"For one thing, I'm interested in psychology."

"Okay. What else?"

"I know how to play the piano, and I can wiggle my ears."

"You're right, I didn't know that." He smiled with amusement. "We don't have a piano, so how about wiggling your ears for me?"

"That's another thing you apparently don't know about me. I'm not a dog that does tricks on command."

He wasn't sure if she was serious or just teasing him. He decided to change the subject. "What do you want to do for the rest of the day?"

"I'm still tired from the trip. Would you mind terribly if we just relaxed this afternoon?"

"Not terribly." He went into the bedroom, switched on the TV, and stretched out across the bed.

"You didn't tell me how your meeting went," she yelled from the other room.

"Great."

The long hours on the plane had begun to catch up with him too and so, they stayed in all that night. He made love to her in front of the fireplace, and they ordered in Chinese food. Welde found an unopened bottle of wine in Allison's cupboard, and they finished it before going to bed.

Chapter 30

A NEW SUIT

Welde was up with the sun and went for a walk across the street and through the park. The cool fall air was bracing, and he never felt more alive. If he could make this deal, and he knew he could, he'd net enough cash to buy his way out of the airplane jam.

He went back to the apartment and tiptoed to the bedroom. His girlfriend was sprawled on the bed. She had pulled the snowy-white comforter over herself. "Hey, hon. How about some breakfast?" he said.

"Good. Are you cooking?"

"No. I thought we could go out. I want to look for a new suit. There are excellent tailor shops a few blocks from here. We could eat and then go there unless you'd rather stay here and sleep."

She slid her legs over the side of the bed. "No, no. I'll go with you. I've never been to London before. It would be a shame to come all this way and miss it."

Down the street, they found a pub that served breakfast. From the outside, it looked very British with a large, divided-light window with dark green muntins. The door was set into a shallow recess and was similar to the front window except for its polished brass doorknob and kickplate. Inside was a long mahogany bar with eight burgundy, leather-upholstered stools sitting on a floor of octagonal terra-cotta tiles. There were six tables in the center of the room and four similarly upholstered booths against the wall to the right side of the door. The aroma wafting from the kitchen could have been of pork sizzling over a wood fire. Two men dressed in work clothes sat at the bar sipping their morning Guinness, and a youngish waiter with slicked-back, brown hair and a handle-bar moustache greeted them as they entered.

"Good morning, folks." He gestured with a sweep of his hand. "Please sit anywhere you like."

Except for the men at the bar, the place was empty. They chose a booth and sat down.

"I'm Gerald," the waiter said as he presented them with menus and flatware wrapped in white linen napkins. After perusing the menu, Welde ordered eggs with ham and a cup of coffee for himself and a blueberry muffin and tea for her. Gerald came back with thick, white ceramic mugs, one filled with rich black coffee and the other with Breakfast tea. He placed a silver creamer and a bowl of sugar cubes in the center of the table.

She poured a splash of cream into her tea and folded her hands around the mug. She put her elbows on the table and let the aromatic steam warm her face before speaking. "James, what are we really doing here?"

"What do you mean? We're having breakfast."

"I mean, what are we doing in London? You didn't come all this way to purchase circuit boards."

"I came here to get financing to buy computer parts, yes."

"With false passports? I'm not stupid, you know. There are rumors about you in El Nido. People are saying you traffic in guns."

"And you believe them?"

"I'm starting to. So, I'm asking you point blank, and I expect you to tell me the truth."

"I'm a businessman, sweetheart. A merchant. What difference does it make if I sell computers or arms? The money is still money. There's a lot more of it to be made in munitions."

"So, the rumors are true."

"To answer your question, yes, we're here because I have a chance to make a big gun deal."

Her face darkened. "A big gun deal? Have you ever stopped for one minute to think about all the people who are killed with guns?"

"People are going to kill each other. It's inevitable."

"You don't think about what your guns are used for after you sell them?" she asked carefully.

"Not any of my concern."

"Who ends up with them anyway? I watch the news and see people in the desert getting killed by the thousands. People in nightclubs being mowed down in cold blood. Are they using your machine guns?"

"I like to think not, but I don't know. People get killed by buses and motorbikes too. Hell, I imagine people have been killed using computers."

"I haven't read about anyone being attacked by their laptop recently."

This was a side of her he hadn't seen before, and he didn't much like it. "Maybe you should just drink your tea," he suggested.

Her eyes hardened, and her jaw flexed. "How do you sleep at night?"

He smiled across the table but sat his coffee mug down

hard. "I have a house on the beach. I let the breeze blow through my windows and listen to the waves as I drift off."

She wasn't amused. "You're getting rich by helping people to kill each other. Dictators and terrorists, and that's okay with you?" She was speaking loudly now. The two men at the bar swiveled on their stools to look at her.

Welde grinned, nodded at the men, and then glared at her. "Well, sweetheart, I thought it was all right with you too. You haven't complained much about the jewelry, the cars, the helicopter, the swimming pool, and the house on the beach. Not until now, that is."

"I guess this is the first time I've realized what you do. For a long time, I wanted to believe you were in the computer business."

He laughed derisively. "C'mon, you're smarter than that.

"Yes, I'm smarter than you think, that's for sure."

"Be honest. It doesn't matter where the money comes from. There's nothing we can do about the actions of other people. The fact is we have it made. Let's just eat our breakfast. I need to get my suit. My meeting is in a few hours." They finished their meal in silence.

Welde paid the check as she shoved open the door and stepped out into the brisk morning air. Her breath formed little clouds that drifted upward into the ubiquitous British fog. A double-decker bus roared by, belching black smoke. The exhaust fumes made her cough.

Welde stepped across the sidewalk and hailed a taxi. The little black sedan wheeled to the curb, and Welde held the door for her. They still hadn't spoken. "We'd like to go to Savile Row," he said to the cabbie.

"Very good, sir." Traffic was heavy, and honking horns accompanied the curses from the driver as he maneuvered the car deftly through the melee that was Central London in the morning.

"This is fine," Welde said. "Let us off right here."

Once out on the street, he pointed to a four-story, red brick building. It was surrounded by a black wrought-iron fence. "This is where The Beatles played their last concert." he said.

"Isn't that a clothing store?"

"It's Abercrombie & Fitch now, but it used to be Apple Studios back in the day."

"I've heard of The Beatles," she said, "but why were they playing for Apple?"

"Forget it."

Savile Row was comprised of brick-and-limestone buildings, mostly the same approximate size and abutting each other for blocks. Located in the Mayfair section of London, it had been the epicenter of bespoke tailoring for almost two hundred years, and its patrons were some of the most prestigious and wealthy men in the world. It was a fraternity that Welde had desperately wanted to join for a long time. It was Sunday morning and many of the shops were closed. They walked under an oversized Union Jack that was flying from a mast tilting over the sidewalk.

A few doors further along, they spotted a shop with an impressively understated façade where they were greeted by a gentleman in a white shirt and black vest with matching trousers. He wore a tartan bow tie, and a yellow tape measure hung around his neck. Thick, horn-rimmed glasses were parked on his wrinkled forehead. "Good morning, sir. How may I help you?"

The shop was small but elegant. A pair of leather upholstered club chairs and a hand-rubbed chestnut side table sat on the polished maple floor. One wall was hung with many suit jackets made from rich-looking fabric, all distinctively tailored to a single style. On the other side of the room, angled mirrors afforded several views of a low, carpeted platform and a pair of short, wooden stools. A heavy antique desk stood in front of two fitting rooms at the rear of the shop.

"I'm interested in a custom suit, and I'm on a tight schedule."

"What do you mean by tight?"

"I need it by tomorrow," Welde said.

The clerk smirked. "Sir, a bespoke suit requires at least four fittings and takes ten to twelve weeks to complete. We sew all our clothing by hand."

Welde's face flushed red with embarrassment. "Of course, but I thought…"

"Perhaps the gentleman would like to see some of our premade suits." He said "premade" the way one might say "processed meat."

"Maybe. Can you show me something in blue serge?"

"Certainly." A few minutes later, Welde had several suits draped over his arm and was escorted to one of the fitting rooms. The woman settled into one of the oversized leather chairs and waited for what seemed like an hour before he finally emerged wearing a navy-blue suit. The unhemmed pant legs dragged on the carpet, and his hands were obscured by the jacket sleeves.

"What do you think?" he asked tentatively.

"It's nice. It looks expensive."

The clerk looked down his nose at her. "If madam is concerned about price…"

"She isn't," Welde interrupted. "How long will it take to have it altered?"

"If we put a rush on it, we could have it ready for you by tomorrow morning." But then he added, "Of course, there is an extra charge for the rush."

"Of course," Welde said brusquely. "Let's get started. I'm in a hurry."

Welde stood on one of the stools while the tailor went to work with the tape measure and a stick of white chalk. He marked the jacket in several places and did the same with the pants before asking Welde to put on his shoes. He pinned the legs to the appropriate length for the cuff.

"That's all we need, sir, except for the deposit."

Welde produced his American Express card and signed the sales slip. "Let's go, honey."

Out on the sidewalk, he checked his watch. "I have just enough time to make my meeting. Do you mind taking a separate cab back to the apartment? I'll meet you there later."

"No, that's fine. I'd like to take a bath anyway. Take your time."

He gave her cab fare and the key to Allison's apartment and tried to kiss her. She turned her head so that his lips barely brushed her cheek. He stepped into the street just in time to stop a passing taxi, leaving her alone in the heart of London.

Chapter 31

A WARM BATH

t was cold, even colder for a woman from the Philippines. She had been cold ever since she got off the plane. She remembered the store she had seen called Abercrombie something just down the block. She walked in that direction and soon found herself staring through a huge window at an endless array of clothes. Maybe there was a warm coat in there somewhere. She went inside. It was the biggest store she had ever been in. There were shelves and shelves of sweaters and shirts stacked to the ceiling, and there were coats and jackets hanging from rods lining the walls.

"Looking for something in particular, miss?"

She turned to find a young woman with several facial piercings beaming at her. "I'm looking for a warm coat."

The salesclerk led her to the center of the store and motioned toward a rack filled with dozens of coats. "There should be several in your size." she said.

She picked one that was nylon on the outside and fleece on the inside. It fit her perfectly. "I'll take this one" she said as she handed over one of Welde's credit cards.

"Excellent choice. It looks smashing on you."

Back out on the street, she made several attempts to hail a cab before one stopped for her. She wrapped her new coat tighter around herself and slid into the back seat. She gave the driver the address and stared out the window. It was a vista alien to a woman who had never been out of the tropics. The street was lined with trembling, ashen trees. Some were clinging to the last vestiges of their golden gowns, and others were stripped naked by the cold, crisp wind that coursed insistently along with the fitful flow of traffic. She saw a young girl with her hands in the pockets of her green wool coat, red hair streaming wildly behind her as she stood at the crosswalk. An imposing cathedral rose from behind an iron fence on the left, stained glass windows lending color to the otherwise monochromatic sandstone walls. She recognized the leaf-strewn lawn of the park on her right and knew she had arrived at the apartment.

"Six quid" the cabbie announced as he rolled to a stop.

She had no idea how much that was, so she held out all her money, and he took two bills from her hand, tipped his cap, and thanked her. The elevator took her to the fourth floor. She unlocked the door marked 4D and went inside. In the bathroom, she twisted the faucets to start filling the tub. She found a box of bubble bath and emptied it into the warm water, peeled off her clothes, and settled into a mountain of snow-white foam. It was the first time she had been truly warm all day.

Chapter 32

THE MEETING

Sasher Global Investments occupied the entire third floor of an impressive building in the SoHo District. Like most of the buildings along the street, it was constructed of aged red brick, except the first ten feet of its façade was veneered in white marble. The entrance was the width of three doors, all constructed of stainless steel frames holding green-tinted glass. As Welde approached, one of the doors swung open. He took the elevator to the third floor and stepped out in front of an imposing marble desk. It was Sunday, so he hadn't expected to see a receptionist, but here she was, and she was ravishing. She looked up from her computer and smiled. "May I help you, sir?"

"James Welde here to see Bruce Sasher. I have an appointment."

She checked the appointment book. "Yes, Mr. Welde. We have you scheduled for one o'clock. Would you care for a cup of tea?"

"No, thanks."

She could see that he was annoyed. "It will only be a few minutes."

Welde checked his watch. Twelve thirty-seven. "I can wait," he said, although he was irritated. *Like Sasher is so busy he can't see me twenty minutes early? On a Sunday?* He sat on a green leather chesterfield and perused a *Fortune 500* until, at last, the woman at the desk announced, "They will see you now."

He pushed open an imposing oak door and stepped into an expansive but elegant office. Oil paintings of stern-looking old men stared from one of three walnut-paneled walls. The Sasher precedents, he presumed. The back wall was all glass, affording a view of the verdure outside. Three men in suits were seated in leather armchairs before a massive walnut desk. Sasher was behind the desk. He rose and shook Welde's hand. "Good afternoon, James. Sorry to keep you waiting."

"Nice to see you, Bruce."

"These are my associates, Smith, Barnes, and Chase." The men remained seated but nodded in turn.

"It's a pleasure, gentlemen."

Silence. It was as if the very room itself was waiting to hear Welde's presentation.

He turned back to Sasher. "I'll come right to the point. When the United States pulled out of Nam in 1973, they left a large number of M16s behind. They are still there in a warehouse, wrapped and crated. I'm talking NOS. New old stock, Bruce."

"Do go on," Sasher said.

"I'm buying three thousand of these rifles. I already have buyers for them. All I need is a little operating capital, and I'm offering you a chance to get in on the deal. You'll see a healthy return on your money."

"And you'll see an even healthier return on yours, I presume. How much of your own money are you investing in this little venture?"

Sasher noticed Welde bristling at the words, "little venture". It was the desired effect.

"It doesn't matter. All that should matter to you is your net return."

"I'm more concerned with how much we can lose than with how much you say we can make, frankly."

Welde could hear the creaking of the leather chairs behind him and imagined the approving gestures being offered by the three men occupying them. He didn't want to admit that he was putting up none of his own money, but his answer was of no consequence to Sasher. He already suspected Welde was desperately broke. Otherwise, why would he offer such liberal terms?

"Give us the numbers, James."

"All I need from you is two hundred thousand. As soon as I flip the guns, I can repay you three fifty."

"On the phone, you said I could double my investment."

"There's overhead." He turned and glanced at the blank faces of Sasher's associates. "I'm covering the shipping, and, of course, certain people will have to be paid off."

"Exactly who are you dealing with over there?"

Welde grinned. "C'mon, Bruce, I can't tell you that."

"But it's a solid deal?"

"Rock solid. You'll see your money in thirty days." He instantly regretted saying he could repay the money in thirty days. The truth was he had buyers for maybe five or six hundred M16s, and he'd have to find someone to take the rest. The Africans were desperate for arms, but they liked to trade. If he took diamonds for guns, he'd still have to fence the diamonds. The timing could be problematic.

Sasher and his three partners stood up, signaling the meeting was over. "We'll discuss it James, and let you know."

Welde had come all the way to London, and he wasn't about to leave before he had a commitment from these guys. "What's to discuss, Bruce? You know I'm good for it. And where else are you going to get a one hundred and fifty percent return on a thirty-day loan?"

Sasher took a cigarette from a silver box and lit it with a matching silver lighter. He sat on the edge of his desk and took a couple of long, deliberate puffs. He was reading his partners faces over Welde's shoulder. "It's a tempting proposition, James. Give us a few minutes to talk this over, will you? You can wait in the outer office."

"That's fine, but don't give me time to change my mind. I'm crazy to be making this deal, and you know it."

He went back to his seat outside. The heavy door clunked closed behind him. Thirty minutes passed. He cooled down a little. He tried flirting with the secretary, but she ignored him. *A nonreceptive receptionist.* He chuckled to himself at his own joke.

Eventually the door opened, and the man who had been introduced as Barnes said "Please come in, Mr. Welde" before taking a place next to Sasher's other two associates who were standing to the left of the door.

Sasher lit another cigarette and took a puff. "We like your offer, James. We agree to your terms."

"That's great." Welde took two steps forward and extended his hand. Sasher clasped it loosely, and the two men shook on it. A gentlemen's agreement.

"Come by tomorrow, and you can pick up a check."

"Bruce, you know better than that. I can't deposit a check for two hundred thousand dollars. I'll need a wire transfer to my Swiss account."

"All right, we can do that, I suppose. We'll draw up the

papers, and when you get here tomorrow, we'll sign them."

"That sounds real good." Welde turned to the three men standing behind him. He shook the hand of each one of them as well. "I really appreciate it, gentlemen. Thank you."

He found his way to the street and started to look for a taxi back to West Carriage Drive. He was elated.

———

BRUCE SASHER PICKED UP THE PHONE. HIS RECEPTIONIST answered. "Get me Ambassador Grey."

"Yes, sir."

"Hello?"

"Grey, this is Bruce Sasher. We've just met with your new partner."

"Brilliant. How did it go?"

"Just like we planned. Well played, Ambassador."

"Thank you. I haven't lost my touch."

"We'll front him the money, and you'll make the deal. Our half of the sales and seventy-five percent interest on the loan should be a tidy payday for all of us."

Grey was elated. "Sounds easy enough."

"Easy enough, but there is one thing."

"What is that?"

"You had better make sure James never finds out what you're actually paying for the rifles or that we are partners. He's a frightfully vengeful man, and he won't like to think we're taking advantage of him."

"No need to worry, Bruce. He'll not find out from me."

"Oh, and one more thing. Thank your man, Trang. He did a fine job setting this up for us."

"Right. Goodbye."

Chapter 33

A DISCOVERY AND A PLAN

Meanwhile, on West Carriage Drive, as she was about to drift off to some much-needed sleep, the doorbell rang. Her first inclination was to ignore it, but then she remembered that Welde didn't have a key. She climbed out of the tub, wrapped herself in a blue satin robe that was hanging on the back of the door, and found her way out of the steam-filled bathroom. "I'm coming," she called.

Without looking through the peephole, she opened the door. But it wasn't Welde. Instead, there were two men staring at her from the hall. They were wearing suits, and one of them held a leather wallet displaying a badge.

"Miss Welde?"

"No."

"You aren't Allison Welde?"

"I already told you, no I'm not. Who are you?"

"We're with the police, ma'am, and we'd like to ask you a couple of questions. Mind if we come in?"

"Yes, I do. I'm taking a bath." She didn't believe they were the police. The badge didn't look real, and they were frightening her. She tried to close the door, but one of the men blocked it with his arm. He wedged himself into the doorway.

"Look, lady, we know who you are, and we know your father is here. We need to speak with him. Right now."

She didn't want these men to know she was alone. "You have the wrong apartment, and my husband and I are the only ones here."

But the man blocking the doorway wasn't buying it. He was halfway in the apartment now and he was staring at her cleavage. She clutched the robe tighter against her body. "If you aren't Welde's daughter, then you must be his girlfriend. That means you flew in here with him the other night. We know about his arms business, and we know what he's up to." The man craned his neck and glanced around the apartment. "You can tell him we were here and that we'll be back." She felt his eyes sweep over her body, from her eyes to her feet and back again. "Tell him I admire his taste in women."

He stepped back enough for her to slam the door in his face. She shuddered slightly. She wasn't sure if these men were who they said they were. Did they want to arrest him, or were their motives more sinister? Either way, they represented a threat to her plans. She moved to the bedroom window and watched them get into a large, dark-blue sedan. The car rested at the curb for a few minutes before moving into the street and disappearing down the block.

She was heading back toward her bath when she noticed the open door to Allison's closet. She ran her hand along the row of garments hanging from the upper bar. So many wonderful things. One dress in particular caught her eye. It was almost sheer and had gold and silver appliques sewn in patterns that afforded the wearer some degree of modesty. She dropped her robe and slipped the dress over her head. It was gorgeous and sexy at the same time, but she doubted she would ever have the nerve to wear it in public.

She got on her knees and searched the bottom of the closet for shoes to match. Before she found them, however, she discovered a box. It was long and narrow with three silver latches along the front. She pulled it out and laid it on the bed. It looked like it might be a guitar case. She clicked open the latches and lifted the lid. Inside was a rifle. A Remington Model 700 with a scope. The etching on the barrel indicated that it was a 30.06 caliber. She took the gun out and hefted it to her shoulder. She pointed it out the window and sighted through the scope toward the park across the street. Her pulse quickened. At that moment she knew what she was going to do.

She put the Remington back in its case and placed the case on the closet floor where she had found it. She took off the dress and hung it on its hanger before closing the door, revealing a full-length mirror screwed into the wall. She stood for a moment, gazing at her naked body. Her skin was like silk stretched over amber. Her face had a honeyed glow with deep, brown eyes and full lips. Her beauty had been her only weapon. Until now.

When Welde got back to the apartment, he found the door unlocked and the young woman asleep in the bed. He stood in the bedroom and stared at her. He was glad he had brought her on this trip. She was young and beautiful, just the way he liked them. Ever since his wife divorced him, he'd had a penchant for young women. If he were honest, his desire for them had begun even before that, but Welde was seldom honest. With himself or anyone else.

He left her sleeping, hung his overcoat on a hook by the door, and went to the kitchen where he found eggs and ham in the refrigerator and croissants and honey in the cupboard. He warmed the croissants in the oven while the eggs and ham fried on the stove. The girl appeared in the doorway wearing socks and his sweater. "You can cook," she said.

"I thought you might be hungry."

"I'm starved. Thank you."

They sat at the table and ate in silence. She drizzled honey over a warm croissant. He tried to make small talk. "What did you do today after I left you?"

"I came home and took a bath." She had no intention of telling him about the two men who came looking for him.

"Do you want to know what I did?"

"Not really, but I can guess."

"Are you still upset with me?" he asked.

"I'm not upset with you. I'm upset with what you're doing."

"I guess you read one book on psychology, and suddenly you're concerned about my behavior? You're not upset with me. You're upset by my behavior. Should I go lie down on the couch, doctor?"

"You don't have to get nasty."

"Look, I might as well be selling cars. More people die in car accidents every year than get killed by guns."

"Don't be absurd. The people who die in third-world wars are the poorest, most desperate people on earth. You give them the means to be cruel to one another. It's not the same as car accidents."

"How come you never brought this up before?"

"I don't know." She kept her head down, she didn't want to look at him. "I guess I thought it was none of my business."

He was beginning to raise his voice. "You were right about that, at least. It's not any of your business."

"So. You don't like it if I don't ask, and you get angry when I do. What do you want from me?"

"Some respect would be nice."

"Respect? People are being killed all over the world, and you and your friends are their accomplices. That's not being respectable. And I don't respect you. I know who you are, James."

"You don't know shit about me."

"I know more than you think. Those trips that we made to that training camp and you made me wait in the jeep? I knew you weren't selling computer equipment to those men. They were not soldiers. Now I am sorry I said nothing."

There was that self-righteous side of her again, and he still didn't like it. "All of a sudden you think you're so moral. We fucked a few times and that's all. I don't want to hear your shit."

"You go to hell. I'm not your whore. You want respect, you must give respect. But you are not respectable. You're a murderer," she screamed.

Welde pushed his chair back from the table and stood over her. She ducked her head lower, afraid he would strike her. But he just glared down at her.

"I want to go home," she said quietly.

"Go then. I don't give a damn." He was yelling now. "Girls like you are a dime a dozen, and I'll always be able to find another one just like you. Except maybe she'll appreciate me."

She remained quiet for a long moment and then said, "I'm getting a flight back tomorrow."

"Fine." He stomped off into the bedroom and slammed the door.

Everything was going according to her plan. She settled onto the heavy brocade of the sofa, pulled the cashmere throw over herself, and fell asleep.

Chapter 34

24 OCTOBER

Soft sunlight was streaming through the windows, casting a glow across the room. She woke to the clatter of dishes and the gurgle of the coffee pot in the kitchen. The warmth of sleep slowly faded into the chill of early morning as she slid from under the sofa throw. Clad only in Welde's sweater and her socks, she shivered as she brushed past the brass telescope and shuffled to the window. The sun was struggling behind a curtain of clouds, pink just above the horizon but turning to gray overhead. A light mist drifted gently in sheets, forming silver puddles on the glossy street below. At the curb sat the dark-blue sedan. She gazed at the park. A few defiant leaves clung stubbornly to the brown, twisted limbs in a stand of ancient elms, a sharp contrast to the brilliant green of winter grass. She turned to find Welde standing in the doorway, holding a coffee cup.

"Are you still planning to leave today?" His voice was almost kind. Almost conciliatory.

"Yes," she said coolly.

His eyes narrowed, and his voice hardened. "I left your ticket on the dresser. Don't be here when I get back."

She didn't turn to meet his gaze but stared out the window. "I won't."

Welde sat his coffee on the table, took the overcoat hanging in the hallway, and stormed out the door. She fixed herself a breakfast of fried eggs and toast, took a leisurely shower, and got dressed. She wiped every surface she could recall touching, took her plane ticket from the dresser, and packed her bag. The rifle was waiting in its case on the closet floor. She left her suitcase in its place and took the back stairs up to the rooftop. It had stopped raining, but the tarpaper was still wet. She picked a spot that was away from the puddles and that afforded an unobstructed view of the street in both directions. She rested the Remington on the parapet and positioned the case so that she could lie on it and stay dry. She slid back the bolt and inserted a 180 grain, soft-point cartridge into the chamber. She slammed the bolt shut and locked it down. Now there was nothing left to do but wait.

Chapter 35

4 NOVEMBER, AFTERNOON

Kincaid was feeling pleased with himself as he parked the jeep at the El Nido docks. His day had been productive. Now all he needed to do was pick up his things at the resort and get back to Jillian's house. He purchased his ticket and chose one of the two-seater units on the periphery of the ferry. There were only a few people onboard the big catamaran. No one had ascended the stairs to the upper deck. In his purview were two Philippine women dressed in maid's uniforms, a young couple with a small child, and a group of ten American tourists. It was easy to tell they were Americans by their clothing and boisterous behavior. He took one last look around the lower deck and propped his legs on the seat opposite his. When he was satisfied no assassins were making the trip this afternoon, he closed his eyes. Maybe he could grab a short nap on the ride over. A soldier slept when he could, because he never knew when his next chance to rest may come.

When the ferry finally landed at Oceania's dock, it was 4:00. Its last trip back to El Nido was scheduled for 5:30. Enough time to get his things and check out of the resort. He headed toward the stand of bamboo that marked the entrance to the villas. The boards on the walkway creaked, and his footfalls echoed off the white cement walls in a rhythm that suggested a marching gait, betraying Kincaid's true persona. He was military through and through. He arrived at Suite 20 and slid his card through the lock. The door clicked open, and as soon as he stepped inside, he knew someone was there. An instinct born of dark jungle nights and starlit dusty plains informed him of a presence. He placed his hand on his pistol and stood motionless. A faint sound was coming from the direction of the bathroom. As he stepped softly and carefully across the room, a voice called out.

"Kincaid, is that you?"

It was a woman's voice. He held the gun in front of his face, finger on the trigger, clenched his jaw, and flung the door back against its stop. It was Lucia. She was in his bathtub, surrounded by mountains of bubbles. Her broad smile slipped away at the sight of the big gun and the narrowed eye that was peering down its barrel at her. Kincaid tucked the .45 in his belt and stared at her in silence, his anger tempered by concupiscence.

"You said I am welcome to take a bath in your bathtub anytime I want. I thought I could slip in and out before you returned."

"I might have shot you."

"That is not necessary. If you want me out, I will leave." She stood up. The fluffy, delicate foam stuck to her and covered most of her body. Patches of caramel skin, wet and glistening from the bath, peeked out here and there. Pouty lips consorted with her raven hair to complete her exotic aspect. But it was her eyes, those deep, dark eyes filled with mirth and passion that had attracted him from that first day at check-in to this penultimate moment. Kincaid stood transfixed. Lucia returned his stare with a seductive gaze. The foam was turning to liquid and had begun sliding down her bronze legs. It was more than a man could resist, but more than a man, Kincaid was a Ranger, and a Ranger never abandoned his mission.

"I don't want you out, Lucia. I want you to stay and enjoy your bath."

"Will you like to scrub my back?" She cooed.

"More than anything in the world, more than you could possibly know, but right now, I can't. I have other obligations, I'm afraid."

"What's her name?"

"It's Jillian Welde, but it's not what you think. I'm helping her find her father, and I believe our search may have exposed her to a serious threat."

"Jillian Welde?" Lucia looked surprised. "I know her. What's happened to her father?"

"We aren't sure. Maybe nothing."

Lucia's expression darkened. "That is a creepy man. Somebody may have it in for him." The suds were dissolving and abandoning large parts of her body now.

Kincaid's resolve was weakening. "I think you should sit back down in your bubbles. Welde was creepy in what way?"

"I'm not sure." Her voice was barely above a whisper. "He was always flirting with me and…I shouldn't say this," the girl's eyebrows came together and wrinkled above her nose, "but I think he may have been abusing Jillian's sister."

"You mean sexually?"

"M-maybe."

"How do you know?"

"I don't know for sure. It was more of a feeling. The way

he used to look at her, and she always seemed kind of scared of him." She paused and stared at the ceiling for a moment. "Anyway, how does any of this keep you from coming in here with me?"

"I promised Jillian I'd stay at her dad's place for a while. Welde is mixed up in something nefarious. Jillian and I have been poking around, and I think we may have upset some bad people."

"So, you will leave me here and go to live with another woman?"

"I'm not living with her, Lucia. I'm staying at her place."

"Then I will go with you. Maybe I can help with the bad people." She stepped out of the tub and wrapped herself in a big, white towel.

Kincaid had begun gathering his belongings. "Don't be ridiculous."

"I'm not being ridiculous. You're hurting my feelings."

"You know I don't want to hurt your feelings, Lucia, but I can't leave this woman unprotected. I don't believe you want me to do that, do you?"

Her brow wrinkled slightly, and her lips formed a tight pout. "No, I guess not."

"I didn't think so. If you want to help, you can check me out of the resort. At least for now.

"For now? How long are you going to be gone?"

"As long as it takes."

She had never considered that Kincaid would turn her down. The fact that he had taken up with Jillian Welde was even more hurtful. She was unaccustomed to jealousy. Kincaid headed for the door, but she grabbed his elbow. "Will you at least call me and let me know what is going on? I'm worried about you. Don't forget, the PISF is looking for you too. You can't kill three terrorists and not expect their brothers to retaliate."

He didn't tell her about the fourth man. The one he stabbed and threw off the ferry. "There's no reason to worry. I'll call you."

She locked her arms around his neck and kissed him deeply. "But I do worry about you, baby."

A searing fire pulsed through him, but a smile crept onto his face as he pulled away and, without a word, disappeared through the door.

Chapter 36

DADDY'S GIRL

24 October was a drizzly fall day in London. Three miles north of the city center, at a friend's apartment, Allison Welde was thinking about her father. She hated him. She had every right to hate him. *Shouldn't a child be able to trust her own father?* She had trusted him until she was twelve years old. That's when he started molesting her. At first, it was just fondling, and she told herself that it was merely normal parental affection, but it didn't feel normal. Later, he made her undress and touch him while he touched her. He said that if she told anyone, it would be the end of the family, her parents would divorce, and it would be her fault. So, she didn't tell anyone, not even her sister. But her parents divorced anyway, and when her mother and sister went back to America, they left her in the Philippines with him. She pleaded to go with them, but she had become a bargaining chip in the settlement. Why hadn't she told her mother about him then? She was ashamed. She felt guilty. Had she somehow encouraged her father's abuse or just tolerated it? She hadn't told anyone. That fact only exacerbated her feelings of guilt.

Her father apologized and begged for her forgiveness. He even cried and told her he would make it up to her, but then it only got worse. When she was left alone with him, he started raping her. It happened so often that she became numb to it. She would close her eyes and try to think of other things. Happier times and other places. After a while, she was able to temporarily detach herself from the reality of what was happening to her, but she became determined to get away from him as soon as she could.

School became her only escape. She joined every afterschool club. She was a good athlete and played for the volleyball team, the basketball team, the softball team, and the soccer team. During football season, she was on the cheerleading squad. Anything to avoid being alone with her father.

That's when she met Lucia. Lucia became her best friend. Allison invited her to her house every day, and Lucia came a lot. She felt safe as long as someone else was in the house. Sometimes Lucia would spend the night, but then her father began to flirt with Lucia. Allison wanted to tell her what was happening and warn her about him, but she didn't have to, because Lucia stopped coming.

Allison was a good student and she studied hard. Her grades were outstanding, and when she graduated high school, she applied to schools in England, America, and France. Anywhere far from El Nido. She was accepted to several colleges but was offered a full scholarship from Durham University in London. She left that summer. The money from her scholarship afforded her the independence she so desperately needed. Her nightmare was over, and she hadn't been back home since. It had been two years, and except for when he came to visit last year, she hadn't seen him at all. During his visit, her sister had been there too, so she felt safe. Her father had apologized for all of it and promised her nothing like that would ever happen again, but Allison didn't believe him. She had heard it all before. That's why she had invented the story about going to France while he was in town this time.

But, despite all that he had done to her, she still loved him the way all girls love their fathers. Maybe she should go and see him. He did say he had brought someone with him. *Surely he won't try anything with another woman in the house, and besides, wouldn't his girlfriend keep him occupied?* Her conscience told her she should go home and visit with him. Perhaps he had changed. She would never forget what he had done to her all those years, but maybe she could forgive him. After all, she was partly to blame for letting it happen.

Meanwhile, on West Carriage Drive, the woman rested behind the scope of her high-powered rifle, waiting. An hour had passed. She didn't know which direction he would be coming from, so every taxicab was scrutinized. James Welde would emerge from the back door and present the perfect target.

Chapter 37

ONLY FOR A SECOND

After his meeting with Sasher, Welde was elated. It was a good deal for him. The money would soon be in his bank account in Switzerland. There was still lots to be done to make the arrangements for the delivery. He'd call Trang as soon as he got back to the apartment. He'd instructed the cabbie to drop him off at the tailor's on Savile Row to pick up his suit. He tried it on, and it fit perfectly. This was his day. He hailed another cab and rode to the park. The rain had stopped, and the brisk autumn air was invigorating. He felt like walking across the green and back to the apartment. He had forgotten all about the argument he'd had there earlier. He was on top of the world. Yes, James Welde was back, and he was a force to be reckoned with.

Allison got into her car, drove to her apartment, and parked in her assigned spot. She noticed a dark sedan sitting at the curb just outside the gate. She hurried through the lobby door and took the elevator to the fourth floor. Her father would be surprised to see her. She opened her door and called, "Hey, Dad. I'm home." There was no response.

She strode to the kitchen. There were dirty dishes in the sink and a coffee cup on the table. She went to the bedroom. There was a suitcase standing in the closet and another open on the floor. It contained a man's clothing and shaving kit. There was nothing to suggest the presence of a woman. The bed was unmade, but no one was there. She sat down in the lounge to wait. A few minutes passed before she wandered idly to the window and the big brass telescope that she liked to use to observe the joggers and the wildlife in the park. It was a pleasant way to pass the time.

Just beyond her view, behind a stand of oak trees, James Welde encountered an old man sitting alone on a bench. The man appeared to be homeless. "Could you spare a couple of quid?" he asked.

Welde was feeling charitable and reached for his wallet, but it wasn't in his back pocket. He checked his coat pockets. No wallet. "Sorry, old man, I seem to have misplaced my money."

"Sure you did, governor, sure you did."

Welde thought he must have left his wallet in the cab. He'd call the taxi company as soon as he could get to Allison's and find the number. Any concern he might have had about his wallet disappeared when he spotted two young women jogging toward him. They were in tights and sweatshirts that bounced provocatively with each stride. "Morning, girls. You're looking good." They ignored him.

A few yards along, and he was almost to his daughter's apartment. Just through the small wood and across the street.

She peered through the eyepiece and adjusted the focus. A familiar form came into view. The perfect haircut, the navy overcoat, the chiseled features of an impossibly tanned face. It was him, and he was alone. Her heart beat faster, she felt her pulse in her ears. She was having second thoughts. Where was his girlfriend? He must have lied to her again.

What would she say to him? She felt vulnerable, reliving the old familiar dread she used to feel when she heard his footsteps outside her bedroom door. She thought of running down the stairs and back to her car to get away. But just then, a gunshot rang out from somewhere outside and above.

James Welde had just cleared the last of the trees. He felt a sharp sting in his forehead. But only for a second.

She saw a puff of red mist where her father's head had just been. He folded like a rag doll and collapsed. Allison was numb with shock. Moments passed before reality made its way back into her consciousness. She moved to the phone and dialed the emergency number.

"Nine nine nine. What is your emergency?"

"I've just witnessed a murder."

"What is your name and address?"

"I'd rather not give you my name, but the murder took place in the park off West Carriage Drive. A man was shot, and I'm sure he's dead."

"Are you the person who shot the man?"

"No. Sorry."

"Did you see who shot him? Are you still at the scene?"

"I'm sorry. I have to go now."

Allison threw the phone on the table and ran out the door. She wasn't sure where she was going, but she had to get out of that apartment. The thought of going across the street to stay with the body frightened her. It was too gruesome, but wasn't that where a daughter should be, waiting for the ambulance to come and get her father? Or what was left of him? Instead, she got in her car and swung out of the parking lot and down the street back toward her friend's apartment. She heard the blare of the siren before she met the ambulance speeding toward the park. Allison was ashamed to admit, even to herself, that instead of grief, the most prevalent emotion she felt was relief.

Tears filled her eyes and streamed down her face as she replayed the horrific scene in her mind. Her father, whom she loved yet loathed, pitied yet feared, had been gunned down violently as she watched. She heard the blare of a second siren somewhere behind her. Maybe it was the police speeding toward the park. She glanced at the rear-view mirror through her tears and missed the traffic light in the intersection.

The lorry driver was checking the address on his delivery order. Neither one saw the other. There were no screeching brakes, no honking horns, just the hollow, metallic sound of the crash that could be heard for blocks, followed by a thick silence. Gasoline trickled from under the wreckage. There was no movement in either vehicle. Then came the explosion and the fire. The witnesses could do nothing but watch it burn.

Lucia de la Rosa put the rifle back in its case, picked up the spent bullet casing, and calmly walked down the stairs. She used her key to open the door to apartment 4D and went inside. She uncased the weapon and carefully wiped it clean of her fingerprints before putting back in its place in the closet. Then she wiped down every surface she had touched in the apartment. She left the key on the table and rolled her suitcase to the elevator. There was no one to see her as she stepped out of the building. The few people who were about had fled for cover or were gathering around the man lying in the park.

On the plane bound for home, she stared out the window. Clouds rose like wispy, snow-covered mountain peaks rising from a misty, gray sea. Her heartbeat had returned to normal. She relived the moment she pulled the trigger: a few calming breaths, then one deep one, held as the target moved toward the crosshairs of her scope. A gentle squeeze, and her mission was accomplished. She had waited a long time for this day, and the price she had paid was steep. Once she found him, she flirted, took meals, slept, and had sex with James Welde for months, waiting for the perfect chance to kill him. Every kiss made her want to gag. The sight of him repulsed her, but she persisted. And when the opportunity presented itself, it was almost too perfect. The weapon, the logistics, and her years of target shooting with her uncle comprised the lethal trinity. Her only regret was that she wasn't able to blow him to pieces. She had dreamed of Welde climbing into his car to drive home to his family. In her dream, he would turn the key, and the explosion would vaporize him. Just the way he had killed her father.

Welde had been investigated in her father's death and cleared by the military inquest. The case went unsolved, but there was one fact that the military never uncovered. Maybe they didn't think to ask. Days before his death, Lucas de la Rosa told his wife that he had discovered Welde's secret. Welde was stealing arms from the government and selling them to terrorists and despots. When de la Rosa had gathered enough evidence and was set to expose the operation, Welde rigged a bomb to his car and killed him. Her mother, God rest her soul, had been afraid to speak to the authorities in fear of retribution. But Lucia knew James Welde was guilty of murdering her father, and she had vowed to make him pay.

She smiled softly at her reflection in the glass. Her sacrifice had paid off, and it was worth it. Her father's death had been avenged at last.

Chapter 38

INTERPOL

The receptionist looked up just as the door swung open at Sasher Global Investments. Two Asian men walked briskly to her desk, and one of them produced a badge. "Good afternoon. My name is Sato, and this is Mr. Nakamori. We're from INTERPOL."

"Good afternoon, officer. How may I help you?"

"We'd like to speak with Bruce Sasher, please."

She smiled at him as she lifted the telephone to her ear. "I'll see if Mr. Sasher is in."

"We know he's in, miss. Just tell him we're here."

"Mr. Sasher, two gentlemen from the police are here. They'd like to speak with you," she said pertly. She hung up the phone and said, "Go right in, sir."

Bruce Sasher was gazing out his office window with his back to the door when it opened. He swung his chair around, stood, and offered his hand to Nakamori. "Gentlemen, please sit down." He motioned to the chairs in front of his desk.

Sato displayed his badge. "I'm Agent Sato, and this is Agent Nakamori." They sat.

"What can I possibly do for you this afternoon?"

"A Mr. James Welde was here last Sunday, and we wondered if you could tell us the reason for his visit."

"James? He's an old friend. He happened to be in town last weekend, and he stopped in to say hello. Is there a problem?"

"We have reason to believe Mr. Welde may have been in London on some business. Was he here on a personal visit, or does your firm have an official interest in Welde Technologies?"

Sasher could see that this was more than a polite inquiry. The problem was that he didn't know how much they knew. He had no intention of providing anything that might be useful to them. "I think we may have made a small investment in his computer enterprise a few years ago, but other than that, no. Sasher Global Investments has no business connections with James at this time. May I inquire as to what this is all about?"

"You're a personal friend of Mr. Welde then?"

"Yes, that's right. Why all the mystery, officer?"

Sato leaned forward in his chair and loosened his black necktie. "I'm sure you're aware of the recent shooting that occurred in the park?"

"I read about it in the papers." The agents sat motionless and didn't speak.

A chill went up the back of Sasher's neck. *That's why I haven't heard from Welde since Monday.* "You don't mean to tell me that was James?"

Sato spoke softly. "I'm afraid so, sir."

"I can't believe it. Who would do such a thing?"

"We were hoping you might be able to tell us. You may have been one of the last people to see him alive."

Under his desk, Sasher's foot was tapping uncontrollably. "Well, no. I'm certainly not aware of any enemies he might have had. James got on with everybody as far as I know."

"Obviously, he had enemies, Mr. Sasher."

"I see what you mean, but the paper said the victim was unidentified. Are you certain it was James?"

"There was no identification on the body, so it took some time to run the prints. Welde was in the military, so his were on file. They matched. It was him, no question about it."

Nakamori, who had sat stoically until now, stood. "Cut the crap, Sasher. Welde was a gunrunner, and you know it. You financed his operation in the past. What do you know about a planeload of munitions flying out of Egypt a couple of weeks ago?"

Sasher pounded his desk. "This is outrageous! I have no idea what you're talking about, sir. Welde Technologies is a legitimate business, and all our dealings with them have been strictly along those lines, I assure you." He took out a handkerchief and mopped his brow. "I'm afraid you're going to have to excuse me now. This news about James is most distressing. I need some time if you don't mind."

Sato stood and bowed. "I am so sorry to be the bearer of such bad news, Mr. Sasher. You have our sympathy. We can continue this discussion at another time. Thank you."

"There is nothing further to discuss, gentlemen. I'm afraid I've told you all I know on the subject."

Nakamori approached Sasher's desk. "I think you do know more. A lot more. I think you might be involved in killing Welde. We'll be back," he added, menacingly.

As soon as he was certain the agents were gone, Sasher was on the phone to Grey. "Grey? I'm afraid I have bad news, very bad news." He proceeded to tell the ambassador the details of his visit from INTERPOL.

"You're certain that Welde is dead?"

"Quite certain. You must've seen it. The papers were full of it."

"Yes, but just this morning, they were saying the man in question was as yet unidentified."

"Probably because they are still investigating. They don't have the killer. More alarmingly, INTERPOL seems to think I may have had something to do with it."

"Preposterous. Why would they think that?"

"Who knows? They're aware that he was here on Sunday last, but that's all they have. I can prove my whereabouts all that day."

"That explains why he hasn't contacted us. What about the money?"

"I don't know. It depends whether his Swiss account is known to his estate. If it is, we will put in a claim at the appropriate time. I do have a signed promissory note. However, if we can't prove the existence of the account, it will sit, unclaimed, in Switzerland and we shall be out of luck, I'm afraid."

"A devastating loss for you."

"That's putting it mildly. I was afraid he might try to double-cross us some way, however, I could never have foreseen this."

"What shall we do now?" asked Grey.

"If you're still willing, I'd like to carry on. I'm not keen to report to my stockholders that I made a covert deal and lost one hundred fifty thousand pounds."

"Of course, I'm willing."

"Excellent. As far as the gentlemen in Palawan, I suppose you could go there and consummate the deal yourself. Wasn't that the original plan?"

"Yes, I suppose I could. My contact at the El Nido police

station was going to set up a meeting for me. I assume he still can."

"Good. Let's get that transaction done and go from there. Maybe Trang can give us some information as to Welde's other clients."

"I'll keep you apprised of my progress." He paused. "Bloody awful about Welde though. I heard the poor man got it in the head. No warning."

"That's how the paper put it."

"Who do you suppose did it?"

"Could be any number of people. The bastard was not well loved."

"Given the tone of my meeting with him, I can see why," Grey said. "Well, goodbye."

"Goodbye. Keep in touch."

Chapter 39

A MISTAKE

The ferry ride back to El Nido was as uneventful as the one to Oceania had been, and the jeep was parked where he had left it for the drive back to Jillian's. He was still as awestricken with the scenic grandeur of the drive along the coast highway as the first time he'd driven it. No place on earth was more beautiful, he thought. The sea. Once again, he was taken by that familiar magnetism he had felt most of his life. Sixty percent of the human body was water, but more than that, his father had been a navy man. He served in Vietnam and for several years afterward before being lost at sea in a training accident when Kincaid was ten years old. His body was never recovered. He was still out there somewhere.

His melancholy was cut short by his SAT phone ringing. It was Alex. "Hey, man, I've got some news about your boy, Welde."

"Let's hear it."

"He's dead. He got shot about ten days ago by a sniper in a London park."

"Ten days ago?"

"Yeah. More or less. He didn't have any ID on him at the time. It took the local authorities a while to identify him.

Shot in the head with a lead point of considerable caliber."

"In London. Who did it?"

"This is where it gets interesting. They suspect his daughter."

"That's impossible. She's been with me, looking for him."

"Different daughter. This one had an apartment overlooking the park, and they found a Remington 700 rifle with a scope in her closet. Allison Welde."

"That's crazy."

"Yeah. Even if she didn't do it, she had to have known about it. She looks guilty as hell."

Kincaid's mind went to an obvious question. *If she did it, why didn't she get rid of the gun?* "Maybe her gun wasn't the murder weapon."

"It was her gun all right. The ballistics matched up."

"Still, it must have been a pretty long-range shot."

"About five hundred meters."

"Who kills their father? From five hundred meters? That's a hell of a woman if you ask me. Where is she now, in custody?"

"No. Are you ready for this? She apparently fled the scene and got into a traffic accident a few blocks away. Collided with a truck. She's at the morgue."

"Dead? This is too bizarre, Alex. I don't like it. Something is missing."

"I don't know. A kid has it in for her daddy, gets the right opportunity, and shoots him. She probably freaked out when she realized what she did, and in her haste to get away, runs through a traffic light and gets hit by a truck. Poetic justice, I guess."

"Why would she do that?" Kincaid thought back to what Lucia had said. *Maybe Welde had been molesting his daugh-*

ter, but even if that were true, there must be easier ways to
bump off the old man than that. And then immediately die
in a car crash? "That would be a hell of a coincidence, even
if there were such a thing as a coincidence."

"It's cold blooded, man."

"I don't buy it. It's too convenient and bizarre. Are you
free right now?"

"Like a bird. What do you want me to do?"

"Will you see what else you can find out? There must be
other suspects. I can't see a daughter shooting her father at
long range like that."

"I see what you mean. I'll do what I can." Alex hung up
before he could be cut off by Kincaid again. A man could
only take so much.

Kincaid thought about his new problem. How was he
going to tell Jillian that her father was dead? And that the
police thought Allison had killed him? Even worse, that her
sister was dead too? At least he had some time to prepare
himself to deliver the news. He was glad he'd left Jillian at
home and that she hadn't been there to overhear his conversation with Alex.

As soon as he turned off the Taytay-El Nido National
Highway into Welde's driveway, he knew he had made a
mistake leaving Jillian alone. The gate was open. He had
emphatically told her to keep the gate locked. The Toyota
was parked in front of the garage. Maybe she had gone
out and, when she came back, forgotten to close it behind
her. He accelerated to the bottom of the stairs, slid out of
the jeep, and moved cautiously up to the porch. The first
thing he noticed was that the curtains were drawn over the
windows. He looked at the door—or where the door had
been. Now it was lying in splinters across the threshold. It

appeared that someone had used a battering ram to bash it from its hinges. Kincaid drew the .45 from his belt and stepped inside as quietly as he could. It took a moment for his eyes to adjust from the bright sunlight to the darkened room, but everything looked normal. No sign of a struggle. He called out for Jillian. There was no answer. He hurried down the hall toward the bedrooms, dreading what he might find there. He found nothing.

"Jillian?" he shouted. "Jillian, are you here?" There was no response, just the gentle whisper of the waves drifting through the opening where the door had been. He searched the rest of the house, but it was empty. Sure, the furniture was still there—the rugs, the clothes, pots and pans, all the artifacts of the lives spent inside its plastered walls—but the house was empty. Empty as only a place can be when the people you expect to be there, who should be there, are gone. He pulled back one of the curtains and noticed blood. Small crimson droplets sprayed across the polished koa floor.

Kincaid's mind raced. Obviously, someone had taken her, and logic told him it must have been the PISF. They probably came there looking for him. Maybe they followed the Toyota and somehow got through the gate. Maybe Jillian heard them coming and closed the drapes and locked the door. The terrorists had broken it down and grabbed her. She would have been panic stricken, easily subdued. Had they bloodied her face, trying to beat information out of her? A vision of Lisa Kittering flashed through his head. But if she had been raped and stabbed, there would be much more blood, and besides, they wouldn't have bothered to move her body. She was still alive. They were holding her somewhere. But where? It was all speculation, but it was the only scenario that made sense.

Just then, he was jolted from his thoughts by voices coming from outside. He edged through the doorway and pressed his body against the wall before peering around the corner. Two men dressed in camo were examining the jeep. They had been waiting for him to show up. He ducked back around the corner just before they looked up in his direction. Kincaid heard them creeping up the steps. He eased back inside and crouched behind the sofa with his pistol resting on its arm. He knew their vision would be limited as they came in, just as his had been. It was all the advantage he would need.

The first man through the door never saw anything. A single round from Kincaid's automatic struck him squarely in the forehead. Bits of his bloody skull skittered out onto the porch as his body slumped to the floor like a sack of grain. Kincaid knew the second man would hesitate before making the same mistake, so he leaped up, ran to the doorway, and stood against the wall. Several seconds passed. They seemed like minutes. Maybe the dead man's partner had thought better of it and decided not to enter the house at all. But then, the barrel of an AK-47 appeared. Kincaid holstered his pistol and waited until the man was almost inside before grabbing the barrel with his right hand and pushing it away. He stepped toward the terrorist and punched him hard in the face with his left fist. Simultaneously, he shoved the rifle upward and grabbed the stock. He raked the barrel down the man's face and twisted it from his grip. He poked the AK into his chest but didn't pull the trigger. He needed this guy alive.

"I hope you speak English, or you're a dead man," Kincaid said through clenched teeth.

"Don't shoot, don't shoot!" the man pleaded.

Kincaid gestured with the gun. "Over there, Mohammad."

"My name is Roberto."

"Okay, Bob. Sit down in that chair."

The Filipino sat heavily into one of the rattan chairs.

"Where's the woman, Bob?"

"What woman?"

"Don't get cute with me, Bob. I don't like cute boys."

Roberto said nothing but stared straight ahead. Kincaid stood over him, still brandishing the AK-47. "The woman who lives here, the woman you took. What have you done with her?" His voice was louder now and menacing.

"I don't know what you're talking about. We were going to steal your jeep. I know that's wrong, but that's it. We didn't do anything to any woman."

His defiance was infuriating, but Kincaid tried to remain calm. "Oh, I see. You aren't part of the gang of punks who call themselves the Piss?"

"Fuck you. It's PISF, and all we were doing was looking for a jeep."

Kincaid lowered the rifle.

The terrorist thought his story was working. The bullet tore through his boot and into his foot. Roberto cried out in pain and pulled his foot into his lap, clutching it in agony. Blood seeped onto his hand and ran down his arm.

"I'm tiring of you. You need to tell me where the woman is. Right now, it's the most important thing in your life. You need to tell me where she is." He rested the gun barrel on the man's left knee.

Tears streamed down his face. "I said I don't know," he insisted.

"Okay. If you don't mind walking with a limp for the rest of your life, I don't mind either."

"Don't you understand, asshole? If I tell you, they will kill me."

Kincaid pulled the trigger. Blood and bone exploded from Roberto's knee. He screamed and grasped at his knee with both hands. Kincaid poked the rifle into the man's right knee. He was stoic, almost detached from the situation. "If you don't tell me, Bob, I'm going to kill you. Only, not as mercifully as the beheading they'll give you. I'm going to make you suffer a little first." Now his voice was soft and calm. His eyes narrowed.

"All right, all right, please." His captive was begging. The pain was unbearable. He craved unconsciousness, anything to escape the agony. "I'll tell you whatever you want to know. Please don't shoot me again."

"Who has the woman?"

"A man called el-Fasil. He is the leader of the PISF here."

"Where is she now? With him?"

"Yes. The camp is about eight kilometers south from here."

"How do I find it?"

"Look for a small road cut into the jungle that turns off the highway. From there, you will turn left. A few kilometers into the jungle, turn to the right."

"How many men are in this camp?"

"About thirty, maybe more, I don't know. You are a fool if you think you can go there without being killed. They are looking for you right now."

"Well, that's exactly what I am, a fool." He pulled the trigger, and the terrorist's right knee exploded. The man rolled off the chair and fell into the blood that was puddling on the floor, holding his legs in the fetal position. He was weeping violently.

"Sorry, Bob, but I need to know where to find you if you're lying to me."

"Fuck you, man. You're going to fucking die!" He screamed with all the strength left in him. "You will fucking die!"

Kincaid could still hear him sobbing as he turned the key in the jeep's ignition. He shifted into reverse and turned around. He rushed down the drive, turned south onto the highway, and sped away.

Chapter 40

TWO GUARDS AND A THIEF

His experience had taught him to detach himself from his emotion. He had to think logically, to make a plan. Thirty men, and they would be well situated against intruders. Probably sentries near the highway and maybe more on the perimeter of the camp. Kincaid glanced at the odometer on the jeep. The terrorist had said the road was eight kilometers down the road. About five miles. That's just about where he saw a gap in the trees. It had to be the road. Kincaid kept driving another hundred meters before pulling off the highway and into some thick brush. He hoped the jeep wouldn't be noticed as he killed the engine and jumped out.

He grabbed the AK he had taken from Roberto, hiked into the forest, and started back toward the road to the PISF encampment. Luckily, the trees were thick, and the undergrowth was dense enough for cover but not so dense as to obstruct his progress. He kept his head low and was careful where he stepped to be as quiet as possible. Most of the groundcover was green and moist from recent rain, and there were few dried leaves or twigs, so he made almost no noise.

He smelled smoke. He stopped and breathed in. Not smoke from a campfire. Campfires gave off deep, rich, woody-smelling smoke. He couldn't see this smoke, and it smelled bitter. Cigarette smoke. He moved forward and crouched behind a fallen bagras tree. He lost the scent of the cigarette, and now all he could smell was eucalyptus. He lay down and was still, waiting, until he heard a voice. It was a man speaking in, probably, Tagalog. The man seemed agitated about something. Another voice answered. His speech was calmer and lower in pitch and volume. There were at least two of them, but how many more? It was common to post two guards in a remote spot like this to make sure at least one of them would be awake at any given time. Kincaid hoped that was the case and there were only two.

He dug under the groundcover and found mud to cover his face. With the AK slung over his shoulder, he advanced on his stomach toward the voices. He didn't go far before he spotted them. They were sitting on the ground at the foot of a tree. The tree had slats nailed up the height of its trunk, ostensibly to facilitate climbing. If they were any kind of soldiers, at least one of them should have been up there keeping watch, but these were not soldiers. They weren't much more than boys, both wearing fatigue pants. One had a black T-shirt with the Adidas logo, and his pants were Vietnam tiger stripe camo. The other was sporting woodland pattern camo pants and a white T-shirt. *What kind of idiot wears white in the forest and expects not to be seen?* Kincaid waited a full half hour to see if they would split up. He figured he could take them one at a time if they did, but they just sat there cross-legged, smoking and talking. He could have easily picked them both off with the rifle, but that would have brought the cavalry, and he wasn't ready for that. Yet. He needed more firepower to take on thirty men. And he knew just where to get it.

Kincaid crawled backward slowly so that he could keep the guards in sight as long as possible. If he turned his back on them and they slipped up from behind as he retreated, he would be defenseless. Which meant he would be dead. When he could no longer see them, he got to his feet and hurried back the way he had come. He was at the edge of the tree line and about to step out toward the highway when he spotted a man in gray sweatpants and wearing a green shemagh but no shirt, inspecting the jeep. He walked all the way around it before searching the inside. He found the bag of Kincaid's belongings and rifled through it. He took the burner phone and the energy bars but left everything else, including the clothes. He opened the glove box and took out some documents. Probably the registration. Kincaid wondered if he recognized Welde's name. He watched as the man looked under the seats and walked back around the vehicle, feeling under the fenders and the top of each tire. Probably looking for the key. When he finished his search, the man stood upright with his back to the forest. Kincaid had no choice; he couldn't risk letting the intruder walk away and report what he had found, and he couldn't shoot him and risk the shot being heard. He pulled his knife and rushed his victim from behind, grabbing him by his head wrap. Then, in one smooth, violent motion, he drew his blade quickly and firmly across the man's throat, slashing the larynx, esophagus, and arteries. Blood gushed, and the man slid to the ground. Kincaid let him fall and then dragged him by the feet into the woods. The man's eyes were frozen wide open, and he made a gurgling sound as he was shoved into thick bushes.

Kincaid wiped the bloody knife and his hands on the soon-to-be dead man's shemagh and moved quickly back to the jeep. He picked up the burner phone and energy bars the thief had dropped and started the engine. He didn't want to be around when the guy's friends came looking for him.

Chapter 41

THEY'RE NOT COMING BACK

At the El Nido police headquarters, the man who identified himself as an INTERPOL agent had just began briefing Captain Belka on the Welde case. He told him what was known about the airplane captured over Iran and started detailing the shooting in London when he was interrupted. Belka jumped to his feet, almost swallowing his stub of a cigar. "Do you mean to tell me you have been investigating here without notifying this office?" he bellowed.

"I'm afraid so, sir. Neither of these crimes were committed in your jurisdiction, so we were not obligated to contact you."

"Not obligated?" Belka's voice went up half an octave. "What the hell is that supposed to mean?"

"Customarily, we solicit the cooperation of the local authorities only when a crime has been committed in their jurisdiction. My coming here today is basically out of courtesy."

The captain bristled. "Courtesy? Courtesy or necessity? Maybe you think we might be able to assist you." He paused to gather his composure. "We've been experiencing an increase in criminal activity here ourselves. Maybe it would benefit us both to share information. Er…what did you say your name was, again?"

"Bautista. Good point. Maybe we can work together, Captain."

Nathaniel Bautista was a well-built man in his forties. He wore his dark hair in a brush cut over a ruddy forehead. He had an air of self-confidence born of a career that consisted of twenty years in America as an FBI agent followed by two years with INTERPOL. He had been working on the Iranian arms seizure when the main suspect ended up dead in a London park.

"When it was illegal firearms confiscated in Iran, that was one thing, but murder of one of your citizens is another. That's why I'm here."

"Right. Welde, you said."

"James Welde of Welde Technologies. We think he was importing weapons to Manila. The Iranians captured the plane. One of the pilots was killed trying to escape, but the other one identified Welde as his employer and the owner of the aircraft along with its cargo. A few days later, Welde was shot by a sniper in London. His daughter is a suspect."

"Shot by a sniper and the police there think his daughter did it? Doesn't that seem unlikely?" Belka's tone was turning sarcastic.

"That's their thinking. At least it was. Her rifle was definitely the murder weapon, but a couple of our guys there interviewed a woman who came into the country with Welde. They were travelling under assumed names. We think she is a more plausible suspect."

"You think she is somehow connected to the guns and that she's from El Nido?"

"That's what we think, yes. Right now, we need to go to Welde's house and see what we can find out there. I'm assuming you know where it is."

"Maybe. What about the factory, Welde's computer business?"

"My partner and I have been out there twice. The last time was this afternoon, as a matter of fact, with a search warrant. It's clean. Some women soldering circuit boards and a flunky with a broken hand. A dead end."

Belka called Cutro's desk. "Sergeant get in here," he snapped.

Cutro hurried through the door.

"Do you know where James Welde's house is?"

"Yeah, why?"

"He's been killed. We need to go out there and take a look around. We'll need a warrant."

It took Cutro a moment to process this information. "Maybe not. His daughter has reported him missing. I guess we can get permission from her when we notify her he's dead." Cutro stared at his feet and watched his toe try to dig into the floor. He recalled that Kincaid had been looking for Welde.

"What's the matter, Cutro? You've notified next of kin before."

"Yes, sir. I'm just a little overwhelmed right now. We've got a lot of murders all of a sudden."

"Who said Welde was murdered?" Bautista asked.

"Nobody, I just assumed…"

"Well, you were right, but he wasn't shot here. He was in London at the time."

Belka interrupted. "Wait a minute. His daughter, whose rifle is the murder weapon, is here reporting him missing?"

"Must be a different daughter. The one with the rifle is in London, Allison Welde. I forgot to mention that she's dead too."

"Now I'm really confused."

"She was fleeing the area right after her father was shot. She was involved in a traffic accident and died at the scene. That's another reason the authorities initially thought she was the shooter."

Cutro said, "This daughter was here the other day. Her name is Jillian Welde. I think she just got into town." He left out the fact that she was with Kincaid.

"Just got into town from where?" Bautista asked.

"I don't know. Maybe London?"

Belka fell heavily back into his chair. "This just gets better all the time. Let's get out to the house before something else happens."

The three officers piled into Cutro's Crown Vic and headed down the highway to James Welde's beach house. When they arrived, they found the gate open and a rental car in the driveway. Bautista was out of the Crown Vic first and walked around to the stairs. At the bottom step, he saw a man lying at the end of a trail of blood. He had been shot, apparently in both legs. He was semiconscious and obviously in great pain.

Bautista called out, "Quick! Call an ambulance!"

Cutro and Belka rushed over and saw the man writhing on the ground. Cutro ran back to his car and called in to the station. "Cruz, get an ambulance out here to the Welde residence as quick as you can."

The officer at the desk asked what had happened.

"A guy has been shot out here. By the way he's dressed, looks like he might be a terrorist. He's been tortured. Probably met up with Kincaid."

When Cutro got back, Bautista was trying to get the man to talk. "Who did this to you? Who shot you?"

Obviously in shock, the man was sobbing and gasping for breath. "That bastard," he said, finally.

"Where is he now? Is he in the house? Do you know where he went?" asked Belka.

But the man had passed out. Attempts to revive him proved futile.

Bautista turned to Belka. "Any idea who he's talking about?"

Belka was silent, lost in thought and chewing his cigar.

Cutro had a sickening feeling he knew. But all he said was, "I guess we just wait for the ambulance."

Bautista had other ideas. He drew his weapon, followed the blood smear up the stairs, and found the second man. Part of his skull was lying several feet from the rest of his body. Blood had pooled two feet in every direction. Bautista cautiously stepped past it and entered the house. There was no one there, just another pool of blood. "Belka, you'd better get up here!" he yelled.

While they waited for the ambulance, the three men did a cursory walkthrough of the house and grounds looking for Kincaid or the Welde woman, but they turned up nothing. The EMTs arrived and loaded both men onto stretchers. They looked through the victims' pockets. Nothing. Efforts to get more information from the survivor were futile, as they could see the life ebbing from his eyes.

"I guess we go back to the station and try to sort all this out," Belka said.

"Somebody needs to stay here to preserve the scene and see if anybody comes back," Bautista said.

Belka thought for a minute. The tip of his cigar glowed a brilliant orange. A plume of blue smoke preceded his answer. "Unless you're volunteering, I'll send someone as soon as we get back to town."

After he hung up from talking with Cutro, Cruz placed a call to el-Fasil. "Do you have men at James Welde's house?"

"Bakar was there earlier and brought back Welde's daughter. Why?"

"Nothing, I guess. I just got a call that they needed an ambulance down there. Did you get the American?"

"No. Bakar left a couple of men behind to wait for him."

"In that case, it's bad news. The ambulance wasn't for Kincaid. He wasn't there. Must be for one of your guys."

"Puta." el-Fasil spat.

"I'd keep an eye out for Kincaid if I were you. He's bound to be looking for the Welde girl."

"He'll never find her, but we'll find him. That's for sure."

"What about Grey? Do you still have him?"

"Yes, but he is proving to be useless. I am quickly growing tired of this whole thing."

"I'm sorry to hear it, because there's more."

"What now?"

"James Welde. I overheard talk. He may be dead."

"May be?"

"I can't be sure yet."

"Keep us informed, Cruz."

"No problem."

el-Fasil turned to Bakar. "Have you heard from the men you left at the Welde house?"

"Not yet."

"They are probably not coming back."

Chapter 42

PREPARING FOR WAR

A few kilometers down the road, Kincaid turned the jeep around and headed back north toward Welde's house. He didn't know if Jillian was at the camp, but he had no other leads. He had to act based on the limited and questionable information he had. Maybe he could extract something more from Roberto if he was still alive.

Moments after the ambulance and Cutro's car left for El Nido, he turned into the driveway and swept passed the still-open gate. A trail of blood smeared down the stairs, ending at the driveway. At the top of the stairs, where a dead terrorist should have been, was a thick pool of dark blood congealing in the hot sun. There was no other trace of the body. Inside, where he had left Roberto, was the genesis of the bloody smear that Kincaid had followed up the steps but no Roberto. Had he found enough strength to drag himself out of the house, and if so, why did his bloody tracks not extend into the driveway? And did he take his friend's body with him? *Not a chance.* Somebody must have discovered the bodies and removed them from the house. The question was who.

Now wasn't the time to think about that. Right now, he needed to see if the house had been searched. He hurried down the hall to Welde's bedroom and opened the closet door. He pushed aside several suits and shirts. All the rifles were still there. He pulled out the Barrett and a box of ammunition. Since he already had the AK-47, he started to leave the other rifles there but then thought about the Heckler & Koch 9 millimeters. One of them was fitted with a silencer, so he grabbed it, along with a box of ammo. There was also a box of tracer rounds. He took a few of them and abandoned the AK in favor of two blocks of PE4.

Kincaid piled his newly acquired arsenal on the kitchen table except for the H&K. He took it and went outside to see if anyone was out there waiting for him. It dawned on him that he might be in trouble. The thought didn't summon fear in him, just an uneasiness. Unease had been an old familiar friend ever since he became a Ranger. He found it comforting in a way. The challenge of matching wits and combat skills with an enemy was exciting, and he felt confident as he searched the house, the garden, and the beach. But he found no one. His thoughts turned briefly to the two missing men, one of whom was dead for sure and one who probably should have bled to death by now, but he wondered about them for only a minute. He had other things on his mind. He grabbed his bag from the jeep and headed back to the kitchen.

He found what he was looking for in a cabinet under the sink: a roll of tape and a box of scouring pads. He opened the door that led from the kitchen to the helipad and cut a square piece out of the screen. Next, he took a water bottle from the refrigerator and drank it dry before cutting off the bottom and making a hole in its center. He rolled the piece of screen into a tight cylinder and placed it into the neck of the bottle before stuffing as many scouring pads as would fit around it to hold it in place. He taped the bottom back onto the bottle, aligning the screen with the hole. He took three lighters from his bag and broke the flame guard off each one. He found two more bottles of water and tossed everything into the bag. He flung it and the H&K over his shoulder and carried the big sniper rifle back down the stairs to the jeep.

Chapter 43

STAKEOUT

As soon as they arrived at the police station in El Nido, Belka jumped out of the passenger seat of the Crown Vic. "No need to park it, Sergeant. Find Sal and send him back to the Welde house. Hurry it up. Somebody's going to turn up down there, and I think I know who it'll be."

"Who's that, Captain?" Cutro asked.

"Have you seen Kincaid lately?"

"No." He lied.

"Well, from the looks of that crime scene, I think he's been there, and he'll probably be back."

"What makes you think he wasn't a victim?"

"You can't be serious, Cutro."

Salvatore Campos was the cop Kincaid had called Fat Boy. He was in his late twenties and had weighed more than 140 kilos since high school. Now he was closer to 160, soaking wet. And in the tropical heat of the Philippines, it seemed like he was always soaking wet. That's why Cutro could always find him in the breakroom under the air conditioner.

"Sal, my car is out front. Take it down to the Welde place on the beach. Wait there until you hear from me."

"Cruz said somebody got shot down there."

Cutro continued, "Don't let anybody in the gate. If Kincaid shows up, arrest him."

"Arrest him? For what, trespassing?"

"Suspicion of murder."

"Murder? Kincaid whacked a guy again?"

"Don't ask questions, Sal. Just get out there and wait for the forensic guys. You'll figure it out."

Sal stepped from the cool lobby into the swelter. His white shirt sleeves were already rolled up, and the pits were gray with sweat stains. He loosened his tie and undid the top button. He always drew the shit assignments. When he joined the force three years ago, it was with the hope that he could land a desk job, but Officer Cruz had that position nailed down. Cutro only used him for muscle or, like today, some security detail that was either dangerous or boring. Or sometimes both.

He often wished he had kept following his dream to be a bass player in one of Manila's dozens of cover bands. The problem was he wasn't much of a musician. He owned a Fender bass and an amp, which made him attractive to several bands. But, unfortunately, his playing didn't. He'd lost every job he ever had, usually within the first month. Sal told himself it was because of his weight. Nobody wanted a fat man in the band. Looks were important if the band was going to be successful enough to make it to America.

He was daydreaming of all the money he'd make and all the girls he'd meet if he were playing on stage in an air-conditioned New York City nightclub. He reminded himself he needed to focus on the job at hand as he drove down Taytay-El Nido National Highway. He wasn't sure exactly where the Welde house was. He knew it was on the beach, so he would have to look for a mailbox on the right. He crept along slowly, which wasn't a problem, as there wasn't much traffic. Twenty minutes passed. Sal concluded that he had somehow missed it. He turned around at the next opportunity and steered the Ford back north. He met a peasant in an ox-drawn cart when, up ahead, a beat-up, old jeep was coming in his direction. He should have recognized the driver, but the mailbox he was looking for appeared in the next moment. He hit the brakes and veered into the Welde driveway.

The garage doors were open, so he pulled inside. It would keep the car cooler for the drive back. He may be out there for a while. El Nido didn't have a forensics examiner, and Sal wasn't sure where one would be coming from. It was going to be a long wait for sure. He wandered back out onto the driveway and started toward the steps. He stopped in his tracks when he saw the long streaks of blood leading up the stairs. He carefully stepped between them to the main floor of the house. He almost walked into the large puddle in front of the door. He felt a little dizzy. There had been a gruesome killing here, but who was the victim, and who was the killer? Scenes like this made Salvatore Campos glad he wasn't a detective. He couldn't stand the sight of blood.

His idea had been to sit inside the house. Hopefully, the air conditioning was working, and it would be cool. The front door was broken onto the floor, and just beyond the threshold was yet another large pool of blood. His stomach churned. Maybe the garage would be cool enough. At least he'd be in the shade.

He'd been sitting on the padded seat of an old wave runner for about an hour before he heard the sound of a small engine approaching. He got to his feet and moved to the driveway to see a red scooter coming through the gate. It was being driven by a woman. She wasn't wearing a helmet, so he could see she was an attractive Filipina. He stepped squarely into her path, raised both arms, and showed her his palms. The scooter squeaked to a stop a few feet in front of him.

"Sorry, Miss. You can't come in here."

"What's going on?" She looked puzzled and concerned at the same time.

"This is a crime scene, and it can't be disturbed while an investigation is going on."

"A crime scene? What kind of crime?" Her concern was becoming worry. Kincaid had said he was coming here to protect Jillian Welde from danger.

"I'm not at liberty to say," Sal said. "Who are you, anyway? You look kind of familiar."

"I'm Lucia de la Rosa. I work at the Oceania Resort."

"No, that's not it." He touched his finger to his chin and thought for a moment. "You're Johnny Rome's girlfriend. I was in his band. That's where I know you from."

"Oh, yeah, that's right. You're the bass player."

"Yeah. Sal Campos."

"Well, Sal, tell me what's going on. You have me worried about my friend, Jillian. Is she okay?"

"I'm not sure. I can tell you she isn't here."

Lucia stepped around the fat man enough to see reddish-brown stains on the stairs. "Is that blood?" she asked, trying to stave off panic.

"Yeah. I think so, but don't ask me who's."

"Do you know a man named Kincaid?"

"Yeah, but I don't think it's his blood, if that's what you're thinking. I'm supposed to be waiting for him to come back."

Lucia decided to try a different tactic. "You're a smart guy, Sal. What do you think happened here?"

Sal glanced around conspiratorially as if someone might overhear. "I think some of those PISF guys came around looking for him, and he killed 'em."

"If that's what happened, where are he and Jillian now?"

"I don't know. The sergeant wants me to arrest him. Maybe they're hiding out somewhere."

"Maybe," said Lucia. She paused. "I guess I'll be going." She thumbed the starter on her scooter and headed back out toward the gate.

"Palaam," he called after her. "Tell Johnny you saw me."

She didn't hear. She was trying to think where Kincaid might be, and she had a feeling she knew. She hoped with all her heart she was wrong.

Chapter 44

HOSTAGE

Grey's satellite phone rang in el-Fasil's tent. Bakar answered it. "Yes?"

"Who is this? I want to speak to the ambassador," Sasher barked.

"Please wait one moment." Bakar crossed the camp and kicked Grey awake. "Your phone."

Grey rubbed his eyes as he took the phone and held it to his ear. "Ambassador Grey speaking."

"Grey, this is Bruce Sasher. I know you're a busy man, so I'll come right to it. Our deal is off. Cancel whatever negotiations you have going. We're out."

The ambassador's heart leapt into his throat. He cupped his hand over his mouth and the receiver. "What do you mean, off? You can't be serious." His hand trembled so violently he almost dropped the phone. He turned away from Bakar, hoping he hadn't heard.

"The situation has changed. INTERPOL has been here twice asking questions. They just left. They're trying to connect me with an arms bust and Welde's murder. It's become much too risky for us, I'm afraid."

"Risky for us? Who is us? I'm the one who is at risk."

"Too risky for Sasher Investments. Tell your clients

that there are complications right now. It's only temporary. This thing will blow over soon enough, and then we can do the deal."

"You mean to leave me here to rot in the jungle until then? I need you to wire me that money!"

"No, Grey. I mean we'll do the original deal."

Sweat was beading on the ambassador's forehead. He lowered his voice to just above a whisper. "You don't understand. They'll kill me if I can't deliver the rifles. You have to let me have that money."

Sasher laughed. "Don't be ridiculous. No one's going to kill you over an arms transaction."

"You don't know these people." His voice was hoarse and quivering.

"You're an ambassador, for chrissake. You haven't lost your touch. Use some diplomacy, and you'll be fine." The line went dead.

Grey turned and faced Bakar. He tried to manage a smile.

"Who was that?" Bakar demanded.

"It was one of my people in London."

"What did he say? Do we have a deal or not?"

"Yes, y-yes," Grey stammered. "Of course, we do."

"When will the guns be delivered?"

"Very soon." Grey's hand was still shaking badly as Bakar took the phone from him. "We just have to work out the logistics. Can you take these handcuffs off me now, please?" He was trying not to sound desperate, but that's exactly how he sounded to Bakar.

"I'll ask," Bakar said with a sneer. He turned and walked away.

I'm a dead man, Grey said to himself.

Bakar pushed through the flap of the command tent. el-Fasil was sitting at the table, pulling at his beard and leering at Jillian Welde. She was duct taped to a camp chair in the corner. "Let me go," she demanded. "Why did you bring me here? I'm an American citizen. You will be in big trouble if you don't release me immediately."

el-Fasil smiled. "Your government doesn't know or care anything about you, Miss Welde, including where you are or what happens to you."

Jillian struggled against her bonds. "You'll regret this" she said, frantically, "you'll see."

He turned away from her to face Bakar, who was smiling broadly.

"What was that about?"

"Grey got a phone call from London."

"And?"

"I'm not sure, but I think there is a problem. A big problem."

"They don't agree to make the trade?"

"It sounded like they didn't. Grey said they did but that there are some logistics that need to be worked out. I don't think he is telling the truth. Do you want me to go and get him?"

el-Fasil thought for a moment and continued to stroke his beard. "No, not now. We'll let him worry for a while."

"Perhaps if we kill the woman, they will see that we mean business," Bakar said.

"My friend, you are always too eager to kill. She is the daughter of Mr. Welde. Besides, it would be a shame to deprive ourselves of the company of such a beauty, don't you think?"

"I see what you mean."

His tone darkened. "What about the American, Bakar? Why isn't he dead yet? He has cost us several lives already. Why haven't you killed him?"

"I am working on it. We are searching for him now."

"I hope for your sake you find him and bring his body to me," el-Fasil stood and looked Bakar in the eyes, "or I will have your body in his place."

Bakar swallowed hard. "I will not fail you, sir." He turned on his heel and hurried from the tent.

Outside, most of the men were working on the new building. Hammers and saws were transforming the lumber Bakar had procured into the framing for walls and a roof. Bakar selected four men from the laborers and instructed them to go and find Kincaid.

"Where should we look? How will we know him? We have no idea what he looks like," one of them protested.

"Search everywhere. He is a large and vicious-looking American. He will probably be the one who is shooting at you."

The men looked at one another as if they couldn't believe what they were hearing. It was a suicide mission.

"Don't come back without him or I will kill you myself."

el-Fasil left the command tent and crossed to the other side of the camp to inspect the progress on his new storage shed. When the munitions shipment did arrive, he would take the guns he needed for his men and store the rest until they were shipped to the other PISF cells operating to the south. If he didn't have the weapons when his superiors asked for them, it would be his life. He was going to make certain that didn't happen.

"Why are you not finished with your work?" he shouted at no one in particular. None answered. They didn't dare even look at him but kept their heads down and hammered more furiously. "I want this done. Soon." He turned and stormed away.

Inside the command tent, Bakar had pulled Jillian from her chair and was standing inches from her face. He slid his hands up and down her sides. He was fumbling with the top button of her blouse when el-Fasil arrived and shoved him violently away from her. "Stay away from this woman," he roared. He gathered his composure and glared at Bakar. "No one is to touch Miss Welde. Not you, not anyone. If her father is foolish enough to try to double-cross me, I will exact my payment from her then." He leered at her. "I'm sure she will be the source of much pleasure for me. But I do not believe it will come to that, Bakar." He turned back to his captain. "I think the fool is our Mr. Grey. He is trying to take advantage of our situation. I think he has done something with Welde. He will regret it, I assure you. Bring him to me."

Bakar hurried out through the tent flap and collected Grey from the shelter. Grey had been sleeping and was disoriented. Bakar pushed him into the tent.

"Have you met Miss Welde?" el-Fasil said.

"No, I haven't had the pleasure."

"Miss Welde, this is Mr. Grey. He's the former British ambassador to Vietnam and currently your father's business associate. Correct, Grey?"

Grey stared at the attractive blonde across from him. "That's correct." He had a sinking feeling in the pit of his stomach.

"Miss Welde is looking for her father. I told her you would know where he is."

Grey said nothing.

"Where is he, ambassador?"

"I'm not exactly sure."

el-Fasil wasn't satisfied. "But you have been in contact with him, correct?"

"I guess so, yes."

Bakar drew his pistol from his belt and poked it hard into the back of Grey's head. "Stop playing games with us or I am going to kill you right now."

Grey looked at el-Fasil for a sign that he would save him, but el-Fasil stared coldly back at him. "Where is Welde, Grey?"

There was no use pretending any longer. The ambassador knew he was doomed either way. "Welde is dead."

Jillian gasped loudly.

"He was assassinated in London just before I came out here."

"You have been playing me for a fool all along," el-Fasil growled through gritted teeth.

"No. I came to honor your deal. Welde's death changes nothing. I will get your guns for you, I swear."

el-Fasil turned to Jillian. "My apologies, Miss Welde. It is regrettable that this has happened. I had no idea, I assure you. I would never have subjected you to such a cruel ordeal as this."

Jillian was crying bitterly. Her sobs came in waves, interrupted only by short pauses to recover her breath. She had doubted that her father was still alive, but to hear the news this way was more than she could bear. Grey had used the word *assassinated*. What did that mean?

el-Fasil's demeanor changed again. He sounded like the ruthless man Jillian thought he was. "We will deal with Mr. Grey in the morning. Return him to the shelter. Take Miss

Welde to my tent and post a guard. Make sure the guard understands no one is to molest her in any way. If she is harmed, you and he will both die."

Bakar stood frozen with dread.

"Do it!" el-Fasil shouted.

Chapter 45

IMPROVISE AND PREVAIL

Kincaid had found the cutoff to the PISF camp. As before, he drove past the road before heading back north. He guided the jeep down a slight embankment and killed the engine. He took the machete into the brush and chopped a few branches and palm fronds to pile onto the vehicle. It wasn't completely hidden, but maybe it wouldn't be noticed. He needed to conserve his strength if he was going to be able to rescue Jillian from a small army. He changed into a pair of camo pants and a green, military-issue T-shirt before loading the cargo pockets with magazines for his pistol and the H&K. He took six rounds for the sniper rifle, along with a few tracer rounds and stuffed them into his pocket as well. The .45 and his knife went into his belt, and he threw his bag and the two rifles over his shoulder. He was ready.

He was startled by the ring of his SAT phone. It was Alex. "Okay, Kincaid, I've got some info for you."

"Let's hear it."

"James Welde had a cargo plane full of munitions headed for Manila that was intercepted by the Iranians in their airspace. INTERPOL was looking for him and encountered a woman who had been traveling with him to London. They were both carrying fake passports, so they don't know who she was. But now the thinking is she might be a more likely suspect in Welde's death."

"They have no idea who this woman is?

"None. Where are you now, Kincaid?"

"I'm in Palawan. Welde's other daughter has been captured by some lame-ass terrorist group down here, and I'm on my way to get her. Maybe Ambassador Grey, too, if he is still alive."

"How many men do you have with you?"

"All I need."

"How many is that?"

"Counting me, one."

There was concern in Alex's voice. "Don't ever underestimate your enemy, Kincaid. Take my advice and go get help."

"There's no time. Plus, I don't think there's anyone here who would be useful. I'm better off on my own."

"Don't be stupid, man."

"Gotta go." Kincaid hung up.

"Shit."

He clipped the phone to his belt and started back toward the camp road when he caught the scent of the dead thief he had stashed earlier. The heat had accelerated the decaying process, and the smell was unmistakable. Kincaid was all too familiar with the stench of rotting corpses. Once he located the dead terrorist, it was easy to find the tracks where he had come out of the jungle after encountering the two lookouts. He cautiously crept back to the spot where he had last seen them. They were still there. The sun was sinking behind the trees, but there was still plenty of light. He unshouldered the H&K and clicked the safety to single-fire mode.

He watched and waited for about ten minutes. One of the guards stepped behind the big tree. Kincaid figured he was going to relieve himself. The one in the white T-shirt was sitting on the ground, smoking a cigarette. He was young, probably not even twenty, but he was the enemy. *The enemy is ageless.* Kincaid took aim at the cigarette and pulled the trigger. The boy tumbled over. The silencer worked better than Kincaid had hoped and suppressed the muzzle flash. The second man zipped up, hurriedly ran around the tree, and picked up his AK-47. He frantically scanned the perimeter but saw nothing. Kincaid's second round caught him just over his right eyebrow. He fell beside his comrade. The two shots hadn't been loud but could have been heard, cracking through the thick stillness of the jungle. Kincaid stayed still, waiting to see if anyone was coming to investigate, but all that came were ants. Great big red ants that began biting him with agonizing results. He had to move.

He checked the bodies of the sentries and found them both dead. There was nothing in their pockets or in the area to help him with his immediate problem. He had no idea what he was headed into. He knew nothing about the camp, not even its exact location. Were there more guards to be dealt with before he got there? He was almost certain there would be, but where?

To the left of the big tree with the makeshift ladder, he noticed a path. Maybe it would lead to some answers. But first, he climbed the ladder as far as it went up into the tree. From there, he went limb to limb until he reached the tender branches at the top. It must have been at least forty feet high, but the jungle canopy was so thick that it afforded him no clue where the PISF encampment might be. Back on the ground, he moved cautiously through the brush along the rocky, narrow trail for about a hundred meters before reaching a steep limestone cliff. Set into the side of the cliff was a small cave. Kincaid took cover behind a pile of rocks that looked to have fallen from the cliff at some point. He sat motionless for a few minutes, listening and watching for signs of life. Nothing. He crawled to the mouth of the cave and tried to see inside, but all he could see was darkness. With his flashlight pressed against the H&K MP5, he stepped in silently. It extended back about five meters and was completely empty except for the ashy remains of an old campfire. He decided this was a good place to hide the sniper rifle. The big 50-caliber Barrett was heavy and too cumbersome to lug through the underbrush. If he needed to take a long-range shot with it, it would be easy enough to come back for it, and if he had to retreat without his H&K for some reason, it would serve as a backup gun. He laid it on a stony ledge along with its makeshift silencer and covered it with a few rocks, hoping no one came along before he could retrieve it.

Back outside, Kincaid found that the path dwindled to nothing more than an animal trail from the cliff. He proceeded through thick brush and over rocky ground, cutting his way along until he eventually met up with the road again. He was reasonably certain it was the same road that led in from the highway.

He followed it, staying off to the side as much as possible. It was risky, but he didn't have the time or the energy to slash his way through the dense foliage with a rusty machete. He had hiked almost two kilometers when he heard a big vehicle approaching ahead. He scurried into the brush and laid low. A black Land Cruiser was slowly advancing toward him. He pushed between the bushes, watching it roll past and straining to see if Jillian was inside. He might as well have been standing in the middle of the road. What he saw were four men laughing and yelling, paying no attention to anything outside the truck. There was no sign of a woman, and the men definitely hadn't seen him, so he continued toward the camp. He still wasn't sure what his plan was, if Jillian was alive, or if she was even in the camp. All he knew was that she wasn't in the Land Cruiser that had passed him on the road. But he was pretty sure the ambassador was being held there. Maybe they were together. He'd do what he had been trained to do. He would improvise and prevail.

Moving on up the road, he gradually became aware of gunfire. Steady and not a single shooter but several guns being fired at random intervals. He left the road again. He'd have to advance on his stomach from there. It was too dangerous to walk any farther. As he got closer to the sound, he realized he wasn't hearing gunfire at all. It was hammers. People were hammering on wood. Building something. But then he heard something else. An engine. Another vehicle was approaching from behind him. He crawled deeper into the brush and peered back up the road. It was a scooter. And Lucia was riding it.

Chapter 46

A CONFESSION

He checked to his right before stepping out into her path. She stopped, killed the engine, and smiled at him.

"What the hell are you doing here?"

His voice was low, but she could tell he was angry with her. She ignored the question. "I'm so glad to see you, Kincaid."

"I can't say the same. How did you find me, and why are you here?" His jaw was tightening.

"I went to Allison's house. There was a lot of blood there, and the police are looking for you." She looked around and behind him. "Is Jillian with you?"

"Answer my question, Lucia. What made you think to look for me here?"

"It's obvious who is looking for you, Kincaid. I may not know you well, but I know you well enough to know that if someone is hunting you, they are likely to become your prey. Don't worry, I'm not being followed."

Her explanation did little to placate him. "How do you know this place?" he persisted.

"I've been here before. I came with Mr. Welde once or twice. There is a camp out here and men who will be waiting to kill you, Kincaid. Maybe I can talk to them for you."

"That makes no sense. Why would they talk to you? Besides, the fact is, there isn't going to be any talking. They have Jillian, and I'm going to get her back. I've already eliminated a few of them, and I'm prepared to send the rest to Jannah or wherever they go after this life." He suddenly realized what Lucia had said. "You were here with Welde? When was that?"

She hadn't wanted to tell him about being with Welde, but now she needed him to take her seriously. "It's a long story, and it's not what you think. Anyway, I can help you. I know the layout of the camp. I know where the guards are and everything. Do you even know how to get there?"

He tried to sound self-assured. "Yeah, I think so."

"You think so? Now who's making no sense? They will find you, and you won't have a chance against them. There are lots of them, and you are one man."

"Okay, maybe you *can* help me, Lucia. You can tell me what you know, but then I want you to go home. This is no place for a girl. You said it yourself. It's dangerous out here, and it's going to get more dangerous before this is over."

"I'm not just a girl, you bastard. I'm a woman, and I can be dangerous too. You have no idea."

He could see that arguing with her was a waste of time, and he didn't have a lot of time. "All right. Let's hide that scooter, and we'll make a plan."

They pushed Lucia's scooter off the road, and Kincaid cut enough kaligag branches to secret it from the road. He backtracked and led her back to the cave. "We'll spend the night here and get an early start tomorrow. Maybe I can catch the camp sleeping and have the advantage."

She bristled at his use of the pronoun *I* but said nothing.

He went into his bag and brought out the water and energy bars. "It isn't much, but that's all I have." he said. He built a small fire at the mouth of the cave, and they set about formulating a strategy for the raid on the camp.

Lucia used a stick to draw in the dirt. "When I was there, this was how their camp was arranged." She showed him where el-Fasil's tent was along with the HQ tent and the crude shelter. "There are a few other, smaller tents here and there," she said "but mostly they are close to the center of the clearing. They had one big campfire right there in the middle of everything."

"The camp itself—was I on the right road to it?"

"If you went a short way farther, you would see a smaller road turning to the right. That road leads into the camp."

"That's what I thought. What about guards?"

"When I was there, there were two guards on the road just before the clearing. I didn't see any other ones besides them." She waited for his response, but Kincaid just bit off a chunk of his energy bar. "What's the plan?" she asked.

He stared into the fire for what seemed to her, a long time. "You didn't tell me how you happened to be at a terrorist camp with James Welde" he said, finally. "And if you knew about PISF, why didn't you tell me before now?"

"James Welde killed my father," she said, simply. "My father told my mother, before he died, that Welde was taking weapons off Clark Airbase to sell. It took a long time for my uncle to find out that my father was killed in an explosion on the base, why we weren't allowed to see the body. It wasn't hard to figure out that it was a car bomb, and there was only one person who had a reason to do that.

"I knew Allison from school, so we became friends. When I started going to visit her at her father's house, he started coming on to me. I realized he had a thing for younger women, and I suspected he was molesting his daughter. After my uncle told me what he had learned, I decided to get close to James. The idea was to use his perversion against him."

Kincaid was beginning to understand what he was hearing, but he didn't want to believe it. This delicate young woman wouldn't, couldn't have been the person who shot Welde. "What did you do then?"

"I killed him, Kincaid. I went with him to London with a fake passport. Allison goes to university there, and we stayed at her apartment. I didn't know exactly what I was going to do or when. I was just waiting for the right chance. I had been waiting for a long time. In London, fate stepped in, and the situation presented itself. I shot him with Allison's rifle."

Could she really be capable of such violence? How else could she know how Welde died? "Where was he when you shot him?"

"Across the street from Allison's apartment. He was walking through the park. I waited for him from the roof."

"And you were able to shoot him from that distance? That had to have been a difficult shot. You must be an expert with a rifle."

"My uncle used to take me hunting in the jungle all the time. We would shoot at targets when we couldn't find game. I was better at it than him. I'm probably a better shot than you are."

"You just might be." Kincaid was only half joking. "More impressively, you got away with it."

"It was perfect. The only thing that worries me is if the police find her gun, but I don't think they will ever suspect her."

Kincaid took a deep breath. *You never really know what someone is capable of.* "They did suspect Allison, I'm afraid."

"Oh, no! Did they arrest her? I can't let her take the blame for what I've done. I'll have to go back to London."

"They didn't arrest her Lucia." He paused. "She was in a car crash. Allison is dead."

"Dead in a car crash? When?"

"The police think she was fleeing after the shooting and ran a traffic light. She was T-boned by a truck in the intersection. She died at the scene." Lucia's eyes welled with tears. Kincaid realized he had been too blunt. He should have broken the news more gently, but he knew nothing about tact. "I'm sorry, Lucia."

She was trying to keep from weeping openly, but the tears spilled down her cheeks and clung to her chin. "I already felt kind of bad about shooting her father, but now I feel terrible. Poor Allison." She wiped her face with her sleeve.

"Was she there when you did it?"

"No. James said she was in France. I don't know how she could have been anywhere near the park. I never saw her anyway."

They sat quietly for a few minutes before she spoke again. "Do you ever regret shooting someone, Kincaid?"

"Not really."

She could see in his eyes that he did have regrets. "Tell me. I want to know everything about you. I want to hear."

"Soldiers don't tell war stories anymore. The wars have gotten too complicated. Hell, most of the time we don't even know what we're fighting for except to stay alive."

"I thought you fought for money."

Kincaid looked like he'd been slapped in the face. "That's right, I do, but I don't merely hire out to the highest bidder. I have to believe I'm on the right side of justice."

"I'm sorry. I didn't mean to be cruel. I wasn't thinking."

He was quiet for a moment. "I had some remorse after I killed my first man in combat, I guess. It was in Afghanistan. We came upon some goat herders. We thought they were friendlies until one guy brought an AK-47 from under his robe. He killed our medic before I shot him. He didn't die right away but cried bitterly until he bled out. I almost felt bad for him until I remembered he killed my buddy. Then, I shot him again. He was already dead by then, but I felt a lot better after I shot him the second time. Every man I've killed since then deserved it. I don't feel sorry about any of them. To hell with them."

"James Welde deserved to die too. He said I was his whore, and I guess he was right. In the end, he paid for what he did to my father." A last, small tear made its way down her face as she stared into his eyes. "You're right, Kincaid. To hell with him." Several more minutes passed. The fire was fading to ashes before she softly repeated, "Poor Allison."

Kincaid saw no reason to discuss it further. "Let's talk about tomorrow." Lucia shifted her gaze from the smoking ashes to him. "A little before dawn, I'm going to go back toward the camp. I want you to stay here with this gun." He pulled the sniper rifle from its hiding place along with the silencer he had made for it. He taped the silencer to the barrel. "This may quiet the shot a little, but it will at least hide the muzzle flash from anyone trying to locate your position. I need you to make sure no one gets in behind me. I know you're good with a rifle, at least. I'm depending on you to cover my ass."

"I want to go with you," she said firmly.

"No. You'll be much more help to me if you stay here. Find a good spot to hide near the road and keep a close eye out to make sure nothing comes in behind me." He handed her the six rounds he brought for the Barrett.

She was adamant. "I'm going in with you."

"No, you're not," he barked. "You'll do as I say. I'm serious." Lucia said nothing. "That's the end of it. Now let's get some rest. Tomorrow is going to be a hard day."

Chapter 47

THE PRISONERS

Bakar returned to the command tent. "I have done as you ordered, sir. The girl is in your tent, and Grey is back at the shelter. Some of our men are there with him. He is secure. What are you going to do with him?"

"I have been thinking about that. If we cannot get the rifles from him, perhaps the British will pay a ransom for him. He could be worth much more to us than we planned on. If that fails, I am giving him to you."

Bakar smiled. "I would then make a video of his beheading. We could post it on the internet. It would bring us much honor and perhaps some new recruits."

"Always, you are wanting blood. I am thinking of the cause. The need for arms and supplies is more important than new recruits." el-Fasil said.

"Yes sir. Of course, you are right."

"What of the American? Why have you not killed him?"

"I sent four of my best men to find him, but they have yet to return."

"And this does not concern you?"

"No, sir. I instructed them not to come back until he is dead. They have been gone only a few hours. I expect it will take some time to find him."

"It makes me nervous to know he is out there somewhere, Bakar. He is our most serious threat right now. If he finds our camp…"

"He will not find it. Even if he does, we have two men at the highway and two more at the road. He will never get past them."

el-Fasil stared thoughtfully. "The men at the highway. What do you hear from them?"

"I have not been able to contact them for some time."

"I do not find these answers reassuring, Bakar."

"Sir, the American is but one man…"

el-Fasil interrupted. "You are a fool! Send two more men to the highway, and make sure they have a radio. I want to know of anything out of the ordinary that happens out there."

"Yes, sir." He waited a moment, but the general didn't speak. "What else may I do for you?'

"Leave me. I am going to spend some time with Miss Welde."

"I understand. You will not be interrupted."

"See to it."

Bakar pushed through the tent flap with el-Fasil following. They walked briskly to el-Fasil's tent. "You are to see that no one enters this tent under any circumstances. Is that clear?"

"Yes sir."

el-Fasil went inside to find Jillian tied to a chair. "I am sorry that you have been treated so poorly, Miss Welde," he said, smiling. He untied her hands. "Would you like some wine, perhaps?"

Jillian was feeling several emotions at once: sadness and shock to learn of her father's death and outrage and terror over her situation. "What are you going to do with me? You need to let me go. I am an American citizen. I demand that you let me go. Right now." She tried to sound self-assured.

"Where exactly would you go, Miss Welde? No, I think you should stay here for the time being. It is for your own safety."

Chapter 48

ACCORDING TO PLAN

Kincaid had no intention of waiting until dawn. He needed to get to Jillian as soon as possible. Besides, the darkness was his friend. *Just ask Paul Simon.*

As soon as Lucia drifted off to sleep, he started back toward the camp. He found the scooter where they had left it on the road. It was almost inaudible at idle, so he decided to take a chance and ride it, at least for a while. He twisted the throttle barely open and crept along the road, keeping an eye on his rearview mirror. He hadn't gotten far before he saw lights on the road behind him. It was a vehicle coming around a sharp bend through the trees. He killed the engine and parked the scooter on its kickstand in the middle of the road. Hiding in the brush, he watched the big Land Cruiser amble toward him. It was the same truck that he had observed going out earlier. *No battle plan survives the first contact with the enemy.*

The driver stopped just short of the scooter. He and the passenger in the front seat opened their doors and got out to investigate. Kincaid shot them as soon as they stepped into the headlights. The two men in the back seat weren't aware what had happened. The pop of the rifle was covered by its silencer and the idling engine of the truck. But Kincaid's third shot spattered the passenger behind the driver's seat with the brains of the man to his right. He panicked, jumped out of the Land Cruiser, and crouched behind the rear wheel. Kincaid needed to eliminate him before he had the chance to fire his weapon. He needn't have worried. In his haste, the terrorist had left his firearm in the vehicle.

Kincaid figured the man would try to flee into the jungle on the opposite side of the road, which is exactly what he did. Kincaid chased him for a few meters before he got tangled in the dense bush. Kincaid shot him in the throat before he could cry out. Back out on the road, he loaded the other three men into the truck and buckled them in place with their seatbelts. After pushing the scooter back into the brush, he climbed behind the wheel of the big SUV. He took a shemagh out of his bag and wrapped it around his head. Maybe the guards wouldn't look too closely and wave the Land Cruiser into the camp. That was his new plan.

He hadn't driven far before he saw tire tracks turning off the main road to the right. Kincaid wouldn't have called it a road, but vehicles had obviously been using it as one. One set of tracks looked to have been made by a heavy truck much bigger than the Land Cruiser. He decided it must be the way to the camp, so he followed it. About a mile along that road, he saw what appeared to be a lantern light. The guards. He drove ahead. His idea was to drive right past, but one of them stepped into his path. He stopped. The guard walked up to the window and peered in. Kincaid recognized immediately that he hadn't been fooled. He grabbed the man by the back of the neck and jerked it violently down onto the windowsill, crushing his larynx. The guard struggled but could make no sound. A minute later, he stopped struggling. He was dead.

Lucia had said there were two guards. Kincaid dropped the corpse and pushed it aside as he got out of the truck. The second guard was lying on a blanket asleep, a few feet into the trees. Kincaid took off his shemagh and kicked the man awake before wrapping it around his neck and strangling him. He decided to turn the truck around and leave it there. An exit strategy was just as important as a plan of attack, and now one had started to take shape in his mind. There was just the small problem of three dead men strapped inside. The jungle heat and humidity were sapping his strength, but the bodies had to be disposed of. One by one, he took off their seatbelts, pulled them from the Land Cruiser, and piled them on top of the two guards well past the tree line. As he worked, he tried to calculate how many of the terrorists he had eliminated already. There couldn't be that many left. He wondered if they had night vision equipment.

Satisfied that the corpses wouldn't be found anytime soon, Kincaid took his bag and rifle and entered the camp on foot. The first thing he saw was the shelter. Several men were lolling about. A few looked to be playing cards; others were lying on cots or sitting on camp chairs. The ambassador was on the ground, handcuffed to the wall on the right. Kincaid wrapped the shemagh back around his head and neck, hoping he wouldn't be noticed outside the glow of the main campfire. With Lucia's sketch in mind, he located what he figured to be el-Fasil's tent. That was most likely where they were holding Jillian if she was in the camp at all. To the left of el-Fasil's tent was what appeared to be the HQ tent, flying the black flag of the PISF. To the left of that was the long, aluminum boat he had last seen speeding away from the resort after the failed attempt to kidnap the ambassador. It was on a trailer, tilted back at a shallow angle to allow rainwater to drain into the bilge and out through the transom. Somewhere out of sight, a generator was idling loudly, supplying electricity to the tents.

Kincaid moved to his right and slipped along the perimeter of the camp, staying in the shadows whenever possible. A two-ton flatbed truck was parked alongside a ditch that ran the length of the clearing. He checked underneath it. Nothing. He inched his way around the back of the truck, careful to keep his back against the tailgate. He peered around to the side next to the ditch. He saw no one, but as soon as he stepped around the corner, he found himself face to face with a man whose long beard cascaded over a ZZ Top T-shirt. Kincaid thought he could have been a Hells Angel, but despite his size, the big man seemed as surprised as he was. He spoke, but Kincaid didn't understand.

"Kamusta," Kincaid said softly and turned his head away. The man didn't reply but kept walking in the opposite direction.

Just ahead, he saw the construction site of what was soon to be a small shed. Boxes of nails and a few hammers were strewn around the wood floor. Two walls appeared to be finished, and there were studs in place for a third. *So that's what all the hammering was about.* He continued his reconnaissance around the outside of the clearing. He passed silently behind the shelter where Grey was being held. Four men were playing cards and laughing while two more were in deep conversation about something. No one was paying any attention to their captive. There were three pup tents between the shelter and el-Fasil's tent. The pup tents looked unoccupied, but the big tent was lit on the inside. A sentry was posted in front. Kincaid crept to the rear wall. He put his ear against it and listened. A man was speaking. It sounded like English, but Kincaid was unable to make out what he was saying. He decided to take a chance and slipped the blade of his knife into the canvas and made a slit long enough to peer through. There was Jillian, seated in a camp chair. A bearded man dressed in camo was standing beside the chair. His back was to Kincaid, and he was doing all the talking.

Kincaid moved on past the tent and the generator toward the boat. A familiar odor stopped him in his tracks. The stench of death. There was no mistake—a dead body was nearby, but he didn't have time to look for it. He climbed into the boat. The outboard motor was fed by one of two portable gas tanks. That's what Kincaid had hoped to find. He shook one of the tanks. It was full of fuel. He carried it from the stern up to the bow and positioned it on its side against the front bench seat. He loosened the cap just enough to let the gas leak out slowly. A small stream meandered down the floor toward the bilge. He clambered over the side and doubled back toward the unfinished structure on the far side of the camp.

He made it back undetected and crouched behind one of the walls. He scanned the darkness and saw no one, so he shielded a small LED flashlight as best he could inside his bag and fished out two of the disposable lighters. He turned the flame adjustment on one to its highest setting and slid it back and forth while pressing downward. After a few cycles, the gas began to leak out on its own. Using a piece of tape, he attached it to the wall facing down at an angle and lit it with a third lighter. He quickly repeated the process with the second lighter. Now time was of the essence. Once again, he slipped past the men in the shelter and the pup tents. The guard in front of the big tent was staring stupidly into the campfire. Totally oblivious.

Kincaid peered through the slit in the back wall. The man was still talking, but louder now. "Your father took my money, and now it seems I can expect nothing in return except you, Miss Welde."

"What is that supposed to mean?" Jillian demanded.

"It means that I intend to make the best of my situation." He stood over her and tore at her shirt.

"Like hell you are," she screamed. She pulled her shirt back over her breast and held it there.

"Don't play coy with me, bitch. I know how you American women are. You want it. We both know it."

"Maybe if you were a man." She spat at him.

"I'll show you a man, and then I'm going to kill you. Slowly."

Jillian grabbed the man's crotch. "Who are you kidding? You can't make it with a woman who isn't crying and begging for mercy. And you won't get the satisfaction from me. I'm not afraid of you. You're as impotent as your fucking army."

The man swept his arm in a violent arch and caught her cheek with the back of his hand, knocking over her chair and rolling her onto the floor. He stepped toward her while unbuckling his belt.

Kincaid pulled his knife blade down through the canvas wall of the tent and jumped inside. He looped his wire saw over el-Fasil's head from behind and yanked it from side to side. Blood pulsed from his carotid artery as Kincaid shoved him aside. Jillian screamed and tried to get to her feet. Blood was spurting onto her blouse, and she made low, gasping noises as she struggled to catch her breath. He scooped her off the floor and tried to calm her.

"It's me, Jillian. It's okay." She was slipping into shock. "It's okay. I've got you," he said in a low, raspy voice. "It's me, Kincaid. It's okay."

Jillian plunged her face into his chest and wept quietly. They stood like that for a few moments. She tried to regain her composure while he waited for the guard to come through the tent flap. But the guard never came. Kincaid figured he mistook her gasps for the general having his fun with his prisoner.

"We have to get out of here," he whispered. "We don't have a lot of time. You have to get hold of yourself and come with me right now."

He led her through the opening in the tent wall and out into the bushes beyond the perimeter of the camp. At that moment, the flame of the first lighter melted its way through the plastic body and ignited the liquid gas inside. It exploded with a bang that sounded like the blast from a large-caliber weapon. The men in the shelter grabbed their rifles and ran into the clearing, searching for the shooter.

"Quick," Kincaid whispered, "follow me." He ran to the generator and flipped the kill switch. All the lights in the camp went out, leaving only the campfire to illuminate the area. He grabbed Jillian's hand and ran toward the Land Cruiser. They were only a few meters away when the ZZ Top guy stepped out of the darkness. He pointed an AK-47 at Kincaid's chest as he shouted something in an angry voice. Kincaid could only guess what he had said. The man pointed first at Kincaid's rifle and then at the ground. Kincaid had no intention of giving up his weapon but gestured as if he was pulling it from his shoulder. At that moment, the second lighter exploded. It was enough to distract the terrorist, and when he averted his eyes toward the sound,

Kincaid slid his knife into the back of the big man's neck. He slumped to the ground, gasping for breath and clutching at his throat. Kincaid silenced him with the butt of his rifle.

It was more than Jillian could bear. He could see the panic in her eyes. She started to scream, but he clapped his hand over her mouth. "You have to control yourself" he whispered. You'll be fine, but you have to stay quiet. Understand?"

Jillian nodded. She still had a wild look in her eyes, but he took his hand away. "Take a deep breath," he said. "We're all right." She inhaled deeply. "Good. Now take another." She did. "Feel better?"

She nodded. "I'm okay."

They hastened to the truck. Kincaid opened the driver's door and helped her get in behind the wheel. "All right. Do you know where we are?"

"Vaguely."

"Do you think you can find your way back to your father's house?"

"I-I guess so."

"It's easy. Take this little road until you come to a bigger one that intersects it. Then turn left to the highway. You'll know where you are then. Take a right."

"Okay. Let's go."

"Why do you think I'm giving you directions, Jillian? I'm not going with you. I have to go back for the ambassador."

"Are you kidding? It's not possible."

"I can't leave him there. They'll kill him."

"If you go back now, they'll kill you both."

"No, they won't. Listen to me, and don't argue. We don't have time. The police are at your house. Hurry and bring them back here as quick as you can." There was an urgency in his voice that told her there was no use trying to change his mind. He slammed the door, leaned in through the window and kissed her forehead. "For luck."

She turned the key.

At the edge of the camp, the gasoline had filled the bilge of the aluminum boat. The float on the electric pump bobbed to the surface. The contacts on the relay made a small spark, and the gasoline erupted into an intense fireball. That explosion ignited the second fuel tank. Flames shot forty feet into the dark sky. Several trees in the jungle canopy caught fire, and suddenly, the PISF camp looked like the set of *Apocalypse Now*.

"Go!" Kincaid shouted.

Jillian punched the accelerator. The wheels of the Land Cruiser sprayed dirt and rocks in its wake and propelled the big SUV desperately away.

When he got back to the clearing, men were scrambling in all directions. el-Fasil's tent was ablaze and so was the guard. He ran in circles, screaming, but no one was coming to his aid. The noise from the fire, coupled with the frenzied shouts of his comrades, ensured that a rifle shot would go unheard, so Kincaid put him out of his misery. He picked off another man who was standing frozen at the front of the shelter. It was pandemonium to the left as several men tried to douse the fire on the boat with buckets of water.

Kincaid crouched behind a fallen tree and assessed the situation. He realized he had seriously underestimated the size of the force he was going up against, and he knew he had to act fast before order was restored in the camp and they came searching for him.

THE BINTURONG, OR PALAWAN BEARCAT, IS A RARE animal found only on Palawan Island. It stands about two feet tall on four legs and is about four feet in length, including its tail. The animal is agile enough among the tree branches, with its sharp claws and prehensile tail, but on the ground, it's slower and plodding. For this reason, it was hardly ever seen on foot. And yet, there it was in the middle of the road. Jillian saw it just in time to swerve to the right, missing it by inches. But the problem for her was that the road was narrow, and the tree she hit was massive. The impact drove the steering wheel into her chest and chin. Blood spurted from her mouth. The airbag hadn't deployed, which may have been a good thing. The pain wasn't too bad in her chest until she inhaled. Probably a broken rib or two. She got out to survey the damage to the front end of the truck, but when her right foot touched the ground, her leg buckled under her.

She grabbed the door as she was falling and held herself up off her right leg. It was clearly broken, maybe in more than one place. The firewall had probably crushed it against the seat. It had been numb until this moment, but now searing pain shot from her ankle to her thigh. She held her foot off the ground and hopped around to the front of the truck. Water and steam were pouring from behind the grill. The right front wheel was bent at an angle to the fender. The Land Cruiser was out of commission, and so was Jillian. Walking was out of the question. She'd have to get back into the vehicle and wait. The bearcat ambled into the brush on the other side of the road.

Chapter 49

IF YOU'RE NOT SHOOTING, YOU'D BETTER BE MOVING

Kincaid hurried back toward the shelter. He made it past the truck and to the storage shed. Careful to stay out of the light from the fires, he took a brick of plastic explosive from his bag and placed it atop one of the unfinished walls. He paused to survey the situation.

Bakar was rushing across the camp toward el-Fasil's tent, which was now nothing more than embers floating on a warm updraft emanating from the remains of the canvas floor. There were at least a dozen men fanning out in every direction in search of intruders. Incredibly, there didn't seem to be any interest in the ambassador at all. He sat remarkably still, staring at the melee occurring before his eyes.

Kincaid slipped up to the side of the shelter and spoke through the space between two timbers. "Grey!"

The ambassador, startled, jerked his head in Kincaid's direction. He couldn't make out the face on the other side of the wall.

"Grey, it's Kincaid from the resort. Move over here as far as you can and give me your hands."

EE Sample

The ambassador did as he was told. Kincaid produced his handcuff key and removed the cuffs. "Now slowly slide around the front and back here to me. Don't stand up, and make sure no one is looking before you move."

"I don't need to be told that. Do you think I'm a bloody moron?" the ambassador hissed.

"Never mind what I think of you. Just do it."

The ambassador made it into the darkness behind the shelter. "Let's go," Kincaid whispered. "Stay close to me and keep low." They moved back toward the shed but stopped short. Two men had discovered what was left of the two lighters and the scorch marks on the wall. They yelled frantically in the direction of the other men who were moving toward them.

"We have to go back the other way," Kincaid said.

"Let's just go into the jungle."

"We'd never get through there. They'd be on us before we got ten yards. Follow me if you want to stay alive."

They doubled back to the shelter. It was still abandoned, but beyond it, behind the row of tents, men were slashing into the underbrush, searching for what they believed were several invaders. Kincaid unshouldered the H&K. "Wait here."

The ambassador didn't have to be told twice. He collapsed to the ground, frozen with fear.

Kincaid circled back around the shelter again and crawled as close to the storage shed as he dared. Several men were searching the area around it now, certain that their quarry must be nearby. He was. He ejected a round from his rifle and inserted a tracer round into the chamber, took careful aim, and hit the plastic explosive. It erupted, splintering lumber and taking out at least four or five terrorists. Other men took cover. They had no idea where their attackers were or the size of their force. Some were panicking and running into the jungle. Bakar screamed at them to stand and fight, although he wasn't certain where to stand or who to fight.

The ambassador was trembling on the ground when Kincaid reached him. The men who had been behind the pup tents were nowhere in sight. "Let's go, Grey," Kincaid whispered. The ambassador didn't respond, so he said, "Let's go, old man, or I'm leaving you here."

Grey staggered to his feet. Kincaid grabbed him by the collar and rushed him toward the still-burning boat. Three men emerged from the jungle. They looked surprised. Kincaid sprayed them with his rifle, and they didn't look surprised anymore. They looked dead. The shots attracted the attention of the rest of the camp. Kincaid dove into the brush behind the boat, and the ambassador followed.

"Oh, my god!" He had landed on a rotting corpse.

"Be still," Kincaid barked.

But the ambassador wasn't listening. Terrified, he stood and ran into the clearing. He was immediately taken down by a barrage of AK-47 fire. Not only was he dead, but he had given away Kincaid's position.

He had to move. There was a large tree trunk lying a few feet away. Gunfire followed him as he made a dash for it. Once behind cover, he could see muzzle flash from three rifles in front of him, but bullets were also coming from his right flank. That was especially bad because not only was he vulnerable from that direction and taking fire, it also meant there were soldiers between him and the road, blocking his only escape route. He returned fire at the enemy he could make out in front of him. He sprayed a few rounds to his right, hoping to at least discourage the shooters he couldn't see. He was expecting return fire but instead heard the report of a large-caliber weapon. Then a second and, a few seconds after that, a third. Then no more shots were coming from his flank. Someone was firing from the direction of the road. *Lucia.* It had to be the .50 caliber Barrett. He decided to move again. *If you're not shooting, you'd better be moving.*

This time, he ran to the right. The three shooters in front of him continued to fire at the dead tree. They didn't have night vision. He stopped, emptied his rifle at the muzzle fire, and got all three. Now he had a clear path toward the road, and Lucia was out there somewhere covering him. He clapped a fresh magazine into the H&K and moved off in that direction.

Chapter 50

CONJOINED TWINS

Bakar was as confused as anyone in the encampment. Explosions and gunfire were erupting from all directions. They were under attack, but from which direction and by how large a force? His men, undisciplined and unseasoned fighters and still scattered in all directions, were discharging their weapons, seemingly at random. He had to establish order and concoct a strategy if he was to save what was left of his force. They had suffered many casualties, and el-Fasil was among them. That was certain.

He called out to the survivors to cease firing. As they did so, it was apparent that they were no longer drawing fire. Bakar was able to muster them into a column and move toward the road. His scheme was simple: the road was the only clear route out of the camp. If he and his men caught them from behind on the road, they would be easy targets in the open. If they could get ahead of them and waited in ambush, the enemy would eventually wander into their field of fire. Either way, they would be decimated in a matter of minutes. He sent two scouts ahead and left one behind to guard the rear as the column advanced toward the main highway.

Kincaid had no way of knowing he was just ahead of Bakar and his men. They were all moving in the same direction now.

Lucia emerged from the jungle carrying the big sniper rifle and wearing a broad smile. "You thought you didn't need me, Kincaid, but I saved your ass."

"Yeah, I guess you did."

She told him how she had awakened to find him gone and decided to bring the rifle along and follow him. She had seen two men heading for the road and hid behind some rocks. When the men turned back and began firing on Kincaid, she set the Barrett on its dipod and took aim at their backs. When she had found the range, she took them both out.

"I heard three shots," he said.

"There wasn't much light, and I already said I had to find the range."

"Wasting ammo. That means you only have a couple of rounds left."

"You're welcome," she said sardonically.

Her sarcasm was lost on him. "Where is the flash suppressor I made for your rifle?"

"Too cumbersome." She knew Kincaid would be impressed that she knew the word.

"You're lucky they didn't find you. Who knows how many more there are around here? We need to get on down the road." Lucia struggled to sling the big rifle onto her shoulder. "Here, trade with me." He offered her the H&K.

"No. I'm fine."

"Suit yourself."

The sun was coming up now, and the humidity, coupled with the early morning heat, made simply walking a chore.

Lucia followed him until he spotted the Land Cruiser sitting beside the road. He grabbed her shoulder, pushed her into the brush, and jumped in beside her.

"What is it?"

"It's the truck I put Jillian in. She was supposed to go to the police for help. Something has gone wrong."

"Do you think they recaptured her?"

"Probably. Listen, I want you to stay here. Keep that rifle pointed back up the road. I'm going to go look in the truck to see who, if anyone, is inside. Can you do that?"

"Of course, I can. Be careful, Kincaid."

He stayed in the undergrowth and edged his way to the back of the Land Cruiser. He looked in all directions before darting out of the brush and crouching behind the truck. Carefully, he peered through the back window. He was relieved to see Jillian in the front seat. She was alone and looked unhurt. He stepped around to the driver's door. "Hello there."

Jillian jumped and hit her knee on the steering wheel. She let out a whimper before she realized it was Kincaid. "What the fuck? You scared me almost to death," she yelled.

Kincaid put his finger across his lips. "Shhh. You want everyone to know where we are? What happened anyway?"

"Something ran out in front of me. It looked like a bear. Whatever it was, I swerved to miss it and ran off the road and into that." She pointed through the windscreen. He hadn't noticed that the front of the vehicle was lodged against a formidable tree. "I damaged the radiator and the right wheel. I'm afraid I'm stuck here."

"At least you're ok." He searched her face. Her pupils were big as dimes and she was breathing rapidly. Her lip was split, and a trace of blood was caked in the corner of her mouth. It was evident she was still on the verge of shock. His intention had been to get her out of danger and home, but now he realized it had been a mistake to send her out on her own. "You are okay, right?"

She was trembling slightly. "I'm afraid I've broken my leg. Maybe some ribs."

Lucia saw Kincaid talking to someone in the SUV and decided it was safe to join him. "What's going on?"

"Jillian, do you know Lucia? She was a friend of your sister's."

Lucia had almost forgotten that Allison was dead. Tears welled up in her eyes.

Jillian nodded to Lucia. She hadn't noticed Kincaid's use of the word, *was*. "Nice to meet you."

"You, too. I've heard so much about you. Are you okay?"

Jillian stared at the ground.

"She has a broken leg, Lucia." He closed Jillian's door, and they climbed into the back seat behind her. Kincaid saw the tears in Lucia's eyes and could only imagine what must be going through her mind. He tried to reassure both women that everything was going to be okay.

Only a few minutes had gone by when Jillian suddenly shrank back into her seat. "Someone is coming," she whispered urgently. Her eyes were wide with fright and glued to the rearview mirror.

"Get down!" Kincaid pressed Lucia's head down and peered over the back of the seat. Two men were striding quickly toward them. It appeared they recognized the Land Cruiser and were expecting to find their friends inside. "Roll down the back glass," he said to Jillian.

"I don't think that's a good idea."

"Do it now," he snapped. The rear window moved silently

into the back door. When he heard the men's feet shuffle to a stop, Kincaid sat up and pointed his pistol at one of them. Both men froze in fear.

"Put your guns down."

They did not move or make a sound. Lucia said, "I don't think they speak English. Let me try." She spoke to them in Tagalog, and they both started talking frantically at once.

"They are terrified of you. They are sure you're going to kill them. I'm surprised they haven't wet themselves." Kincaid saw them for what they were: two boys trying to prove themselves as men by joining a terrorist cell.

"Ask them if they are PISF."

"They say they are, but they had nothing to do with trying to kill you. They are begging for their lives."

"Tell them to shut up."

Lucia said something to them, and they stopped babbling. One of them wet himself.

Jillian asked weakly, "Are you going to kill them?"

"I'm not sure yet. We can't risk two shots in case their friends are nearby. Plus, I can't spare the ammo." He turned back to Lucia. "Ask them where the rest of their men are."

"They say that Bakar sent them ahead as scouts. They are supposed to report back."

"Who is Bakar? Their leader?"

Jillian spoke up. "Their leader was el-Fasil, the man in the tent. Bakar is his lieutenant or whatever."

"How many more of them are there?"

"They aren't sure. Maybe ten or twelve."

Kincaid searched the space behind the Cruiser's back seat and came up with a roll of duct tape. "Here," he said to Lucia, handing her his pistol. "Hold this on them."

He got out of the car and grabbed the first terrorist by the collar. He roughly dragged him into the bushes. His captive was crying and obviously begging for his life. Kincaid taped his wrists together behind his back and shoved him to the ground before taping his ankles. He went back to the truck and did the same to the second boy. He pulled them into a sitting position, back to back, and ran a length of duct tape across their mouths and around their heads. They sat like conjoined twins while he used the rest of the roll to bind them together at the chest.

"That should keep them out of the way for a while. We need to move. It won't take Bakar long to find them, and we'll be sitting ducks here."

"Do you think we can make it to the main road?" Lucia asked.

Kincaid looked at Jillian. "Do you think you can walk?"

"I can try." She winced as she slid off the seat. As soon as her foot touched the ground, she cried out. Her leg buckled under her weight.

"It's no use. Leave me here. I'll be all right until you can get back with help."

"That's not happening, Jillian. We all stay together." He paused, assessing their situation. "We can't stay on the road if they're chasing us, and the jungle is too thick to get through."

"What should we do?" Lucia was beginning to sound desperate.

"We'll go to the cave. It isn't far from here, I don't think. All we have to do is find it."

"No problem. I can find it."

"Good. You lead the way. I'll carry Jillian." He bent over in front of Jillian, and she fell across his shoulder.

It was a hot, grueling walk through the jungle, but Lucia found the path, and they crawled into the cave. Their water was gone, and they were hot and exhausted. "What now?" Lucia asked.

"I'm going to call Cutro. He's our best chance at this point." Kincaid reached for his SAT phone, but it wasn't on his belt. He searched his pockets and looked in his bag. No phone. He must have lost it somewhere near the camp. They crawled farther back into the cave where it was cooler.

"What do you think will happen to those two men? I hope that bear doesn't eat them alive," Jillian said.

Kincaid had other things on his mind. He didn't think there were bears on Palawan.

"I think we're in trouble," Lucia whispered, looking at Kincaid for reassurance.

"I've been in trouble before."

She searched his eyes for a trace of fear but could find none. "Do you believe in God, Kincaid?"

"I do, but I doubt God believes in me."

"I believe in you."

He looked away. "Maybe the terrorists won't find us. Let's wait it out. If they aren't here by nightfall, we'll just walk out of here."

But it wasn't to be.

Chapter 51

BAKAR

About an hour had passed since they had settled in the cave. Lucia heard it first—a rustling noise somewhere outside but very near.

"You two stay here and be quiet." Kincaid slipped silently to the mouth of the cave and drew his knife. A few moments passed before a surprised youth found himself face to face with an intense ex-Ranger. Kincaid plunged the steel blade into his chest once and then again. The boy slumped to the ground. Kincaid kicked him away from the opening and went back to Jillian and Lucia. "They're out there."

Lucia was clutching the Barrett to her chest. "It's just a matter of time."

"You're right."

"What are we going to do?"

"These soldiers are nothing more than a bunch of punks. I need to find Bakar. Cut off the head, and the serpent dies."

The women stared in silence. He could tell Jillian wasn't going to be able to withstand much more trauma. "Can you describe Bakar to me, Jillian?" he asked softly.

"H-he's tall and strong-looking. He wears camouflage with a red bandana tied around his head."

"Sounds easy to spot."

"I guess so, yeah."

"Lucia, I need you to bring your rifle to the front of the cave. Prop it up on one of those rocks and keep guard while I'm gone."

"Are you sure you want to do this?"

"Yeah. I'm sure. If they can keep us boxed in here long enough, we'll die of thirst. Not the way I plan to go."

Lucia did as she was told. Kincaid knelt beside her and surveyed the area in front of the cave. Her voice was low, barely a whisper. "Okay but be careful. I don't want to lose you."

He smiled at her and darted out into the daylight and into danger. He crouched low and made his way from tree to bush to rocks, anyplace that offered cover while he reconnoitered the situation. The PISF apparently assumed their enemy was holed up in the cave and had established a ragged line in front of, but at some distance from it. He was unnoticed as he flanked their position and circled in behind them. If he'd had more than one thirty-round magazine, he would have considered instigating a firefight with them all right then. But he stuck to his plan and continued to search for their leader, Bakar.

It wasn't long before he spotted a tall, gaunt man with a long, black beard and a red headband standing atop a rocky cliff and peering through binoculars. It had to be Bakar, and he was a sitting duck. Kincaid could make the shot easily from where he was behind a fallen almaciga tree, but the problem remained: not enough ammo. If he shot Bakar, he'd have a firefight on his hands that he couldn't win. No, he'd have to climb up and take Bakar in a quieter way. He slung his rifle over his shoulder and started to make his way to the foot of the cliff. The jungle was thick, and he almost stumbled on four men who were huddled together in a small clearing. They were talking softly and smoking cigarettes. Kincaid slipped by silently and unnoticed.

When he made it to the rocks, he could no longer see Bakar. Hopefully, he hadn't left his position but merely moved back from the precipice and out of view. He started to climb. The heat was oppressive, and the cliff was steeper than it had looked from a distance, but Kincaid made it to the top and peered over the edge. Bakar was alone. Surveying the jungle from this height, he was sure he could see anything that moved below. He was mistaken.

There was little cover between Kincaid and the terrorist leader, but he had one advantage. Two, counting the element of surprise. The sun was at Kincaid's back, and Bakar would be squinting into the sun. Kincaid carefully laid his rifle down and stood upright. "Bakar, you're a dead man," he barked.

Bakar's head jerked around instinctively toward the sound of a man's voice. He couldn't believe his own eyes. It was impossible that his enemy had appeared out of thin air, yet there he stood. Bakar was several steps from his weapon, but Kincaid only had a knife.

Probably doesn't understand English, Kincaid thought.

Instead of scrambling for his rifle, Bakar ran straight at Kincaid who was waiting, knife in hand. Kincaid thrust at him and caught the meaty part of Bakar's right shoulder. Bakar grabbed the knife blade, slicing his hand to the bone. He was bleeding profusely, but he held onto the knife. Kincaid let go of the knife and grabbed Bakar by the wrists. Bakar managed to slash at Kincaid with the point of the blade. Kincaid felt a sharp pain in his forearm as he took a couple steps backward, pulling his enemy with him. Then he threw himself onto his back, slamming both feet into the man's stomach. Bakar flew headlong over Kincaid and over the side of the cliff. He screamed when he realized what had happened. His men looked toward the sound in time to see their leader plummet through the trees. They grabbed their weapons and started firing in Kincaid's direction.

He crawled back to where he had left the H&K. He was in it now. He fired at the few targets he could see, which were mainly muzzle flashes. He heard the report of the sniper rifle he had left with Lucia. He hoped she was firing support at the enemy's back and not staving off an attack on her position. He only had about twenty rounds left in the rifle and eight in his pistol, but he did command the high ground. He tried to wipe the blood from his arm with his shirttail and rolled over on his back to check his rear flank. For the first time, he saw it. An easy path leading to the summit from somewhere down below. If the enemy could find it, he'd be trapped.

Before he had time to get worried, he heard heavy gunfire from down below. The jungle canopy was too thick to make out exactly what was going on, but one thing was certain. There were a lot more weapons being discharged than there were moments before, and none of it seemed to be directed at him. Between bursts of fire, he heard angry voices. The only word he could make out was *humpay*, which he was pretty sure meant "stop."

Five minutes later, all was quiet. Kincaid was puzzled until he heard a voice on a bullhorn. "Kincaid, where are you?" It was Cutro. "Kincaid, it's all clear. If you can hear me, come on out."

He made his way down the path to the jungle floor and followed Cutro's voice, which was still urging him to "come on out". "It's Cutro. You're not in trouble, Kincaid, and we have everyone in custody."

He finally came upon an entourage of lawmen that included Cutro, Campos, and several other officers of the El Nido police force along with two burly characters who introduced themselves as being from INTERPOL. "How does it happen that you knew where to find me?"

"A friend of yours who would only identify himself as Alex. He was tracking your SAT phone and called us with the coordinates. He said you had undertaken to round up a terrorist cell by yourself. He was worried about you." Cutro smiled. "Although I don't know why."

"Well, I'd say you came along at the perfect time as far as I'm concerned. Thanks."

"You've been shot," Sal exclaimed, pointing to his arm.

Kincaid laughed. "You should have been a medic. I got a little cut is all. I'm fine."

A few hundred meters away, Lucia had heard the firefight and the bullhorn. She put two and two together and deduced that the battle was won. She stood up and called to Jillian. "I think it's all over now. Come on, let's go find Kincaid."

She was excited and anxious to make sure he was all right, but as she exited the cave, she didn't notice that the man Kincaid had stabbed was still breathing. He was alive, barely conscious but enough to retaliate for his wounds. He took the 9 mm Browning from his belt and fired at Lucia from only a few feet away, striking her three times in the chest. She slumped to the ground.

Jillian had been on her way to the mouth of the cave when she saw what happened. She picked up the big sniper rifle and put a .50 caliber bullet into the man's brain.

Kincaid and the others heard the pistol shots and then the unmistakable report of the Barrett. They raced to the cave where they found a sobbing Jillian holding Lucia's head in her lap. Kincaid rushed to her side. Lucia was awash in blood, but she smiled up at him. "I'm sorry, baby," she said weakly. "I love you."

"I love you too, baby," he whispered. Lucia closed her eyes and was gone.

Chapter 52

ANSWERS

A week had passed since Kincaid's raid on the PISF camp. Jillian spent twenty-four hours in the hospital after having her broken leg set and recovering from the shock of her ordeal and the news of the deaths of Allison and her father. Since her release, she and Kincaid had stayed at her father's house. It should have been a time of relief, maybe even celebration but, instead, it was a time of grief and sadness. They attended Lucia's funeral—a beautiful ceremony that did little to assuage the pain of losing her for her uncle and friends.

KINCAID WAS DRIVING THE JEEP TO THE EL NIDO POLICE department after being summoned by Captain Belka. While en route, he used his SAT phone to call Alex.

"Well, well, look who it is. I was wondering what happened to you."

"Hello, Alex. I've been meaning to call you. I owe you, pal." he began.

"Ya think?"

Kincaid ignored the sarcasm and continued. "I probably wouldn't be here if you hadn't had my back. Thanks. And I mean that."

"Don't worry about it. What happened anyway?"

"I got myself into a little jam. A few guys had me surrounded when the cavalry showed up. They saved my ass is what happened. They said they were working on a tip from you. I had lost my phone, so I couldn't call out. They were heading for the coordinates you gave them when they found me."

"Maybe you can explain how you thought you were going to take on a small army by yourself and come out alive."

"I guess I didn't think about it that way." He paused. "What's going on with you?"

"I'm about to leave for North Africa. There's some serious shit going down out there. The US is involved but strictly off the record. They need men. You interested?"

"Yeah, I think I might be."

"If you're coming, I'll wait for you. When do you think you can get here?"

"I just have a few loose ends to tie up out here. I can probably fly out tomorrow or the next day."

"Okay. See you then." Alex clicked off and chuckled. *I beat him to it again!*

Kincaid parked the jeep just as Sal Campos was about to enter the police station. He smiled and wiped the sweat off his forehead with the back of his hand. "Mr. Kincaid. How are you?"

"You tell me, Sal. Am I about to be locked up?" He was trying to make a joke and was more than a little startled at Sal's answer.

"I dunno, sir. I think you might be in some trouble." Sal

held the door and followed him in.

Kincaid pointed to the empty desk in front of the door. "Where's Cruz?"

"He's in his new place, a cell in the back. That's my desk now," Sal said, with a broad smile.

Cutro appeared and walked stiffly toward them. "Kincaid, we've been expecting you. Please follow me." His manner was a little too professional. They were greeted in Belka's office by the captain and the two INTERPOL agents.

Belka stood up, clenching his unlit cigar in his teeth. He extended his hand across the desk, and Kincaid shook it. "Sit down, Kincaid." He motioned to the two other men in the room. "This is Bautista and Guiterrez. You remember them from the other day?"

"Yes. I guess I forgot to properly thank you," he said sheepishly.

"Don't worry about it," Bautista said. His tone was brusque. "We need you to answer a few questions, Kincaid."

"Okay."

"Who do you work for?"

"Right now? Nobody."

"Who were you working for last week?"

"Again, nobody. I was helping a friend who had been taken by that terrorist cell."

"Jillian Welde?"

"That's right."

"Did you know who her father was?"

"We were in the process of finding that out."

"You had no knowledge of his business activities?"

"Not firsthand, no. My investigation led me to the conclusion that he was selling illegal arms to some unsavory characters."

Bautista exchanged glances with his partner. "Let's talk about Grey."

"What about him?"

"What do you know about him?"

"Not much except that he's dead because he was an idiot."

"How did he die?"

"By not following instructions and exposing himself to hostile fire."

"PISF, you mean?'

"That's right."

"What do you know about them?"

"A terrorist cell that wanted me dead. That's about it. It occurred to me that they have informants at the resort and, maybe here."

"We know about them already. Officer Cruz and a bartender at Oceania named Michael Flores. One of the few surviving members of the PISF gave them up."

Guiterrez stepped in front of Bautista and sat on the edge of Belka's desk. "We counted twenty-five dead men in that encampment, not counting two bodies we found buried in a ditch and the one we know Jillian Welde shot at the cave. How many of those men did you kill?"

"I can tell you I didn't bury any bodies." He thought for a minute. "And I can tell you there was one guy who had been dead for a few days when I saw him. As for the rest, yeah, I probably killed them."

"All in self-defense, I suppose?"

"That's right."

"You know how preposterous that sounds, Kincaid?" Guiterrez was standing now.

"I don't care how it sounds."

"We think at least five or six of those men were murdered."

Kincaid shrugged. "All you have to do is prove it."

Bautista took over again. "We don't want to put you away on a murder charge. We're just looking for a little information. What do you know about a plane loaded with surplus military rifles that was intercepted in Iran?"

"Is that what happened?"

Kincaid told them about the helicopter in Manila and the warehouse on Siquijor Island.

"What about Welde Technologies?"

"I think that's a front for the arms business. You should talk to a guy named Marco out there."

"We did. He's been arrested. Did you know Welde was assassinated in London two weeks ago?"

"Jillian told me. Apparently, Grey told her. She's planning to go there to identify the body."

"We think a friend of yours, Lucia de la Rosa, may have been the one who shot him."

"In London?"

"That's right."

"Impossible. I saw her every day right up until the day she was killed. She couldn't have been in London."

Bautista crossed his arms over his chest and studied Kincaid for a few moments. The smell of stale cigar ash filled the air and punctuated the silence. "Would you excuse us for a few minutes?" He motioned toward the door.

"No problem."

"Make sure you don't leave the lobby."

"Sure."

He sat in one of the plastic chairs in the lobby and leaned back against the wall. He wasn't about to give Lucia up for shooting Welde. She was dead. It wouldn't matter, except he didn't want her memory tarnished for her uncle's sake. And he saw no reason why Jillian should know that her father and, arguably, her sister were dead as a result of Lucia's need for revenge.

Fifteen minutes passed before Belka opened his office door and asked him back inside. "We've decided not to charge you, Kincaid, but I want you off my island. You're here illegally anyway. Your visa has expired."

"Believe it or not, Captain, I was just making plans to leave."

"We're seizing Welde's assets including the factory and his house. I think that's where you have been staying. Is that right?"

"At the beach house, that's right."

"I'll give you until tomorrow at which time you and Miss Welde will have to vacate the premises."

"Like I said, Miss Welde is leaving for London."

Belka stuck out his hand. "Goodbye, Kincaid. And please, don't ever come back to Palawan again."

Kincaid turned and walked out.

EPILOGUE

H e steered the jeep into the sandy driveway, through the open gate, and into the garage of James Welde's house. He could smell the jasmine and awapuhi that grew along the fence. Beyond the pool, Jillian was sitting on the beach, staring out at the azure South China Sea. Kincaid sat on the sand beside her. She was the color of toasted nutmeg, and her sun-bleached hair floated on the briny wind. She was beautiful. This was the serenity he had been seeking in the exotic village of El Nido. And now that he had found it, it was time to go.

She turned to him and smiled an impossibly warm smile. "Hi."

"Hello, how are you doing?"

"Okay, I guess. I've been thinking."

"About what?"

"Won't you please come to London with me? I can't bear to go alone."

"Your mother is meeting you there. You won't be alone."

"It's not the same, Kincaid."

"I can't do it. I would feel like an intruder. It's your father and sister. You should be with your mother, your family."

Her smile vanished like the wispy plume from an extinguished candle. Tears were welling up in her eyes. "You meant what you said to Lucia, didn't you? You loved her."

"She was dying, Jillian. What was I supposed to say? I don't know anything about love."

"Oh, I think you know a lot about love. Somehow, I hoped that you would love me. You make me feel special and safe. I have never felt this way with anyone before." She hadn't meant to open up to him so completely and candidly, but there it was.

His silence told her it was a mistake. He sat and listened to the ocean's poignant, salty whisper, but it had no answers for him. "There is no future for us, Jillian. I can't go with you to London, and I can't live in Connecticut. What would I do there, be your law clerk? And you sure as hell can't go with me. You don't have the temperament to be a soldier." He meant the last part to be a joke, but she didn't laugh.

"I guess you're right."

"Anyway, I have something for you." He reached into his pocket and brought out a small slip of paper.

"What is that?"

"I had almost forgotten this until I started packing up my things. I took it from your father's bedroom that first night. It's Swiss bank account number. You should check it out."

She took it from his hand and stared at it for a moment before asking, "What are you going to do?"

"I hear there's trouble in North Africa, so I'm going down there to see if I can help out."

"Do you really think you can right all the wrongs in this world?"

"Maybe not, but I'll do what I can. It's the only thing I know."

Her stare was soft yet piercing.

The tears had left glistening tracks on her cheeks. "How long do you think you can keep doing that?"

"As long as it takes."